W9-BMV-178

Acclaim for
Shadows of the Night:
Queer Tales of the Uncanny and Unusual

"Creepy, whimsical, and daring, these wide-ranging stories take the reader to weird worlds and stretch the imagination in unexpected directions. Who'd dream that vampires and Harvey the invisible rabbit could cohabitate so happily in the same book? The grand finale is a New Orleans plague tale—a novella by Victoria A. Brownworth—that's as erotic as it is eerie. Fascinating and frightening reading."

—Warren Dunford
Author of *Making a Killing* and *Soon to Be a Major Motion Picture*

"Utilizing same-sex orientation as a thematic thread, editor Greg Herren has woven a fascinating and broad tapestry of things that go bump in the human psyche. The author has selected his contributors with the eerie discrimination of an incubus in search of gourmet soul food. *Shadows of the Night* is a diverse exhumation of the dark side of consciousness that successfully expands the parameters of both GLBT literature and the horror genre. It's eerie, shattering, humorous, sexy, enigmatic, intriguing, macabre, and suspenseful. Thirteen cheers for Greg Herren, an amazing panoply of GLBT authors, and The Haworth Press."

—Michael Huxley
Editorial Director, STARbooks Press

"In the surprisingly conservative world of horror fiction, it always does my heart good to see work that takes alternate sexualities into account without turning them into bugaboos or grosss-out factors. *Shadows of the Night* showcases fine tales from several of today's most promising queer and queer-friendly writers of speculative fiction. Here's hoping they won't keep exclusively to the shadows!"

—Poppy Z. Brite
Author of *Exquisite Corpse,*
The Value of X, and *Liquor*

NOTES FOR PROFESSIONAL LIBRARIANS
AND LIBRARY USERS

This is an original book title published by Southern Tier Editions, Harrington Park Press®, an imprint of The Haworth Press, Inc. Unless otherwise noted in specific chapters with attribution, materials in this book have not been previously published elsewhere in any format or language.

Shadows of the Night
*Queer Tales of the Uncanny
and Unusual*

HARRINGTON PARK PRESS
Southern Tier Editions
Gay Men's Fiction
Jay Quinn, Executive Editor

Shadows of the Night
Queer Tales of the Uncanny and Unusual

Greg Herren
Editor

Southern Tier Editions
Harrington Park Press®
An Imprint of The Haworth Press, Inc.
New York • London • Oxford

Published by

Southern Tier Editions, Harrington Park Press®, an imprint of The Haworth Press, Inc., 10 Alice
Street, Binghamton, NY 13904-1580.

© 2004 by The Haworth Press. All rights reserved. No part of this work may be reproduced or
utilized in any form or by any means, electronic or mechanical, including photocopying, micro-
film, and recording, or by any information storage and retrieval system, without permission in
writing from the publisher. Printed in the United States of America.

PUBLISHER'S NOTE
This is a work of fiction. Names, characters, places, and incidents either are the products of the
author's imagination or are used fictitiously, and any resemblance to actual persons, living or
dead, business establishments, events, or locales is entirely coincidental.

Cover design by Jennifer M. Gaska.

Library of Congress Cataloging-in-Publication Data

Shadows of the night : queer tales of the uncanny and unusual / Greg Herren, editor.
    p. cm.
   ISBN 0-7394-4250-3
   1. Horror tales, American. 2. Gays' writings, American. 3. Lesbians—Fiction. 4. Gay men—
Fiction. I. Herren, Greg.
   PS648.H6S525 2003
   813'.0873808920664—dc21

                                                                    2003002274

Acknowledgments

Shadows of the Night began as a result of an e-mailed conversation between William J. Mann and myself. *Queer Fear,* a wonderful anthology edited by Michael Rowe, had just been released, and I had e-mailed William about his story "The Spark," which I had really enjoyed. Shortly thereafter, during one of my wonderful weekly phone calls with Jay Quinn, senior editor at Southern Tier Editions, I mentioned my own interest in doing an anthology of queer speculative fiction. Jay, bless his heart, was quite enthusiastic about the project, and, thus, *Shadows of the Night* was born.

I would be remiss if I didn't thank my amazingly gifted contributors. Thanks, y'all, for writing such amazing stories and making me look good. As they say, an editor is only as good as his writers, and I have quite a talented bunch here.

I would also like to thank the following people for their love, support, and encouragement: Felice Picano, David Rosen, Michele Karlsberg, Katherine V. Forrest, Carol Guess, Howard Zucker, Julie Smith, Rosemary James, Robin and LouAnn Morehouse, Mark Richards, Greg Gitz, Chris Walker, Heidi Haltiner, Kay Lowe, Michael Craft, Ken Thistlewaite, Krandall Kraus and Paul Borja, Darren Brewer, Stephanie Hartsog, Kelly Smith, Jim Gladstone, Ian Philips, Melinda Shelton, Kathleen DeBold and Barbara Johnson, Mike Smid, Patrick Merla, Jeff Gregoire, Evelyn Rodos, Jameson Currier, Richard Schneider, Marika Christian, and so many others—I am truly blessed.

Seven years ago, I warned Paul Willis that my life was a rollercoaster ride—lots of incredible highs, and some truly frightening lows. He got on the ride anyway, and every day I thank my lucky stars for bringing me my soul mate. Thanks, honey, for making the ride so much more fun.

CONTENTS

Introduction

Greg Herren

I first became interested in horror as a small child. Every day after school, my sister and I would race home to watch *Dark Shadows*. We weren't the only ones; at recess we would gather with our friends to talk about what happened the day before on the show. At that time, most horror films were generally low-budget B pictures with casts that couldn't act their way out of paper bags. But every once in a while, the afternoon movie on our local ABC affiliate would be something truly thrilling for our young minds, such as *What Ever Happened to Baby Jane?* or *Wait Until Dark*. Back then, we didn't identify them as horror films; to us, they were just scary movies. Then *Dark Shadows* was cancelled and the ABC affiliate began showing reruns of *Gilligan's Island* and *The Munsters* instead of the afternoon movies. I discovered Nancy Drew and the Hardy Boys, and scary movies faded from my memory.

It was in junior high school that horror resurfaced for me, this time in the form of books. William Peter Blatty's *The Exorcist* was a runaway best seller, and kids were stealing their parents' copies to read. I was luckier than most kids; my parents didn't censor my reading material, and even bought me my own copy of the book. Yet I was highly disappointed with it; all it did, really, was gross me out. The crucifix masturbation scene was the main reason all the kids at school were reading the book (frightening to think how sex-obsessed seventh graders are), but by that time I was already aware that I liked boys rather than girls, and that scene just struck me as vulgar and disgusting.

Another book was making the rounds at the time: *The Other* by Thomas Tryon. This book truly struck a chord with me. The main character, Niles Perry, was kind of like me; he preferred to read rather than play sports, and he was most definitely different from the other kids. He had an evil twin, Holland, who was quite monstrous; Niles was torn between his love for his twin and his horror at what Holland was capable of. They had a cousin, Russell, that neither twin much cared for; Holland planted a pitchfork in a hay pile and then goaded Russell into jumping into it from the barn loft. Holland continued to commit crimes of this sort, until about two-thirds of the way through the book, when Tryon delivered the true shocker: Holland was actually dead, and had been for quite some time, and Holland's death had driven Niles insane—only no one knew it.

Around this same time I also discovered Richard Matheson's book *I Am Legend*. *I Am Legend* was a truly frightening book about the last human survivor of a deadly man-made plague that killed most of the population. Those who survived had become vampires, with the lone exception of one man. Matheson's simplistic writing style was easy to follow, yet he managed to create a realistic and truly frightening world that gave me nightmares for days. (A film was made of this book starring Charlton Heston, renamed *The Omega Man;* don't bother watching it.) It was still early in the days of horror fiction, however, so there wasn't a "horror" section at the Kroch's and Brentano's I haunted at the nearest mall, and my local library didn't carry Matheson's work. (Much later, I would rediscover Matheson as an adult— Tor started re-releasing his books in the late 1990s, and I tore through them with much enthusiasm.)

The success of these books opened a door in publishing for the phenomenon named Stephen King.

Much has been written about Stephen King, some damning him as a hack, others recognizing him as a literary genius. When I was a freshman in high school, one of my friends had a book with her named *Carrie*. I picked it up, looked it over, and started reading it, ignoring the lecture we were getting in algebra (which was never one of my stronger subjects, anyway). The class period flew by, and my friend, who had not finished the book, graciously offered to let me read it. I could not put the book down. I read it in my last class; I read it on the bus ride home; and once home, I sat on the couch and read it until later that night I finished, put it down, and thought, "Wow." The story of Carrie White, the outsider the other high school students hated and picked on unmercifully, who had psychokinetic powers and exacted a horrible revenge on her high school, deeply resonated with me. I, like Carrie, knew what it was like to have other students hate you for no reason other than being different. By high school, I was very aware of the difference my sexual attraction to other boys had created; somehow, the other kids were aware of it too, and tormented me for it. *Carrie* inspired me to write my first real short story, which was a blatant rip-off. I was too frightened by my difference to write about a truly gay teenager; instead, I wrote a story about a straight kid that everyone called faggot, who finally used his powers to destroy them all. I didn't show the story to anyone, and eventually threw it away.

The aftermath of the huge success of *Carrie* was an explosion of horror fiction—most of them attempting to cash in on King's success. I read some of these books but was disappointed with them all. The characters weren't real, the settings were fake, and there wasn't any real "scare" to them. So I stuck with King and was rarely disappointed.

As I slowly came to terms with my sexuality and took the baby steps that led me out of the closet, I wrote. I was still too afraid to write anything with openly gay content, but King's influence on my writing was undeniable. My short stories were usually sentimental claptrap with a happy ending that even I thought were terrible. Every once in a while I did manage to come up with a truly beautiful little story that even creative writing professors liked; yet no one would publish them. I wrote mostly for myself by this time. Being a writer had been my dream since I fell in love with books as a seven-year-old, but in my twenties I began to think my dream never had a chance of realization.

I don't remember why I started writing horror stories. It wasn't as though one day a lightbulb went on over my head, or lightning struck. I do remember getting the idea for the story. I was working as a bank teller and had no car, so I had to take the bus to and from work. I hated taking the bus. It took me forty-five minutes and two bus changes to get to the bank; on the rare days when I could talk a friend with a car into giving me a ride, it took less than fifteen minutes. One day on my way to work, someone sat down next to me eating a chili dog, and the bus hit a pothole. The chili dog splattered all over my nice white shirt. There was no way my manager would let me work my window in the shirt; as a result, I was sent home (again by bus) and lost a day's pay, which I could ill afford. All the way home I did a slow burn. I sat down, turned on my typewriter, and wrote a horror story set on a city bus, called "Fellow Traveler." It flowed right out of me; I went into the zone. I submitted the story to *Cemetery Dance* magazine, and, although it was rejected, the editor sent me a wonderful letter praising my writing skills and encouraging me to try again. I wrote and submitted about fifteen stories over the next three years. Every time I was rejected, but was again encouraged to continue trying.

In the early 1990s, a friend lent me a book called *Last Act* by Christopher Pike. It was a young-adult horror novel, written for teenagers. I enjoyed it, and began reading all of Pike's work. I decided then to try to write a horror novel for teenagers. I had been writing a horror novel for adults; I decided to adapt it to a younger audience. When I did so, it began to flow much easier than it had before. Over the course of the next three years I wrote four young-adult novels. I was too afraid of rejection to do anything with them; only my closest friend was allowed to read them. (They are still sitting in a drawer.)

After I finished the fourth, I discovered gay and lesbian literature. I was out of the closet by then, and a lesbian I worked with took me to my first gay bookstore. I discovered Andrew Holleran, Edmund White, Felice Picano, and Michael Nava. Suddenly, I realized the reason none of my fictions really worked was because I wasn't writing from my own experience. I started writing gay-themed short stories, and although none of them sold, there was a truth to them that wasn't in my previous work. I abandoned writing horror and started working on gay fiction.

I never gave up reading horror, but I longed for gay horror: horror stories written with gay protagonists and themes, wild flights of the imagination. As I plunged deeper into the world of queer lit, I was amazed at how little queer horror was being written or published. Every so often, I would dig out one of my old stories from the 1980s and rewrite it, making it queer, but ultimately would do nothing with it. Whenever I became aware of a book that could be considered queer horror, I devoured it.

So, the opportunity to edit this collection was, in many ways, the realization of a dream. I invited writers not primarily known for writing horror-type fiction to contribute, and was completely blown away by the quality of the stories I received. For example, J. M. Redmann is primarily known as a writer of lesbian mysteries. Therese Szymanski writes crime thrillers. William J. Mann writes wonderful popular fiction as well as nonfiction about gay Hollywood, but has, like me, an affinity for horror (he was also a fan of *Dark Shadows*). Jess Wells writes literary fiction and edits lesbian erotica collections. Victoria A. Brownworth has written and edited horror collections, but is primarily known for her nonfiction and journalism. M. Christian is best known for erotica. There are also some wonderful contributions by writers at the beginning of their careers, who are undoubtedly destined for literary stardom: David McConnell, Marshall Moore, Carol Rosenfeld, Greg Wharton, and Quentin Harrington.

I hope you enjoy their work as much as I did.

On with the show!

A QUEER HORROR READING LIST

The Living One by Lewis Gannett
Minions of the Moon by Richard Bowes
Queer Fear, edited by Michael Rowe
Exquisite Corpse by Poppy Z. Brite
The Witching Hour by Anne Rice
Grave Passions, edited by William J. Mann
Night Shade, edited by Victoria A. Brownworth
    and Judith M. Redding
Bending the Landscape: Horror, edited by Nicola Griffith
    and Stephen Pagel
Vampire Vow by Michael Schiefelbein
Bound in Blood by David Thomas Lord

The Ghost of Carmen Miranda and Other Spooky Gay and Lesbian Tales, edited by Scott Brassart and Julie K. Trevelyan

This list is by no means comprehensive; it is merely offered as a place to get started.

Country People

Richard Hall

I had misgivings the minute I walked in. The classroom was too small, the desks were for kids, and the blackboard was on rollers. When the first students turned up, my worries increased. I knew that adult education courses tend to attract the odd and the lonely, but this group looked more displaced than most. Taking the enrollment slip from a large, sad woman in her mid-forties, I wondered if my job was just to keep them occupied till they found out what they were missing.

The woman's name was Emilia Quinn. She was wrapped, sari-like, in yards of yellow fabric. Her dark hair was a tangle, but her eyes were beautiful. She gave me a wounded smile and took a seat by the window.

It had started with Ray Stonington last month, August. Ray had been in one of his mild, helpful moods, which should have warned me. We were sitting in his dining room, the candles illuminating the pine table, the Dutch corner cabinet, the spinning wheel in the corner. The dinner had been superb, as elegant as this eighteenth-century tavern in the Hudson Valley that Ray had converted to a residence.

He had spoken too casually: "They're looking for someone to teach a night course in literature for adults." Ray named the college, one of those two-year affairs that Governor Rockefeller had sown around the state—an institution without the distinction of Vassar or the sectarian rigor of Marist or the blue-jean cheerfulness of Bard. "Why don't you ring up the dean? He's a friend of mine."

I shook my head. I was through with all that. Twenty years in the New York City public school system was enough. "Why do you think I moved up here?"

"This won't be anything like New York, Michael. One night a week, no knives, no drugs, sweet country people." I looked skeptical, and he continued, "It'll help with the shop."

Ray was manipulating me, but I fell for it. Since retiring from teaching, I had been living out a lifelong fantasy—running an antique store. The hardest part of selling antiques is finding the damned things. Suddenly I could imagine the students inviting me over to look at Grandpa's sea chest, at Great-Aunt Letitia's sewing dummy. I gave a reckless laugh.

"The only course I'd consider would be a gay lit course. That's what I couldn't do in the city."

Ray had given me another mild look and changed the subject.

A young man with fluffy sideburns under a blue Civil War cap handed me a class chit. The rest of his outfit was also vaguely military, though I spotted the edge of a beaded vest. He looked at me with wide brown eyes, unsmiling. This country person didn't look so sweet, though he gave off a sexy glow. His name was Cornelius Graef.

Yes, I'd proposed the course as a lark, an after-dinner joke, but a few days later Ray had called back. "I talked to John Sterling at school. Would you write up a proposal for a gay lit course? He'd like to get it approved—on a noncredit basis."

I hung up the phone, quite stunned. I'd meant it when I said I wanted to get away from all that—not only from teaching but from the old preoccupations. Too much despair, too many deaths. Besides, a new literature was being born, post-AIDS, coming from the generation after me. Did I really have anything to say about it?

Daniel Boone was standing in front of me. Where did these people get their clothes? Maybe I could expand the antique-clothing department in my shop. ("Care to see something in a designer deerslayer, sir?")

Daniel Boone's name was Nicolas Hillebrant. He was seriously handsome, powerfully built. "Question, sir." Greenish eyes played over me, calmly judging.

"Have a seat, Nicolas. We'll have questions later."

He didn't stir. He was beyond taking orders from teachers. "I have no money for books. I hope they won't be required."

"We'll discuss that in a few minutes, if you don't mind."

Nicolas turned at last, looking disgusted, and sat down next to Cornelius. They were friends, apparently. I felt an old vulnerability stab against me—if I wasn't careful I'd give them too much attention, work for their approval, even flirt with them. My palms started to sweat. There were unexpected pitfalls in teaching a gay class.

The rest of the students straggled in. There were two more women—Millie Herkimer and Teage Dane—looking butch and paired, in short hair, work shirts, slacks. There was Israel Solomon, an elderly man with a pouter-pigeon figure and clouds of cottony hair. He took the front seat eagerly—a red-hot, as we used to say back in grad school. The remaining two—William Astbury and Bradford Gower—were pale youths, no more than twenty, both afflicted with shyness. They slunk, more or less, to the back seats.

I waited for more latecomers. Eight pairs of eyes studied me. Not friendly, not unfriendly, just waiting. Maybe the sweetness would come later, I thought.

I began the introduction as planned. Michael Littman, formerly of New York, now of Livingston. Please call me Michael. I had never given a course like this. I owned the Den of Antiquity on Route 22. We would explore together. I would need their help. We would be reading and discussing selections from several thousand years of gay and lesbian literature.

I paused for questions. Nicolas Hillebrand spoke up. "I have no money for books, Michael. Neither does he." He jerked his head at Cornelius. A few others murmured in agreement.

"I'll either circulate my own books, borrow extra copies, or make Xeroxes. You won't have to buy anything."

A little relaxation—legs spread forward, sighs released, glances exchanged. It had been a problem for everyone. "Let's talk about the material," I began. "Also what period interests you—classical, medieval, nineteenth century, modern." I paused. "I'd like to make the course as democratic as possible."

Cornelius Graef spoke up. "Did any of them write about war, comrades in war, that stuff?"

I mentioned Whitman and the Civil War diaries, *Billy Budd,* then worked up to *Amis and Amile* and the Theban Band. Cornelius's face lit up. "You gonna give us all them?" He smiled at Nicolas. *They're lovers,* I thought.

Millie Herkimer, the older of the two butch women, asked if there were stories about women living in the countryside. At first I could think only of May Sarton, then recalled *Patience and Sarah*. I sketched the tale, and her eyes glittered.

Gradually, everyone spoke up. Their interests were varied. The Bible, Oscar Wilde, Sappho, South Sea natives. The women liked poetry; the men wanted true stories. Only Israel Solomon was interested in political essays.

At last, when we had more or less settled on the shape of the course, which would meet once a week for twelve weeks, I asked them why they had signed up. Their reasons tended to be vague. Indeed, many of their comments were bewildering.

"People around here won't talk." Emilia Quinn shifted her bulk in the ridiculous child's seat. "Pretend they didn't hear you and clam up if they do."

William Astbury in the back spoke up. "We hear things've changed, but you'd never know it in the valley. They keep us in the dark."

I wondered who was keeping whom in the dark, but I said nothing. Millie Herkimer took her girlfriend's hand. "We want to borrow some of that pride."

We broke up early. Israel Solomon walked me out to my car, informing me that he hadn't sat in a classroom for forty years, had run the apothecary shop in Livingston all his life, and was now retired. The shop, he said, had been founded by his grandfather. Israel had modernized the place but finally sold out to August Hardwick, the present owner.

He hesitated, shuffled, leaned into the car after I got in. He wanted to tell me something else but couldn't quite manage. Well, there'd be plenty of time. I'd probably hear everyone's story before we were done.

As I drove off I saw them all standing in a knot by the road in the front of the building. When I waved, eight hands shot up. A surge of hope and, yes, sweetness barreled across the space. A ball formed in my throat. There were pitfalls, but there were pleasures too.

During the following week, I looked up every time my shop bell jangled, hoping it would be a student, but no one showed. In fact, the bell barely rang. My one sale consisted of a pine blanket chest, the milk-based paint still intact, which brought $135 from a New York dealer.

Only one event reminded me of my class—near Putnamville I saw a sign pointing to the Herkimer School. Ray Stonington informed me it was a home for problem kids—part reform school, part psychiatric hostel. No doubt a member of Millie's family was involved in some way.

The following Thursday six Bibles were produced on my instruction—most of them small, old, and giving off musty smells. We started on Genesis 19, which most of them knew. After we got through with the fire and brimstone, I started on some of the new theories. The sin of Sodom might be inhospitality to strangers. "That we may know them" could be interpreted in many ways. The dogma of several thousand years was being questioned nowadays.

They hardly stirred as I spoke, their eyes wide. When I finished, Israel raised his hand. "They taught us if a man lieth with another man as a woman, that's an abomination."

Cornelius sputtered. "That's just a slander."

"There are no Sodomites," Nicolas chimed in. "There never were."

"We need new words then," Teage Dane said.

"Let's call ourselves squinchies and frimsters." It was Bradford Gower in the back row. Everyone hooted.

By the time the discussion ended, we were one awareness, one crew aboard the good ship *Revision.* The notion of unlocking minds had lured me into teaching twenty years before, but I had never released excitement like this.

After class, everyone bustled into the hall with me, still throwing out ideas. Emilia Quinn took my arm—her eyes fiery, her hair damp across her forehead. "You should have come up here a long time ago, Michael. Everything would have been different."

"A lot of things had to happen first."

"Well, thank God they did." She squeezed my arm.

I left them, as before, in a knot in front of the building. I wondered if they would walk home. More than likely a van would pick them up. Livingston was loaded with vans.

As I drove home, I speculated about their living arrangements. The class chits hadn't listed home addresses, and we hadn't given any personal histories yet. A new thought struck me. Could there be a commune tucked in the hills around here, something left over from the sixties? That would explain the costumes, the occasional swap of odd decorations. It would also explain their ignorance. I pictured them reading *Godey's Lady's Book* and Mark Twain by kerosene lamp—an oddly gratifying image.

My thoughts moved on to the Herkimer School. Millie said her father's sister, her aunt Millicent, had started it as a seminary for young ladies. Millie didn't seem surprised when I told her about its conversion to a home for juveniles—her family had sold it years before. She only smiled when I said I was going to take on some of the school's antique fixtures on consignment. She said they should fetch a good price.

Now, turning into my own driveway, I was filled with contentment. I recalled my old habits, lying awake in the New York night, converting the screech of fire engines and ambulances into something more harmonious—the rattle of coaches, the echoes of past horns. Those fantasies always produced sleep. Now they were all around me—in my shop, the countryside, the classroom.

I unlocked the front door. I had just four rooms on one floor, not fully furnished yet, but I was more settled than I had ever been on Thirteenth Street. For a moment, coming in, I had the crazy notion that some of the original air from 1819 had been trapped under the floorboards and I was actually inside the last century. Then I laughed, fixed myself a drink, and flicked on the TV.

Nobody had bothered to read the *Symposium* clear through, despite the trouble I had gone to in Xeroxing it. In fact, nobody even brought a copy to class. When I asked why, they got fascinated with the dust on the floor and molding on the walls. At last Emilia Quinn spoke up. "We like to hear you preach, Michael."

"She means lecture." Nicolas laughed. "You do really fine at that."

I started on responsibility, the contract between student and teacher, then decided to can it. If they didn't want to read then I'd preach. They must have seen the surrender in my face, because they settled back, grinning.

By the time I got to my favorite passage, everyone was paying close attention. "For they love not boy, but intelligent beings," I read from the Jewish translation, "whose reason is beginning to be developed, much about the time at which their beards begin to grow. And in choosing young men to be their companions, they mean to be faithful to them and pass their whole life in company with them, not to take them in their inexperience and deceive them . . . and observe that open loves are held to be more honorable than secret ones, and how great is the encouragement which all the world gives to the lover."

A pause. The words, so simple and so radical, did their work. I could feel a chunk of the twentieth century breaking off and dissolving.

"That's very interesting, yes." Israel Solomon was mashed down, quivering, in his seat. He half turned around. "Some of you remember David . . . David Whitmore." He looked up at me again, breathing hard. "He was just that, my companion for life. But he didn't realize it." A strange sound came from his chest. "I'm not sure I did either."

I put down the Plato. Here it was.

Israel and David had been classmates in Albany, both studying pharmacology. Then they had worked together in the drugstore founded by the first Mr. Solomon. But in a long lifetime Israel had never told his friend how he felt. "There was once," he said, "when David was sick—meningitis, very common in those days—when I almost did tell him. I thought it was my last chance. But his wife came in, and I lost my nerve." Israel studied his hands for a minute. "If I'd known about Plato, I could have quoted him. It would have made everything, well, respectable."

He closed down. Heavy, unsaid things washed around the room. I let the silence lengthen. Wasn't this why we'd come together—to know our history, to make sure it didn't happen again?

At last Emilia spoke softly. "It's never too late to mend things, Israel."

He didn't reply. There was a scuffling of feet. Time to move on, I thought. Nothing can be changed, only corrected in the mind.

Israel came up after class and finished the story. David Whitmore hadn't died of meningitis but of a fall two years later while climbing Overlook Mountain. "I had a second chance," he concluded, "but I didn't have the nerve then either. I sold the pharmacy. I didn't want to work if David wasn't there."

I patted him lightly, resisting the urge to hug him. There's nothing wrong with hugging, but it can't undo a lifetime of secrecy. "Try reading the Xerox," I said as I got into my car. "It'll help." He looked pleased and dubious at the same time. How could Plato help, really?

The drive to the Herkimer School took me through the center of my town. Downtown Livingston is only a few blocks long, but it offers all your basic services. I was interested in some extra-strength Tylenol. Last night had not been one of my better nights—due more to financial worries than Israel's history, however. The drugstore—now the Livingston Rexall—had been established in 1912, according to the script on the window. I stepped back to check out the brick building. I wasn't surprised to see a familiar name stamped on the iron plate just under the eave . . . *Solomon*. And below it, 1868.

A middle-aged man in a pharmacist's jacket sold me the pills. "Mr. Hardwick?" I asked.

"That's me, John Hardwick."

I introduced myself. He had heard about the Den of Antiquity. He was glad to make my acquaintance. I started to tell him that I knew Israel Solomon, grandson of the Solomon upstairs, then checked myself. Hardwick might ask how we met. It wasn't my job to yank Israel out of his hometown closet. I thanked him for the Tylenol and left, with a final glance at the plaque up top.

The Herkimer School was a rambling building in the Dutch style. Now it showed signs of abuse—torn screens, tarpaper patches, dying shrubs. It was as mismanaged as the lives of the boys within, I thought. The manager, an Irishman named Scully, with a varicosed face and a slight limp, turned me over to the caretaker. As we descended to the basement of the building it occurred to me that my antique hunting always took me to places where people no longer lived.

The gem of the collection was a pewter chandelier, eight branched, in good condition. I put the date at 1780 to 1790. There were also some light fixtures—tulips of amber glass, three to a stem, with rotten wiring, and an imitation Tiffany lamp. Not a bad haul, I thought as we lugged the stuff upstairs.

I was waiting for the manager to reappear to sign the consignment papers when I noticed the founder's plaque to one side of the front door. *The Herkimer Institute for Young Ladies,* read the florid script—an incongruous touch, considering the male adolescent snarls coming from upstairs. The first name on the plaque was faint, oxidized, but I managed to make it out—*Millicent Herkimer, Headmistress.* I pictured her as a tall maiden with a spine like a ruler and an immutable sense of right and wrong. Nothing like her confused niece. My eye ran down the names of the original faculty—each introduced with a cursive *Miss*—but I was interrupted by Mr. Scully. We chatted about the fixtures, my job being to keep his expectations low. Most people who consign antiques think they'll make a killing.

Again that night I had trouble getting to sleep, but not because of financial worry. I had convinced myself by bedtime that it was unrealistic to expect a shop to turn a profit the first year. Something else was tugging at a corner of my mind. Finally it let go of me, and I drifted off.

The class began to go more smoothly, although their reading was patchy. I had the impression that one of the women—Emilia or Millie—read the text and did summaries for the others. We progressed from the Greek poets to the medieval ones, from Michelangelo to

Shakespeare to Byron and Edward Carpenter. We managed Emily Dickinson, Radclyffe Hall, Djuna Barnes, and Gertrude Stein.

It was hard to catch them at their goofing off. At least one member of the class was always up on the homework. Sometimes I caught references to materials not under discussion, which made me wonder if their reading was wider than they let on.

But one night, when it was apparent that Teage Dane had read the Willa Cather story and everyone was taking their cues from her, I recalled my commune theory. "Do you all live together or something?"

Cornelius, usually so guileless-looking, coughed and turned away. Nicolas filled in. "We've known each other a long time."

"It's not a commune, is it?"

Emilia stared at me hard. "How did you know?"

I tried not to sound pleased. "It wasn't that hard. The clothes, the way you always leave together, somebody does the coaching for the next class. Where is it?"

"Just off Sisleytown Road," she replied.

I paused, expecting an invitation to visit. A slight unease swept through the room. "What do you grow?" I asked finally.

William Astbury piped up. "Timothy, sorghum, alfalfa, bluegrass." He laughed briefly. "Plus a lot of weeds."

"You sell it to the dairy farms around here?"

He nodded. "Or they pasture right on our land, though it's against the bylaws."

Well, that explained it. It might explain some other things too—their insularity, their timidity. "Don't you miss traveling, seeing the cities?"

Millie Herkimer replied in a reproving voice. "Americans are one thing today and another thing tomorrow. We prefer a settled life in one place."

Who was I to blame them? Hadn't I taken refuge in the past, which was a community of sorts? The room was quiet. They were waiting, slightly embarrassed. I got the clear message that the urge to include me in their lives had been neutralized by something else. Were they growing a secret cash crop on that land of theirs? They wouldn't be the first around here. Well, I might or might not find out eventually.

In the meantime, "Paul's Case" by Willa Cather was waiting. They took a dim view of Paul's suicide, once they heard about it.

Little by little, as the weeks went by, their stories came out. I kicked things off with my own. I told them about teaching in New York, my increasingly desperate search for a lover until, ten years before, when I was thirty-three, I met Tom Ritenour at a bar in Greenwich Village. They listened as I told about setting up house, our five years of fidelity, the difficult "open relationship" that followed, Tom's illness and death.

After this had been absorbed, Millie had a comment. "Maybe if you'd lived in the country, you could have been more content with each other." She glanced at her friend Teage. "Not so many temptations."

"Maybe so." I agreed. It was a moot point, and it didn't matter anymore.

Emilia Quinn weighed in next. She had lived with her mother. They took in summer guests—city people mostly. "So, you see, Michael," she scolded, "we weren't as isolated as you like to think." She had a lover, a woman neighbor who managed her own farm and raised her children alone. But it had been difficult—not only the fear of gossip but the presence of the children and the elder Mrs. Quinn. At last her lover's farm had failed, the furnishing auctioned off, the place repossessed, and the woman herself committed to the state hospital at Wingdale.

"Our difficulty," Emilia said finally, brushing the tangle of dark hair from her eyes, "was fear. They were all lined up against us. We didn't know there had been others before, just like us."

I got a bright idea. "Why don't you bring your friend to class next week? If she can get a day release?" Emilia looked shocked. "She might learn something, feel better about herself."

Emilia took a deep breath. "It's too late for that, Michael." There was so much death in her voice I let the matter drop. Everyone else chimed in to cover my stupidity.

It was the week we were doing *Maurice,* near the end of the course, that Nicolas, looking mischievous, produced a photo. He waved it around. "Recognize him?" I had no trouble. It was a sepia print, mounted on cardboard, of Cornelius Graef. Cornelius, a bewildered eighteen, was posed in a fake Civil War uniform, with a fake musket in his hand. I turned the photograph over: "W. A. Reed, Artistic Photographer, Copying a Specialty, Negatives Preserved."

Nicolas let out a teasing chuckle. "We took it in Rensselaer one afternoon. There's a photographer who lets you strike old poses."

I gave the photo back. Nicolas kissed the bewildered young face. "I think he's embarrassed," he said.

Cornelius sank down in the seat, pulling his cap—maybe the same one—over his face.

"Try to think of Plato," Israel remarked. "An open love is more honorable than a secret one."

"Shove off, Israel."

"If Plato is beyond your grasp," Israel went on, "try to think about Edward Carpenter and George Merrill. Or Gertrude Stein and Alice Toklas. Or Maurice and . . . what's his name."

Millie Herkimer clucked. "Cornelius, you always were a bad sport."

"Yeah?" The cap came off. "Why don't you tell us your happy story, Millie?"

Millie flushed and turned away. But everyone was waiting.

"I was a teacher until a few years ago," she began.

"Like your Aunt Millicent," I added.

She nodded. "A family weakness. But at school I met another teacher who forced me to face certain things." She reached over and touched Teage's hand. "I wasn't made for marriage, children, all that. It was my antagonism toward the opposite sex." She smiled apologetically. "Toward some of them anyway. We . . . this other teacher and I . . . wrote several letters. The letters were discovered, we were both discharged." She paused. "So here we are, trying to understand what happened."

"The heterosexual dictatorship," Bradford Gower remarked. He had become quite fond of that phrase.

"Also the male dictatorship," Millie amended. "They often go together."

Nobody disputed that.

We broke early that evening. *Maurice,* for all its Edwardian passion, had paled beside the pain in the classroom.

When the final session rolled around, we were deep in December. The fields were rusty, the trees like frozen bolts of lightning. We had all pulled closer, huddling around the lives we discussed, drawing warmth from old passions. I hoped I had given them more than literature, though—courage maybe, or freedom. I asked for comments, suggestions, evaluations. But for some reason the old reserve was back tonight. The course had been "interesting," "informative." My suggestion that we all repair to the Maverick Inn for a last drink was met with an embarrassed shuffle. Finally, irritated, I asked point-blank what they'd gotten out of the course.

Bradford Gower broke the silence. "Now I won't be ashamed if people call me names." A nod from William Astbury. "We won't run away."

Emilia spoke next. "You've given us ammunition, Michael."

"Pride too, I hope."

Cornelius started to speak. I could feel the words forming, wild thing under the moon, but he beat them back. Pride wasn't in his vocabulary—at least not yet—but at least he had tried.

When the class ended, each student filed forward to shake my hand. Teage Dane kissed my cheek, then pressed a few strawflowers into my hand—dry and lavender. I laughed and thanked her.

Outside they huddled against the cold, knotted up as usual, as I struggled with my ignition. I let the engine warm up as we traded a last long look. I was full of sadness. We would never be a group again, never merge into a whole, examining prejudice, hunting justice. We might run into each other at fairs or auctions, but we'd never be a family again. It is the nature of every enterprise, I reminded myself, and might stand for the impermanence of all human connection. Still, as I drove off with a final wave, I felt a lash of the old rage. Why must all meetings end in parting? This was another, muted version of Tom's death. Good-bye, I thought, is the saddest word in the language.

I was due at Ray Stonington's for dinner the next night—a small celebration to mark the end of the course, he'd said. I was grateful even if the students had vetoed the idea of a party, Ray had come through. I really didn't want to be alone, not even inside my favorite year, 1819.

I drove carefully into Ray's driveway—he'd just put in more bluestone. Maybe, I thought, heading up the walk, I'd give the course again. Do it better the next time—different selections, sharper commentary. But luckily, I spotted this as a fantasy, a bad habit from the old days. Courses often got worse rather than better. And these students, for all their quirkiness, had given all they had to give. I had no complaints.

Ray had other guests: a young stage designer visiting for the week; the real estate agent who had sold Ray his house; an assertive middle-aged woman named Jane Snow, who was helping Ray plan a garden of eighteenth-century produce—not an appetizing idea, I thought, unless you like gourds.

We talked a little about my course. Ray had filled them in before I arrived. "You were right," I said to Ray at some point. "They were sweet country people. But it was harder to get to know them than I thought."

"That's often the way." Ray removed his glasses and rubbed one eye. "But once you know one another, it's for life."

I laughed. "I hope so."

It was a typical evening at Ray's—good food, good company, and everybody had to wear a lady's hat to dinner. "That's a Lilu Dache,"

Ray said approvingly when I chose a snappy little number in black velvet with an eye veil. "It would have cost you a fortune in 1940."

We were still at the table, lingering over coffee, when Ray passed around his latest treasure, found in a box of miscellanea purchased at auction. It was a photo of his own house before the north wing had been added. "I can date it quite easily," he said. "About 1895. They'd already cleared the land for the new wing."

It was sepia, with a familiar border. Something stirred in me and I turned it over. "W. A. Reed, Artistic Photographer, Copying a Specialty . . ." and the street address in Rensselaer.

I let out a whoop. "One of my students just had his picture taken there."

Ray looked disapproving. "Somebody's pulling your leg, Michael. That place closed fifty years ago. There's a Burger King there now."

The next instant a shudder went through me, and the knowledge uncoiled from the place it had been waiting. Teage Dane's name was on the founder's plaque at the Herkimer School. I had seen but not seen. Israel Solomon had sold his store to the Hardwick family in 1912, the year his friend David died. The farm woman at the state hospital couldn't visit our class because she was no longer there. Cornelius Graef had been snapped in a studio by a photographer in the style of the day.

I tried to pay attention after that, but it was difficult. My head was buzzing, and my palms were wet. I left as soon as I could, apologizing for my behavior. "That's okay, Michael," Ray said at the door. "We know you teachers are hopeless when you lose your precious students."

I drove the little car as fast as it would go. A half-moon was climbing as I parked on the shoulder of Sisleytown Road. Luckily, the stones faced west. I'd be able to read them.

It took me a while, but I finally came to the last row. I had collected them all, every one. "Okay," I said aloud, the wind whipping my voice, "why didn't you tell me?"

I walked back to Cornelius's grave, then ran my hand over the granite marker, touching the dates. All except Emilia and Israel had died young. Why? Suddenly, I knew—and also knew why they disapproved so harshly of Willa Cather's Paul.

Snow began to drift down. *They died of the plague,* I thought, and the plague was ignorance. Maybe that was the worst of all, because it brings darkness to a living soul.

Snow settled into my collar. I hunched down, into myself, as far as I could go.

But they had overcome it, because all plagues end sooner or later. There's no telling how or when, but they end.

It was too cold to stay out now. I turned and walked back to the car. The moon shone through the brightness, illuminating the stones. I got in, started the engine, and drove home, thinking about the course I would give next time.

The Morning After

Therese Szymanski

And now I lay me down to sleep,
I pray the Lord my soul to keep
And if I die before I wake,
I pray the Lord my soul to take.

Lee Becker cursed as the TV flickered off and then on again, as did the lights and stereo. She turned off the electronics before more permanent damage could be done, but left a light on so she'd know when the power came back on.

She used her hands like a blind person to feel around the room, searching for the candle she knew was on the cluttered bookshelf. The one good thing about being a smoker was that she at least knew where her lighter was.

She found the vanilla-scented candle, lit it, and went in search of a flashlight. She really wasn't surprised that the power had gone out, and she should've been prepared for it, but she wasn't. It had been storming, complete with thunder and lightning, since before she left work at five, and she did live in a remote old house several miles north of Ann Arbor, which was itself not exactly a metropolis by any standard.

Usually she enjoyed the fact that she had no close neighbors, but tonight, looking out at the darkness from the darkness, it gave her the creeps to see absolutely no lights, to be so alone.

There was no one to hear her if she screamed.

She wished she had neighbors she could invite over to tell ghost stories with. The thunder, lightning, and darkness were totally conducive to such a situation, but she had no neighbors. Having grown up in the Detroit metro area, she had really looked forward to getting a house where she'd have space and privacy. She had loved the old farmhouse since the first moment she had first seen it, but the darkness and remoteness did little to soothe her on this night.

She found her flashlight (she had known all along that there was a spare in her car if she needed it), and had two candles lit, but still she had to keep reminding herself that nothing would come out from under the bed, or couch, or closet to get her.

She had to keep reminding herself that she was butch and that butches don't get the creeps, didn't worry about creepy crawlies and bad guys hiding in dark places during the night. They didn't worry that something was going to come out of their dreams and kill them. They knew nightmares weren't real.

Why did she ever decide to rent so many horror movies? She had been in the mood. It had been a long week at work and she just wanted to come home and crash in front of the TV and veg for a while. She wanted to forget everything, and had simply been drawn to the horror section in the video store. She loved the adrenaline rush such movies gave her.

A flash of lightning lit the house, making Lee look around, wondering if all the figures she saw belonged there, if everything she saw was merely furniture and stuff, or if there really was someone else in the house with her. She thought she heard breathing. Someone else's breathing. Someone else in the house with her.

The burst of thunder that followed, rocking the old structure down to its core, did nothing to help her mood. She couldn't feel any strange movements or creaks if the house was being rocked. She wouldn't be able to feel anything that was wrong. The noise covered any other noises, any other people.

It was a spooky night, and now Lee had demons and men with knives for fingers running through her mind. She was afraid to sleep, lest something get her while she slept—either through her dreams, or some madman breaking into her house.

Why had she ever bought such a big, remote house to begin with? She really didn't need all this room . . . all this empty space. All her possessions still couldn't fill the void. All they did was make her feel even more alone.

There was a movement in the corner and Lee jerked in fright.

The candles flickering did nothing for her mood. They only gave more shadows to the space. There was a sudden deep gong, followed by another, and another. . . . Her old grandfather clock chiming midnight. The stroke of midnight. The witching hour. When all bad things happened.

Her last lover had died at midnight two years before. Exactly two years before. The stroke of midnight on Valentine's Day. Her car had crashed off a bridge in the city that Lee had run from. Carrie had drowned in that car. Lee wanted the city and all its evils behind her now.

There was really no one she could call at this hour. What would she say anyway? I'm scared? It's dark, inside and out, and the candles, the flashlights, just make it scarier? I miss Carrie. Why did she ever have to die and leave me all alone?

She should just take something and go to bed. She really knew she'd be perfectly safe, totally fine, and all she needed to do was sleep so that she could awaken in the morning with the electricity back on and the sun shining, and the world would be back to normal. Everything would be fine then. She'd be safe. And she'd take all the horror movies back to the video store and rent some nice, friendly, romantic comedies.

But she didn't want to sleep.

Actually, she was afraid to sleep. She couldn't sleep. The monster under the bed might get her then, no matter how ludicrous it sounded.

But there were no monsters, no demons, no ghosts, no weird noises in the night that came to get you. Lee lived in a safe, rational world and knew that her own worst enemy was her mind, her imagination. Everything bad that she thought might happen, worried about, was simply a product of her mind.

She grabbed her feather comforter and pillows from the couch, picked up the flashlight, pocketed the spare, small flashlight, and blew out the candles. She made her way slowly, carefully, toward the steep staircase, glancing all around her each step of the way.

Everything was in its place and there was nothing extra, no shadows that should not be there. Except for the storm raging outside, it was a totally normal night. There was nothing strange going on. Carrie had always taught her to be careful about security, and although so many people in this area didn't lock doors, didn't watch for strangers lurking about, Lee had been raised in a suburb of Detroit and did such things without thinking about them. They just came naturally, especially tonight.

Okay, fine, her lover had died, drowned, two years ago, and maybe she watched horror movies tonight because she wanted to think that there were worse horrors than that—even thought Carrie and she had only been together for a year before the shooting . . .

Lee entered the bedroom. She stopped. She threw her pillows and comforter onto the bed from across the room. She shone the flashlight down, as far under the bed as she could, ensuring there was no one there, and then jumped onto the bed, fully clothed.

She lay back and realized just how ridiculous this all was. She reached down, unzipped her jeans, and slid them off her body. She threw them toward the chair on the other side of the room . . .

. . . and saw Carrie's white face staring up at her from her coffin. The eyes were closed, but . . .

She covered herself with the comforter, pulling it up over her head, hiding herself from the world, praying for sleep to come quickly, to hide her from everything . . .

And another rumble of thunder burst through the night, again rocking the house. Lee tried to bury herself further from reality, but she thought she heard something . . . something different.

The thunder collapsed under itself, dying out, and the house was still. But that same sound came again . . .

A knocking. A distant knocking.

There was nothing horrible about a knocking.

And then Lee realized that her doorbell wouldn't be working and anyone who came to her door would have to knock, and that was what she was hearing—someone knocking at her door.

At least that's what she thought she heard—someone knocking at her door. She sat up, found her flashlight, turned it on and looked around the room. Everything was in its place. Everything was normal.

The knocking came again. Who would be knocking at her door, in the middle of nowhere, in the midst of such a terrible storm?

Lee sat up in bed, then stood on it and leapt from it, so that she would land a few feet away from the bed. She knew it was ludicrous, but the scary boogeyman under the bed couldn't grab her if she didn't give him the chance, now could he? She grabbed her jeans and pulled them on. Barefoot, she went downstairs, carefully looking around while she made her way down, watchful for anything out of the ordinary. At the front door she peered out and saw darkness. Then she made out the shivering woman standing in the darkness on her porch, knocking.

Actually the woman looked harmless, femme, small, cold, and wet. Lee opened the door.

"I'm so sorry to wake you," the woman said, "but my car broke down on the road, and you were the first house I came to."

She wore only leather boots, jeans, and a blouse, she was soaked down to her skin, with her long, dark hair matted to her head.

"You're soaked," Lee said.

"It's pouring," the woman said.

"I'm sorry; come in," Lee replied, stepping aside.

The woman hesitantly stepped into the house. "Thank you," she said, shivering. "I don't know how far I had to walk, but I was praying somebody was home here."

"We need to get you warmed up or else you'll get pneumonia," Lee said, realizing she sounded like her own mother. "You're freezing."

"Dry clothes and somewhere warm to sleep sound like heaven," the woman admitted.

Lee led her into the great room where she had been watching TV earlier, making sure she closed and locked the door behind her. She was actually grateful to have someone interrupt her evening, for she was sure she would not be able to sleep alone tonight. "If you take off those clothes I'll put them into the dryer and find you something to wear." Her washer and dryer ran on gas.

The woman hesitated. "I hate to do this to you . . ."

"I'm having a bad night, actually," Lee admitted. She looked down at the floor. "I'm actually thankful for the company. Just give me a minute and I'll find you a robe." She relit the candles and went up-stairs.

When she returned from the bedroom with a robe and towel, the woman had lit a fire.

"I hope you don't mind," she said, looking toward Lee, "but I saw this wood and . . ."

"I love a good fire. I'm just not very good at making them myself." She proffered the robe and turned away, trying not to listen to the sounds of this attractive woman taking off her clothes. Getting naked. "I haven't been living here very long, you see, and I never had a fire-place before."

"I'm all done now," the woman said.

Lee turned around and accepted the soaked clothes from her. "Make yourself comfortable," she said. "I'll just toss these into the dryer." She indicated the far wall. "There's a bar over there with cognac and wine, if you'd like something to warm yourself up."

"Would you like anything?"

"Whatever you're having."

When Lee returned, the strange woman had poured them both glasses of cognac and had also found the afghan Lee's grandmother had made, to pull up over herself as she sat in front of the fire.

"I hope you don't mind," she said. "I'm just so very cold."

Lee looked down at her, sitting in her robe, covered with the afghan in front of the fire, and felt a stirring of arousal. She was actually quite beautiful when she started to dry off. Well, she had been beautiful soaked to the skin, but now she was even more stunning. "Not at all. As I said, I'm happy for the company. For some stupid reason I was watching horror movies tonight before the power went out."

"Oh, God, what were you watching?"

"*The Exorcist, Village of the Damned,* and a coupla Freddy movies," Lee said, accepting the cognac from the woman.

"Oh, shit, why were you doing that?" The woman indicated that Lee should sit next to her in front of the fire.

"Stupidity, I guess."

"I'm sorry, you're being so kind to me and I'm being awful rude. My name's Melissa. Melissa Rothchild."

"Well, Miss Melissa Rothchild, I'm Lee Becker. It is Miss, isn't it?" Lee was bold; she took Melissa's left hand and looked at the ring finger.

"Yes, it is," Melissa said, leaving her hand in Lee's and looking up into Lee's eyes. Her gaze was mesmerizing.

"You know, earlier tonight when the power first went out, I was wishing I had neighbors I could invite over to tell ghost stories with."

"Ghost stories can be fun, with the right people. I'm not usually one for scary movies myself, though."

"Usually?" Lee was getting vibes from this woman. In front of the fire she could now tell that her hair was a dark brown, as were her eyes. Her long hair, now that it wasn't soaked, was also rather wavy.

Her body, even hidden as it was by Lee's robe, was slender but well-defined, blossoming in all the right places. She was very much a woman, all woman.

Earlier Lee had thought it might be fun to just lie back and masturbate, but you can't exactly jerk yourself off to a scary movie, and she really hadn't been in much of a mood for sex since Carrie died. She had begun to feel she was dead below the waist.

But now she wanted to kiss this woman who had come to save her during such a dark night.

"Horror movies are scary," Melissa was saying, "and I don't usually think of fear as a positive emotion. But they can fulfill some weird urge." She looked directly at Lee, taking a sip of her cognac. "And if you've got a good shoulder to hide in, they can be quite another experience altogether."

Lee didn't break the connection with Melissa. "What sort of experience?"

"There's a connection when you see a scary flick with a good butch. When she's there to protect you." She looked deep into Lee, as if seeing whether or not she was right.

"Well, you know, that's part of our duty, part of what we give in return for you not letting us go out of the house in plaids and stripes simultaneously. We give you a good shoulder, and we promise to check the locks, look through the house, and look under the bed when you hear something in the night. And we also promise to never be scared."

"So you need a femme around so you won't be scared."

Suddenly the darkness was no longer fearsome; instead, it gave the firelight greater richness when it touched Melissa's beautiful face. Lee had once heard that looking at someone's lips made them want to kiss you, and she was sure Melissa was looking at her lips. She knew she wanted to kiss Melissa, wanted to kiss her like no other woman since Carrie.

"Happy Valentine's Day," Melissa said, still looking at Lee's lips and eyes, somehow simultaneously.

"My lover died two years ago today," Lee said, leaning closer toward Melissa.

"I know," Melissa said, closing the gap, her lips meeting Lee's.

Her lips were so soft, her tongue so gentle yet so demanding. Melissa was soft, yet not. She was a true femme.

Suddenly it hit Lee. "How do you know?"

"It's more than scary movies that have you freaked out tonight." She lay back, covering them both with the afghan as she pulled Lee down on top of her.

Lee had never been one to do one-night stands, and that's what this felt like it might be. In thirty-five years Lee had only ever done one, and had felt so badly after that she promised she'd never do another again.

"My boyfriend was going to propose to me tonight."

"What?" Lee asked, pulling away, looking down at Melissa.

"My boyfriend was going to propose to me tonight," Melissa repeated, looking forlornly at Lee. She swallowed. "He's been waiting for Valentine's Day, thinking of the romance. And I've been fearing it, because I know how wrong it is."

Lee sat up. "I'm sorry . . ."

"Don't be sorry! I've been playing this game, knowing how I am and that it isn't right, but it's easy."

"So I'm just the woman in the night . . ."

"Lee." Melissa sat up, taking Lee's face in her hands. "From the first moment you opened that door . . . You let me in . . ." She placed her hands, with their elegantly long fingers tipped with long red nails, on

Lee's biceps, "you're strong. I look at you and know you can keep anything bad away. I know I can depend on you. Can trust you."

"So I'm an experiment. You're curious."

Melissa grabbed her again. Lee wasn't accustomed to anyone she wasn't lovers with touching her so intimately, so assuredly. "I'm not experimenting. I know what I want. And I know I want you. Do you believe in fate? Destiny?"

Lee looked at her, feeling the heat of her stare, of her touch, as if it was burning her. She hadn't felt so alive in two years.

"Why else would I be driving along, knowing what Greg was going to ask me, and then break down so close to your house? Why else would I pound on a stranger's door in the middle of the night? We're all just players in this divine comedy. We do what we need to, what we have to."

Lee had been an English major. She had once had a dog named Dante. She might've well called him the Bard.

"Right now I need to make love with you."

Lee hadn't been so turned on in two years. She hadn't needed to make love in all that time. To hold someone, touch someone, kiss someone, wake up with someone. But Melissa was so near, so close and . . . she wanted Lee so much. She was seducing Lee with her words, and what could Lee say? No? No, I won't take you because you've never been with a woman? Because I'm afraid of falling in love with you after just one night? Because I'm afraid of ever loving again? I can't love again because you might leave me as well? Leave me like Carrie and my mother and my father and my brother did? The creatures of the night might come and swallow you as well? I can't take you to bed, have sex with you, make love with you—I'd rather lie alone and in fear, in loneliness, because I'm too scared of anything else?

"Lee?"

Lee reached out to run her fingers through Melissa's silky hair.

Melissa took her hand and kissed the palm. "Moments are taken, moments are lost. A moment's difference and all the difference is made." Her eyes were so dark when they looked into Lee's. "Life is to be lived. Experienced. Enjoyed. You've been hiding yourself ever since Carrie's death."

"No, I just can't . . ."

"Be courageous enough? Trust again?" She ran her hand down the side of Lee's face, caressing her. Her voice was like velvet. "We both know you want to spend the night with me."

Lee closed her eyes. She could feel inside of Melissa. She wanted to be inside Melissa. Take her. Taste her. She kissed Melissa's soft hand, took it into hers, and began to make love to it.

Melissa brought her other hand up to caress Lee's hair and face. "It was a dark and stormy night and . . . life happened. Love happened."

It was a place out of space and time. It was a dream. A beautiful, soft dream.

Lee laid Melissa back onto the bear rug. She slowly opened her robe, exposing the creamy white skin underneath. She looked into Melissa's eyes and saw both surety and unsurety there. She had been so cocky a moment before, deliberately trying to seduce Lee . . . but now she was a scared woman, not knowing what the future held.

"Beautiful locket," Lee said, studying the jewelry that lay bewitchingly between Melissa's breasts. She opened it up and found a man and a woman staring back at her.

"My grandfather and my grandmother," Melissa said. "The locket belonged to my grandmother. She gave it to me on her deathbed."

"It's beautiful," Lee said, closing it and laying it back upon Melissa's breast. It made Melissa seem all the more naked—wearing only the locket.

"Lee. I want you to make love to me." She breathed deeply. She pushed her robe the rest of the way open, exposing herself in the light of the fire.

Lee looked down her body, seeing the full breasts with their pert pink nipples, the flat stomach, the way her legs opened just around the patch of dark hair . . .

She ran her hands over Melissa's body, feeling her, enjoying the softness of her skin, enjoying the reactions throughout Melissa, the way she moaned and writhed with each stroke. Resting her weight on one arm, Lee let the other hand have free range with Melissa, knowing that this was a moment out of time.

Her fingertips ran from the smooth edge of Melissa's collarbone, studying its curve, its sensuous nature, the way it jutted forth like a shelf from Melissa's body. Her hand slowly worked down between Melissa's breasts, moving to feel one extended nipple against her palm, then the other.

Melissa groaned and arched up to meet her hand, pushing her breasts up to Lee, toward Lee, giving herself to Lee. Lee cupped one in her hand and leaned down to take the other in her mouth, gently sucking at it with her mouth until she took the aroused nipple directly into her mouth, sucking it, flicking her tongue over it, taking it between her teeth, biting it while running her tongue over it, with increasing urgency . . .

She felt Melissa writhing under her touch. She bit down harder on the nipple and heard Melissa's groans urging her on. Melissa was responding, loving this. This was what she wanted.

Lee ran her hand down to caress Melissa's naked belly, the curve of it, and down further to feel the thatch of hair between her legs. Her fingers toyed with that hair.

"Please, Lee, please . . ."

Lee went down farther with her hand, her mouth still suckling, teasing, Melissa's breast. Her hand stroked the hair, delving into it . . .

She gasped. Melissa was so wet . . . she wanted Lee, wanted her so badly . . . Lee could feel it within herself.

She went deeper still within the thatch of hair, feeling the source of wetness. Melissa felt so good, so wet, so needy and wanting. She was twisting and writhing under Lee's every touch, every feel. Her legs were more and more open, giving herself more fully to Lee.

She wanted Lee inside of her.

Lee obliged.

She thrust a finger inside of Melissa, her mouth working down over her belly, down to her wet center. . . . Melissa groaned and thrust, wanting more. Lee gave her two fingers, the digits sliding easily in and out of the woman.

Her mouth went down between her legs, her tongue finally tasting what it sought—Melissa.

Melissa bucked up, moaning, against Lee, who slipped a third finger into her. She was going to have this luscious woman. She didn't know if it was just for tonight or forever, but she wanted her now.

At this moment she loved Melissa, and it was a glorious moment, even if it was just a moment.

Somehow she knew this couldn't last.

She took Melissa fully into her mouth even as she plunged her entire fist up and into her. Melissa was hers for now, and Melissa was screaming and writhing about in ecstasy. . . . Lee worked her tongue up and down her, sucking at her cunt, eating her, taking her, groaning in ecstasy herself . . .

There was a connection between them, and Lee felt this electricity as she took Melissa, plunging her fist in and out of her. She had never before had a woman to whom she could do such a thing, whom she could take so fully . . .

Melissa spread her legs as wide as she could, inviting Lee as deeply as she could.

"Lee! Lee! Oh God, Lee!"

She tightened around Lee's fist, her body giving itself to Lee, bucking against Lee, and then she grabbed Lee's face, pulling her up, and kissed her deeply and totally.

She was crying when Lee pulled her into her arms, when Lee held her tightly.

"Thank you," she said. She lifted Lee's head from her bosom. "I wish I could spend eternity with you. We were meant to be together," she said, pulling Lee's head down to lie on her breast.

Lee gave it up. The warmth of Melissa's body, the patterns of the fire on their bodies, the thrill of the cognac in her veins, the smell of Melissa on her hand, all around them. She wanted her forever.

Lee rolled over. She wasn't in bed. She was alone. On the bear rug in the great room with the dying embers of a fire in front of her.

She thought of the night before, smiled and rolled over, looking for Melissa.

She wasn't there.

Lee wrapped her grandmother's afghan around her and stood up, looking around the barren room.

The furniture wasn't nearly so imposing as it had been in the darkness of the night before. Now sunlight streamed cheerfully through the front windows.

"Melissa?" she called out, but was greeted with only the echoes of an empty house.

She went to the laundry room, but apparently Melissa had already collected her clothing: The clothes were gone and Lee's robe was on the dryer along with the towel she had given Melissa.

Lee knew there was something she was forgetting, but the house was still. She glanced around for any note from Melissa, but found none.

The front door was unlocked. Melissa was probably from around here, so had thought nothing of leaving it unlocked. The only thing that was weird was the lack of a note.

So Lee had been so tired that morning that she didn't recall Melissa waking her up to say good-bye, to give her a kiss. She had the memories of last night to live on until she saw this incredible woman again, after all. She lifted her hand up to again smell Melissa on it. She smiled at the scent of her.

Lee knew Melissa would not marry her boyfriend. She couldn't, not after last night.

She went to her front door, opened it and collected the newspaper off the front porch. Being a big-city girl, she still subscribed to the *News/Free Press*.

She immediately looked for anything on the power outage of the past night, hoping that her small community rated high enough to make it to the paper. She was pleasantly surprised to find a special section on the power outage.

Apparently, over 100,000 people had been without power for some time the night before, and, as with any such outage, there were some fatalities. Lee slowly made her coffee with some difficulty. It was as if there was something wrong with her left arm, her left hand, because it wasn't working quite right. She ended up sitting down with the paper, glancing through the section on the outage, but something drew her to the listing in the obituaries:

> Melissa Rothchild, 28, died in a fatal car accident Friday night when her car apparently spun out of control on a bridge in Dexter at 12 a.m. She is survived by her parents, Gordon and Virginia Rothchild. Services will be held Tuesday at the Silvester Funeral Home in Troy.

Lee felt a burning in her left hand, the hand of the arm she had been unable to use today. She lifted the hand. The arm worked. She pulled it up to the table. It felt as if a leaden weight were holding it down. The burning grew more intense until finally Lee had to throw open the hand.

It held a silver locket.

She brought her right hand slowly to it, to open it.

And was faced with a picture of Melissa on the left side of it . . .

. . . and a picture of herself on the right side.

Sic Gloria Transit

Marshall Moore

When Julian Gray's mother first brought him home from the hospital, her own mother, Nadine, a rambling creature of thick ankles, mismatched eyes, and scarves that rustled with or without a breeze to inspire them, held the child in her arms and said, "He'll go far." Lisette Gray rolled her eyes and wondered if she could convince her mother to sit with baby Julian for an hour or so without anointing him with any oils more exotic than Johnson & Johnson. Long enough for Lisette to drink the tall cold gin and tonic she'd spent the last nine months looking forward to. Grandma Nadine muttered in French over the little boy, then closed her eyes, crossed herself, and handed him back to Lisette. Lisette could hear her husband Gordon filling the tub with hot water; she wanted a hot bath almost as much as she wanted that glass of gin. Down there, she still hurt from the delivery.

"He'll go places," the old woman said. She kissed Julian on his forehead. "I see a bright future for him."

He gurgled, then wet his diaper.

Lisette wondered what had gotten into her, whether asking Nadine to come down from Canada had been a good idea. Gordon's parents would have been delighted to fly over from Newcastle to help with the newborn. But geography won out. Down came old muttering Nadine from Trois-Rivières, crazier than she had been the last time Lisette had seen her. Her hair stuck out in all directions. When Lisette looked inside her mother's open purse, a litter of colorful Canadian banknotes left her blinking in surprise. A fair number of drab American greenbacks were interspersed with the Canadian currency. Little branches and packets of herb-scented things lay in there among all that money. Dried leaves. An entire desiccated jonquil.

"I'm going places, too," Lisette said. "To the washroom. Then to bed. Love you, *ma mère,* but I can barely stand up."

"Go far," said Nadine. "Yes, he will."

As an adult Julian Gray remembered his mother's home-from-the-hospital story at odd times. He kept odd hours and had an odd profession, so the prediction his grandmother had wrapped around his life like one of her camphor-scented wool scarves seemed to have some merit.

The fascination with travel first manifested itself as a fascination with trains. In particular, subways. The idea that trains roared through tunnels below the surface of the earth intrigued the boy Julian beyond words. *Tunnels down there,* he'd tell his parents in the morning as they ate breakfast. *They're digging tunnels down there, and I can hear them at night.*

"We can hear them, too, darling," Lisette Gray said, holding her coffee mug with trembling hands. Without her makeup she looked a bit like a scarecrow.

"The Metro Authority promised the people in our neighborhood they'd be quiet. They said they were digging far enough underground that we wouldn't hear anything," said Gordon Gray, also sipping coffee.

"When will the trains come?"

"Not soon enough," said Lisette. Would this be a good day to tell Gordon she had started smoking again? And how soon could she sneak outside for a nicotine fix?

Gordon knew about his wife's tobacco habit and, being English, had no intention of confronting her. He ate a grapefruit section, then a spoonful of muesli, then another grapefruit section. Poor Lisette hadn't slept three hours last night. They all believed the Red Line tunnel was being blasted into the rock directly beneath their suburban Maryland house. For Julian, this was a source of endless fascination. The idea that in another year or two one might walk up the street a few blocks to the station, board a sleek electric train, and zoom underground to the museums and monuments of Washington set him to jiggling. His parents had taken him to New York for a vacation when he was six, and the clatter and roar of the subways turned him into a pitcher full of excited jelly.

"I don't think they're using dynamite," eight-year-old Julian said. "I think it would be really loud if they were. I mean, really loud. I think the tunnels are just growing that way. Like blood vessels in the ground."

Gordon and Lisette exchanged a look.

"That's an interesting idea," Gordon said, to counteract the look of vague horror on Lisette's face. She looked like she'd like to add a slug of vodka to her coffee.

"Well, it's true, isn't it? The train tunnels just grow down in the earth, like blood vessels. The trains are the blood. The people are the blood cells."

Lisette looked at her hands. Sniffed them. Julian knew they would smell like rosewater. She applied a floral lotion every morning when she woke up in an attempt to ward off something she called liver spots. Julian couldn't understand how a pretty-smelling lotion on her hands would keep her liver from developing spots, but then, much of the world didn't make sense to him yet. Everything seemed to be governed by rule books everyone but he had read.

"I assure you, Julian, they are blasting down there, and using a gigantic boring machine to dig the tunnel through the deep rock layers," said Gordon. This conversation was making his stomach feel acid. A glass of milk would be just the thing.

"The machine is boring?" Julian asked. He could just see it. The kind of thing Mrs. Brock droned on and on about in science class.

"No, it bores holes. It digs. We will have to visit the library and find you a picture."

Julian stared at the wall, contemplated the smooth expanse of white. He saw tiny capillary tunnels worming their way through the plaster, trains the size of baby caterpillars zipping through their little tubes, transporting micropassengers from floor to ceiling and back. Maybe the trains were magnetic. If he held a strong refrigerator magnet against the wall at the right time, the motion of the train would lift him up. He'd be pulled toward the ceiling as his parents looked on with their mouths open from shock.

Who could say where he might end up?

Julian saved his money through college and spent the year after graduation riding the rails across Europe. He'd settle for a month in some city picked more or less at random, then jump on a train every chance he got, exploring the surrounding area. In London, he rented a flat in Brixton and rode around on the Underground with a notebook, scribbling details about the faces he saw, the outlandish clothes, the rainbow hair, the previously unexplored cosmetic potential of safety pins and glitter. He chugged through green countryside on chronically delayed BritRail trains and got to wherever he was going later more often than sooner. As he would later see in America, suburbs were metastasizing their way out of city cores, beyond once-sacrosanct greenbelts. They were eating the landscape, digesting it, excreting little houses with two-car garages. He lived in Barcelona and took long walks through the overwhelming city, where buildings tended to look as if they were constructed out of cookie dough and sequins, designed by hallucinating architects who had washed down their acid tabs with shots of absinthe. Every corner he turned, his breath was taken away at some new vista, some oddity in tile and stone and brick. The Mediterranean Talgo took him along the coast, across the French border into Montpellier. Down the coast he went to Alicante and Valencia. Late at night, the party trains made stops at the beach discos; crowds of drunk screaming university students climbed on, blissed out, threw up, wound down. He went to Zagreb and Naples, Berlin and Budapest, Zürich and Prague. And wrote a book about it all, more by accident than intent. Before Julian was twenty-five he found he had written the definitive guide to post-collegiate wandering: *Europeregrinations*.

There are advantages and disadvantages to doing something wildly successful by accident before the age of twenty-five, far more of the latter than the former. Julian's book sold out its first print run in three weeks, then sold out the second, the third. . . . His publishers rejoiced, sent him a telegram in Malta instructing him to do whatever was necessary and *spend* whatever was necessary to repeat his success. In the meantime, how soon could he come back to the United States for a book tour? Student audiences in Berkeley and Ann Arbor, Austin and Boston, Chapel Hill, and any number of other cities were clamoring for him.

Julian stepped off a plane from Heathrow to a three-ring media circus, organized by his publishers.

The speaking engagements at universities led to appearances on talk shows.

His chat with David Letterman led to an appearance in a couple of indie films, and then a big-budget, star-studded Hollywood bomb.

Between these projects, he quietly reclaimed both Canadian and British citizenship (his American passport being rather more of a hindrance than a help in some of the places he wanted to write about next) and traveled to South Africa and Australia. His goal: to turn his success upside down by exploring the bottom half of the planet.

The second book sold more copies than the first, and this time the college students accused Julian of being a sellout. Sure, the auditoriums filled up, but as many professors showed up as students.

No matter where he went, at the back of his mind, he could hear his grandmother speaking to him: You'll go far. You'll go far. You'll go far.

In Amsterdam an old woman approached Julian in a café. She wore a loud yellow raincoat and thick granny glasses. Like his grandmother, this woman's eyes tended to point in different directions. He couldn't decide which one to look at.

"I read your book," she said in an accent as thick as her ankles. "I'm a fan. And I know your grandmother Nadine."

She pressed a book of what looked like tickets into his hand.

"You said such funny things about Utrecht, where I live," she said. "You gave me a good laugh. I think you should have these."

Julian opened the booklet and looked at the tickets.

MULTI-PASS was printed in big capital letters, sans serif, on green paper. On the back of each ticket, Julian saw a magnetic stripe.

"They're something new, shall we say. They are a useful gift. They're widely acceptable, compatible with all ticket machines, and you can use them to go wherever you want."

Without waiting for thanks, she waved a hand at him, much the same gesture as if she were shooing a chicken, and waddled away.

MULTI-PASS.

What is this travel thing, anyway? Julian finished his espresso. He had been given various gifts—plane tickets, other travel books, clothing, the occasional plate of home-baked cookies—in the three years since his first book came out. Often these items were intended as a quid pro quo: endorse us and we'll hook you up. Or: you're so cool, and if I give you this, then you'll be my friend. But this was the first time he had really questioned himself, why he traveled, how he got here.

It was also the last. He just didn't think the subject warranted that much self-talk. When you found your groove, you kept dancing as long as you could. If you had any sense at all.

Julian's first spectacular failure was the Antarctica book. He got the idea driving to the bottom of South America, through Patagonia. The farther south he went, as civilization seemed to be petering out, he expected to see the land burning, *gauchos* in high-heeled boots stepping on little blue jets of flame to put them out, scorched llamas everywhere. A permanent pall of smoke, eternal late fall. Why else did the place get the name Tierra del Fuego?

He booked a trip to the frozen continent. His ship sailed from New Zealand, dodging icebergs and chasing penguins. Corporate sponsors outfitted him in the latest subzero-wear, and supplied him with a photographer instead of just turning him loose with a camera this time.

Julian imagined the place colonized in an overpopulated future, subway tunnels carved in the ice, clear trains whisking white-clad urban Eskimos through the frozen South Pole metropolis. Silvery icicle rocket-turbo-jets taking off from glacier runways, their afterburn knocking over penguins like so many bowling pins in tuxedos. It would be like Sweden, only more so. And farther south.

Antarctica is not, in itself, a living entity; regardless, it single-mindedly attempts to kill anyone or anything not already equipped by nature to survive there. Julian's documentary efforts took on a patronizing tone, his critics pointed out. He was losing his focus, his fire, his relevance. His arrogance turned away the college students who had been his mainstay for the past several years, and the more affluent older travelers kept buying their trusty guides from Fodor's and Frommers. Julian slipped through a crack in the publishing ice sheet. His niche closed.

When the Antarctica book sold half its already-low first print run (he hadn't said anything new about the place, and there was no night-life), Julian's publisher suggested he take some time to think about what he wanted to do next, where he wanted to go.

Julian traveled back to Barcelona to collect his wits. Barcelona has always been a good place to recuperate. The sun shines all year (once the morning fog burns off). The locals are pleasant (if you can find them among all the tourists). Julian rented a flat in the Eixample, bought furniture, and tried to figure out how to put down roots. This was a new thing for him; he'd never stood still long enough to stick to one place.

A couple of weeks after arriving there, he found himself at a metro station without pesetas to board the train. He'd left his wallet in his apartment, and he had no change in his pockets. Rather than turning back to rush home and retrieve the thing—he'd be late for a coffee date with a man he'd met a few days before—Julian stuck a MULTI-PASS ticket into the gate to see what would happen. He kept the booklet with him at all times, for luck, he supposed. For the novelty of it.

A click.

He collected the ticket from the turnstile and walked through. A train pulled up to the platform just as he stepped into the concourse, and it must have been an express: it skipped several stations (other passengers protested, and one woman pounded on the doors) and dropped him off at the Port Olimpic station, where he was meeting Antonio.

Does the magic carpet have to be serviced every 3,000 miles, like your Honda or Peugeot or Saab? Does the genie in that bottle you found demand paid sick leave, public holidays off, and regular training opportunities? Does the magic coin lose its power if the exchange rate is unfavorable?

Some questions cannot be answered. Julian did not stay up tossing at night, trying to guess at the truth behind his MULTI-PASS metro trip. The ticket had worked. It might work again, but if he was careless in his experimentation, he'd be likely to waste a trip. Just like the thing with Antonio could be said to be working, after a few months, as long as it worked, leave well enough alone. There was no telling what the future would bring. For now, things could be what they were. He kept the booklet of tickets in a strongbox with his passports, some emergency money in stable currencies, and his publication agreements. Now and then he'd take out the tickets and look at them, pensive, as if he could be putting them to better use if he'd just think, if he'd just see things from the right perspective.

Julian took a small part in a Spanish film and mostly escaped public notice. The director's boyfriend was a friend of Antonio's penultimate ex, and had lost an actor at the last minute. Time dragged by. Julian lived at the periphery of a dream, in a state of fringe celebrity, the sort of person café coffee-sippers ask one another about: where they've seen him, what he's done, why they should know his name. It's difficult to be miserable for long in Barcelona, a city where many buildings look like surreal confections of Play-Doh and jewelry, but Julian was suffering. The money from his first successes seemed to be dwindling, despite his financial manager's best efforts. Julian found himself teaching English with the distracted air of a professor twice his age, and desperate for another idea he could turn into a book.

I should be riding around New York and London in limousines.

I should be at the Oscars, walking across that red carpet holding hands with Antonio.

I should not be struggling with mediocrity.

Julian burned.

Miserable in Barcelona, a hybrid photo essay and travel guide, aroused vague editorial interest on three continents. Julian's Spanish-language publisher in Madrid enjoyed the chance to poke fun at the capital's rival city and offered a contract with enough money to restore some of Julian's battered confidence.

"You really want to photograph the worst of the nightlife there?" Juan, a great gelatinous sphere of a man with a walrus moustache, clasped his belly and laughed like a Latin Santa Claus. "The underworld of Barcelona? I thought it was tossed into the Mediterranean before the Olympics came, and never allowed within sight of Montjuïc!"

Julian nodded.

Vomiting club kids, fucked-out trannie hookers crawling the curbside at six in the morning, street urchins in the Gothic Quarter vandalizing cars, graffiti on the walls of toilets and metro stations.

Juan, a staunchly civic-minded *madrileño,* loved the idea.

Aaron, his British agent, who would also handle rights for Australia, New Zealand, Singapore, and South Africa if a publisher could be found, seemed reluctant but was at least willing to talk. Julian hopped on a plane to London and met Aaron, an effeminate, rail-thin Scot who chain-smoked French cigarettes, coughing as if a lung were about to come unstuck, at a dark pub in Kensington.

"You have to realize, you're on thin ice in the publishing world. After a few failures, it's more difficult for you to convince a publishing house to put out a new book than it would be for a first-timer."

"Tell me something I don't already know."

Aaron named a large, reputable publishing house. "I called an editor there and pitched your project. Pitched? Listen to me; I sound like a bloody Yank."

"I am a bloody Yank," Julian said. "If you want to be technical about it."

"Well, yes, there is that." Aaron stared at the black paper of the cigarette in his yellowish hand. Even in the dim light of the pub, Julian could see Aaron's jaundiced skin. Aaron continued: "In any case, I think we'll be able to do it. Your photographs were strong, and the text you submitted was funny enough. The book will appeal to a certain readership. Maybe even the same ones who made you so popular in the first place."

An ember of hope glowed in the center of Julian all the way back to Barcelona. Antonio met him at the airport and, on hearing the news, surprised him with a weekend trip over to Ibiza.

Julian spent the next three months trolling the seediest places he could find in the coastal city, camera in hand, extra rolls of film in his pockets. Danger loomed: one night an angry man he'd photographed kneeling before a cop in the woods atop Montjuïc, near the Palau Nacional, shouted and gave chase. The cop zipped up in a hurry and joined the pursuit. Julian dashed down the unmoving hillside escalators, frantic, camera banging against his side like a metal fist, and reached the Espanya metro station at the bottom of the hill just as the attendant was shutting the gates. About twenty paces behind, shouts and imprecations could be heard. Racing footsteps.

"We are closing," the attendant said.

"MULTI-PASS," Julian said, tearing off a ticket.

"Step inside."

The attendant shut the gate behind Julian, and when he descended to the platform, a train was waiting. The conductor asked Julian's destination and took him straight to Universitat, the closest Eixample station to Julian's home.

Most of the work necessary for the New York media behemoth to publish *Miserable in Barcelona* could be done via the telephone and the

Internet, but Julian's U.S. agent and editor wanted a face-to-face meeting when the time came to sign contracts. From New York, Julian would travel to Toronto to complete a similar transaction with his Canadian publisher. Antonio kept Julian up late the night before the trip, celebrating in the best Spanish tradition, and as a result, Julian, sore in various places and woefully hung over, missed his plane to New York.

He disembarked from the train at the airport station and stared in horror at the clock, then out the window at an aircraft climbing toward the clouds. No way to know whether the flight was, in fact, his intended; it could have been bound for London or Berlin, Rome or Toulouse—anywhere, really. The moving walkway between the train station and the airport terminal stretched like elastic, elongating the distance to the Iberia check-in counter, where a Spanish girl was going to shake her head at him in disapproval.

"Please tell me my flight is delayed," he said, when he surrendered his suitcase and his tickets to the Iberia agent.

"No, señor, I cannot tell you that, because your flight departed on time."

"When is the next one to New York? I have to . . ." Julian stopped himself and shook his head. "But you must hear that all the time when passengers arrive late. Of course I have to get to New York, or else I wouldn't be here and upset because I missed my flight."

"That was our only direct flight. We can route you through Madrid if you want to fly Iberia, or through Paris if you want to fly Air France. They will honor your ticket, but there will be an additional charge."

"Are you sure this is the only direct flight?" Julian asked, surrendering another MULTI-PASS ticket.

He fully expected the Iberia agent to scorch him with a laser-beam glare, but she nodded and picked up her phone to place a call. After a short exchange in Catalan, she rang off and smiled at Julian.

"Just one moment," she said.

Julian was led down a corridor he hadn't noticed before, in all the times he'd flown in and out of this airport. (BCN is not a sprawling metropolis like LAX or Heathrow.) The uniformed Iberia attendant explained, "There has been a change of schedule. This plane was supposed to go to Havana, but you're just in time to board. It will depart once you are safely on board."

Julian did not stop to ask questions, because he didn't care about the legal issues such a change might entail, nor did he want to know anything more than his estimated time of arrival at JFK. Let the American immigrations people worry about the Cubans, their visas, and all the rest. He still had several MULTI-PASS tickets left, and a contract to sign in New York. He crossed the Atlantic trying to decide how he would follow *Miserable in Barcelona,* what his next project ought to be, what would be the next logical step.

The book landed on shelves in the Borders and Kinokuniya and Chapters stores of the world, and the critics began to pounce like hyenas:

The New Orleans *Times-Picayune* called *Miserable in Barcelona* "Further proof that Julian Gray has passed his sell-by date."

According to the *Christian Science Monitor,* "While his first two books were minor masterpieces combining travel, wit, and social comment, Gray's writing has deteriorated into tedious navel-gazing. Now struggling for relevance, Gray subjects his readers to close-up views of the dissipated and disgusting."

The New York Times said, "Slapdash and haphazard. Julian Gray writes as if he were in a state of arrested development, still holding on to his sophomore year of college, still writing as if unsure who his readers are. The quality of the photographs suggests they were taken with a generic drugstore disposable camera. Flip through this one in the bookstore—there are a few bright spots—but don't buy it."

The *Toronto Star*: "Utterly meretricious."

The entire English-speaking world seemed to unite against Julian's book. There were a few dissenting heretics: Vancouver, Sydney, and Dallas. Melbourne chimed in with a damning breath of faint praise. The book's sales were rather strong in the antipodes—God bless Australia and New Zealand, Julian thought, feeling otherwise as if a pack of vampires had been feasting on him for the last couple of weeks.

Outside Madrid, the Spanish-language papers weren't much kinder. Positive remarks seemed only to be the editors in Mexico City, Buenos Aires, and Sevilla heaving sighs of relief: someone had finally shown that Barcelona, for all its glitter and polish, did in fact have a dirty underbelly. The book itself? "Unfinished." "Sophomoric." And, worst, from Caracas: "If you want to see antics like these, then you should watch an Almodóvar film. He knows how to make low life lovable. He knows how to make you care. Sr. Gray does not. He disdains his subjects. Yes, this is a book and not a movie, but the point remains, this is a pale and embarrassing imitation. If we are lucky, Sr. Gray will find something else to do."

Julian couldn't be sure whether the resulting public humiliation killed his parents, and, since they were dead, he couldn't ask them. He thought of consulting mediums or trying his hand with a Ouija board, but discarded both ideas. He flew back to Maryland for the joint funeral. The car rental agent at the Baltimore airport blushed when she recognized him and said, "Sorry about the book, man." Julian elected not to reply, "My parents died within three days of each other, and I know they subscribed to at least three of the periodicals that gave my book a drubbing. Write a fucking letter to the editor."

Antonio had changed the message on his answering machine to indicate he would be in Naples for the next week. What the hell was that? Naples? Antonio had an ex there, a man he had never quite gotten over. Julian opted to believe he had been dumped *in absentia*.

He celebrated his entire life going down the toilet by taking a cab from his parents' too-quiet house down 16th Street into Washington, getting drunk out of his mind in a Dupont Circle club, stumbling over to Georgetown to keep drinking, and trying to pick up a cute blond fraternity boy dressed head to toe in Ralph Lauren. The frat boy, whose name was Toby and who was a political science major and had a girlfriend named Lily and who was going to law school like his father and his grandfather had before him, and who was being groomed for a career in politics, and who had never ever ever touched another man sexually in his entire life (well, there was that time with

John after their initiation, but they were drunk and it didn't count because it was just mutual masturbation and anyway, no one would ever know), beat the shit out of him. Imagining the criminal charges Julian might press, Toby decided to make it look like a mugging. Julian lay in an alley on top of several boxes and bags of garbage. Toby emptied Julian's wallet and was looking at the booklet of MULTI-PASS tickets when Julian came to.

"Give me that!" Julian said in Spanish first. He remembered where he was and tried again in English.

The language choice might have helped. It at least confused the frat boy enough to buy Julian a little time. He grabbed at the book of tickets. It tore.

Toby took off as fast as he could run.

Julian was left holding one ticket, the last in the booklet.

His parents were good and properly buried, all prayers said, all tears shed. Relatives Julian barely knew had flown in from Canada and England, and had since returned.

Antonio did not return any of Julian's calls.

Copies of *Miserable in Barcelona* languished on bookshelves across the globe, being flipped through, their pages smudged with thumbprint oil and crumbs of food, but not bought. The book had cost quite a lot of money to produce and it wasn't going to break even, at least not on any of its English-language editions. (Well, there was always hope for Australia and New Zealand.) The Spanish figures looked better, but then, it was hard to look worse. How long until his publishers remaindered it? How long before he found it lining somebody's cat box?

Julian made arrangements to sell his parents' house and do away with their belongings. After a week, his bruises from the mugging faded. They passed through an alarming spectrum of visible pain, first purplish-blue, then a bilious sort of green, and finally a terrible shade of deli-mustard yellow. Julian's spirits faded like his bruises. He could still pick up little roles in obscure Continental films, if he felt the need to remain in the public eye. At the very least, audiences in cinemas didn't hiss and storm out when he appeared on the screen. He could try his hand at writing under a pen name, something modest in scope, something ultimately redeeming. There was always the teaching gig.

Julian was having these thoughts as he drank a coffee—despite the saunalike weather of the American capital—on a sofa in a cozy caffeine bar in Adams Morgan. He watched the international bright young things around him chatting animatedly, in several languages. Some studied. Others read. Still others seemed to be waiting for someone to come, for something to happen.

He finished his coffee, stood, and walked outside. The humidity was like walking blindfolded into a brick wall. The breath was knocked out of him. But on the inside, despite the warming effects of his espresso, a deep interior chill remained.

Julian hurried home, then paid the cabbie an extra $20 to wait while he packed his bags. (Both cars were to be auctioned with the rest of the estate.) At the Baltimore airport, Julian presented his last MULTI-PASS ticket at the British Airways check-in counter. (He was changing planes at Gatwick. Or rather, that's what his tickets said. Without Antonio waiting for him in Barcelona, there seemed to be no point in going home, because where, after all, was home?)

"What is your destination, sir?" asked the girl in her handsome British Airways navy uniform.

Julian gave her the last MULTI-PASS ticket with a twinge of regret.

"That's in the hands of the gods, I guess," he said. "I just want to go somewhere I can roast in the sun and not think at all. Alicante? Bermuda? Faro? It doesn't bloody matter."

The British Airways check-in girl gave him a polite nod and directed him to his gate for boarding. Very unusual in its usualness, that. Julian waited with the rest of the passengers on his Gatwick-bound flight, boarded with them, endured the safety spiel, acceleration, lift-off.

The plane kept climbing, though, and the pilot never announced they had reached their cruising altitude of 39,000 feet. Julian's ears kept popping. Centrifugal force pressed him into his chair. Fortunately he was flying first class, so he wasn't suffering as much as the passengers back in economy.

Night seemed to have fallen. Julian looked outside and saw the Earth receding, even as the plane gained speed.

"But I was supposed to transit through Gatwick," he thought stupidly, when he began to realize what he had done.

He'll go far, his grandmother Nadine had said.

For some reason the windows did not burst out of the plane; the aircraft held together as if protected by some exterior power, some kind of force field, traveling faster and faster through a black void Julian accepted, finally, as space. The 777 gave a great swerve, once, dodging Venus. *I need a drink,* Julian thought. *Planes, trains, they're all the same thing. Rule Britannia. I need gin.* He ordered a Bombay Sapphire and tonic from a strangely calm but very handsome flight attendant, and noticed that the rest of the passengers seemed to be asleep.

It was getting warmer in the cabin, much warmer, hot.

Julian had just a moment to sip his drink and think, *The sick glory of transit,* when he arrived at his final destination.

Rabbit Rerun

Carol Rosenfeld

I was walking down Horatio Street, crossing Eighth Avenue, when she passed me. I turned my head to continue admiring her confident stride, well-cut, graying hair, and bomber jacket, and—I tripped, of course. The curb caught me by surprise and I fell forward into a white, fuzzy mass. Two paws steadied me and set me upright.

As a New Yorker, I pride myself on appearing blasé when encountering celebrities. I didn't get excited when I recognized the actor who played Arnold, the young choreographer in *The Turning Point,* in a stationery store. And I didn't even look twice when I passed Tony Randall up near Columbus Circle. But this guy was big.

"I—I know you!" I said. "You were in that movie with Jimmy Stewart. You're—no, don't tell me—you're Harvey!"

I couldn't believe that I was looking up at a real, live movie star. Well, maybe real and live weren't exactly the right words, but there was no denying the large lapin was a bona fide big name. Okay, Bugs Bunny had a longer filmography and Roger Rabbit's name appeared in a movie title too, but they were just 'toons, while Harvey, well, he was a pooka. One might even say, *the* pooka.

"This is quite an honor, Harvey," I said. "Thanks for catching me. I'm not drunk; I missed the curb 'cause I was checking that woman out. Did you see her? Hot! But I wonder why she was wearing sunglasses at night."

Harvey fell into step beside me like we were old friends. I thought about asking him what he'd been doing for the last fifty years, but I knew movie stars could be sensitive about being a one-film phenomenon. So I told Harvey he hadn't changed a bit.

Harvey said the world had changed. The evidence was all around us—every other block had a Starbucks and the street was filled with SUVs.

I wondered if Harvey was on the Web. I suggested that we go on-line and do a search.

"Excuse the mess," I said as I opened my apartment door. "Hey, Harvey, I don't suppose you could wiggle your nose like Samantha on *Bewitched* and have all this clutter organize itself?"

Harvey said I shouldn't believe everything I saw on television.

I sat down in front of my computer. Harvey stood behind me.

"It's a funny thing about the Web, Harvey," I said. "Sometimes you can't find the information you want to find but you stumble on something that's so interesting you don't really mind. Just like when I look up a word in the dictionary. Sometimes on my way to the word I'm thinking of, I find another word—it may even be a word I know and use—and I realize it's a funny-looking word."

By now my home page was up so I typed "pooka" into the search box and clicked "go." I think I was hoping for a message just for me, the way the asylum attendant found "And how are you, Mr. Wilson?" when he looked up the definition of pooka, but the screen just showed the usual assortment of search results. Some had an obvious connection to the query, others seemed inexplicable.

"Well, there's a Boston rock band called Pooka Stew."

Harvey frowned.

"And there's an Irish musical group called Pooka. Here's Pooka—Our Cat. Good Lord, The World of the Postmodern Pooka: Science Fiction and Tori Amos. Harvey," I said, "You've got to get yourself on the Web. Where is the Web page devoted to the greatest, the most famous pooka of them all?"

Harvey began hanging out with me. I worried about keeping him amused. I wouldn't let him come with me to the office, even though I thought the place could do with a little mischief.

"I know you spent a lot of time in bars in the movie, Harvey, but I'm not much of a bar person. I like the idea of bars, but I can't go to a bar alone."

Harvey pointed out that I wouldn't be alone if he was with me.

"The bar I'm thinking of is a lesbian bar, Harvey."

He said he wouldn't go with me to any other kind of bar.

It did help, knowing Harvey was behind me when I opened the door and walked into the smoky, noisy room. I forgot that no one else could see Harvey. When I asked him what he wanted to drink the bartender wasn't as understanding as the one in the movie.

We finally settled ourselves at a small table in the corner. I figured if I faced the wall no one would be able to see me talking to Harvey, but he said I wouldn't be able to do much cruising. He suggested that I take out my cell phone and pretend to be making a call.

"That's a brilliant idea, Harvey," I said.

Harvey and I began haunting the bar.

Cruising sounded simple, but in practice I quickly became overwhelmed. A pair of lips could entrance me; I would meditate on a curl of hair. I yearned to make passes at all the girls in glasses.

"I fall in love too easily," I explained to Harvey.

He thought I should be more selective, but I argued that since none of the women I was interested in seemed to be interested in me, it didn't really matter. "And," I said, "maybe it's a good thing that no one's interested. Have you seen the personal ads? Everyone knows what they don't want. No alcohol," I said, and sipped my wine. "No flab. Women with baggage need not apply. And you know, Harvey, I'm not exactly toting a model's makeup case. I'm lugging a steamer trunk."

Harvey didn't reply; he just walked over to the jukebox. Since I saw him standing in front of it, I wasn't all that surprised when the Supremes started singing, "You Can't Hurry Love." But the cluster of Goth girls lounging beside it were very startled, and the bartender frowned.

"I haven't heard that song in so long," I said.

"I don't remember seeing that listed as one of the selections."

I looked up. She was almost as tall as Harvey. In her black jacket, black turtleneck, and black chinos, she was a solid dark form in the smoky darkness of the room. Leaning up against the wall beside our table, she glanced down at me and asked, "Who's your friend?"

"You can see him?"

"Of course I can see him. He looks familiar."

"He's a movie star," I said.

"Oh, yeah, now I remember. Harvey."

He indicated his approval by getting out of the chair so she could sit down. He said he was going to take a stroll and would see me later.

Her name was Kim. We talked for awhile, and then I had to ask her, "You're real, aren't you, Kim? You're not a fantasy, an illusion, or a pooka like Harvey?"

"Come home with me," she said, "and I'll show you how real I am."

Harvey was waiting outside the bar, but he didn't come with us. He said he wasn't one of those guys who gets off on watching two women getting it on, and headed downtown.

That was the last time I saw Harvey. But when Kim and I celebrated the anniversary of our first night together, I made a carrot cake.

The Mask

David McConnell

A FULL-HEAD LEATHER MASK made of the finest hand-tooled cowhide, triple-stitched with a heavy duty "no pinch" nylon zipper in the rear. PERFECT for scenes of all kinds.

DEPERSONALIZE your lover, partner, slave, or "victim." SENSORY DEPRIVATION—no ear or eye holes in this deluxe model. A nose hole allows breathing for safety. A leather gag snaps over the mouth to silence whimpering (may be removed for play). Optional penis gag also fits this mask. Durable, attractive, top-quality item—Remember, bondage/S/M is a form of love. NO Jeffrey Dahmers, please.

A grotesque tragedy occurred on a gay beach. It was midday, sunny. An old woman danced by herself on the pavementlike, damp sand by the water. Her dance was slow—something Asian about it. Her fingers meditatively riffled the air. Her chin turned right, then left. Higher on the beach, under the palms, only one pair of slender boys was out. Coffee skin and black hair, pink skin and blond, they were both naked. Far offshore, a shrimper puttered in the Gulf of Mexico.

The old woman danced. Though the boys ignored her, she, while still dancing, seemed to concentrate on them. Her hands often snaked in their direction. They were some two hundred yards away. She was evidently a local. Wearing black sweats, she couldn't have cared anything about a suntan. Both her hands suddenly splayed toward the boys. It was a gesture children use when they play at magic. And at that moment a bulky raceme of green coconuts, loosened by the previous day's storm, cracked and fell with a dry cacophony of palm fronds. The coffee-colored boy just had time to half sit up before the mass landed on him, crushing his head.

57

The pink boy started screaming. He ran partway toward the old woman, who'd finished dancing. Then an idea came to him, and he ran off the beach. Near where he'd parked the car, beyond the sea grape and palms, was a phone on a pylon next to a streetlight. While he was gone, the old woman calmly approached the body. She removed the dead boy's watch, the only thing he'd been wearing. She opened a clear plastic beach bag and took out a wallet, which she flipped open to glance at a blurry photograph of the boy himself as a real boy, a little boy (nostalgic icon), and some business cards. At the bottom of the bag was a black leather mask. She took that, too.

Before the survivor got back, the old woman had disappeared with her trophies. A faint siren could be heard from the beach. The blond boy later recalled that an old woman had been on the beach, but it was thought unnecessary to contact another witness to the horrible accident. The victim's things weren't missed. His friend was simply too distraught.

The incident became big news on the island for a while. A few hand-printed warning signs were taped to coconut palms that leaned over paths and public areas. Friends of friends of the boys grieved with the brief intensity of the circuit party set. And even those who didn't know them were chilled by the freak of sudden death. When persistent fine weather and the island's business of pleasure had almost put the tragedy out of mind a week later, something brought it all back with a new sourness. Leaflets appeared with the heading "He got what he deserved" and a crude drawing of a limp-wristed figure next to a palm. If you bothered to read it, the text spoke of "sodomites who parade their sin" and "the hand of God." These signs were duly torn down. And the fine weather and the island's business of pleasure continued.

         *   *   *

Bayard wore a brilliant white shirt open three buttons down. His amber and lapis lazuli beads could be glimpsed and—what he was more proud of—his tanned pecs like rising gingerbread. It was a common look, he knew, but he'd worked long and hard developing the gay boy's gingerbread body. He couldn't bear to keep it under wraps. He loved the curious sexiness of gay uniformity. It was like an advanced stage of coming out: the deepest way to be yourself was to be nobody in particular.

Raptly, he watched the old woman, Mitzi. Her eyes were closed. Her fingertips were on a photograph on the coffee table. She was speaking in a hoarse whisper, a little louder than she wanted just to be heard over her bungalow's decrepit air conditioner. "The boy knows he was wrong now. It's one of the things that put him in the middle ground. There's a sort of field outside a palace, a beautiful place. He has to stay there—outside—for a long time . . ."

"Wrong about what?" Bayard asked.

Wincing slightly Mitzi said, "The afterlife. He wasn't a believer. But I'm also getting the strong sense again that he wants to get this message to you . . ." Her eyes crinkled tightly. "I wish . . . Felix!" she called in the most attenuated voice.

"A message to me? That's what I don't get."

"Maybe you had something in common?" Mitzi ended with the half-inquiring lilt of a practiced spiritualist.

Bayard let his imagination wander. It was how he thought he could connect to the psychic energy. Because he really did believe that you had to be open. You couldn't let the psychic do all the work. The one with the questions had his part to play as well. Although he hadn't known he had questions until Mitzi approached him several weeks ago. Anyway he was fully involved now. "OK, we know it's not the gay thing, because that's too . . ."

"No. Something special in common," Mitzi said firmly.

"Could we have been alike in—you know—sexually? I mean, I really didn't know the guy."

"Hmm. Top or bottom?" Mitzi inquired clinically.

"Mostly bottom, I guess," Bayard said, blushing in spite of himself.

"I know it's not that simple." Mitzi smiled, full of understanding. "But I'm just trying to get a sense of why he chose you, what it is he wants to say."

"Mostly bottom," Bayard repeated in a whisper.

"Probably still not specific enough," Mitzi said with a dissatisfied moue. She summed up, "Well, let's see. I've gotten the sense that he's in the middle ground. That he hasn't passed over yet. That often means they have to perform a service for the living. Could you have had a lover in common? Somebody he wants to tell you about?"

"I guess it's possible," Bayard said, thinking of Rob, a nomad waiter he'd met a week or so before. "But I heard Felix was together with his boyfriend for months before it happened." Bayard's face went lax as it did when he was hiding something.

Mitzi prompted the confession with a mere flick of her eyebrows.

"There is this guy Rob I've been seeing."

"Rob." Mitzi's peach-painted mouth tasted the name for emanations. Unsuccessful, she lifted one bony shoulder. As if beginning to lose interest in the whole investigation, which made Bayard quite anxious, she asked, "Do you think Felix could have a message for you about this Rob? How well do you know him?"

"Well, we've been seeing each other. It's true he doesn't say a lot." Mitzi had hit on a sore spot. If the dead boy Felix had a message for Bayard, what could be more likely than some sort of warning about Rob? Bayard knew this but was still reluctant to speak about Rob, no matter how anxious he was to please Mitzi. Mitzi saw through him and disapproved.

"Rob," she repeated. One matching peach fingernail tapped the face of the smiling coffee-colored child in the photograph. "Could be they weren't lovers. Felix could have learned something about him in the middle ground. That happens. I have to ask—safe sex?"

"Of course," Bayard said. Safe-ish, he was thinking. And he didn't want to mention the restraints, the no-questions-asked, no-personal-details nature of the affair, or the fact that he had yet to meet with Rob before nightfall. It sounded too unhealthy. But it was fun unhealthy. He wasn't sure Mitzi would be able to make the distinction, though she seemed pretty casual about the mechanics of gay life. She was an old woman, after all. Perhaps, also, for his own peace of mind, he didn't want his fun unhealthy dalliance touched by this serious psychic business. The truth was, he got off on the thrilling note of fear when Rob, without a word of greeting, undressed him and pushed him onto the bed. He thought of Rob's slight, genteel roughness, as stylized as a matador's cruelty. Bayard didn't want Rob resolved into either the namby-pamby sweetheart or the monster. The doubt was what was sexy. He didn't want to talk about it. "What could it be? What could it be?" he murmured to fill the loud, air-conditioned silence. "It could be anything. Not necessarily Rob."

Mitzi eyed him steadily.

"We could try again," Bayard offered, looking at the objects on the table, the blurred photograph, the worn wallet, the cheap BOY watch, and a business card with a stolen image of Felix the Cat and the words "studio photography" next to the phone numbers.

"I don't know. I don't know if I want to contact Felix again. Have to say, I find this one especially exhausting." Mitzi pulled her legs up onto the couch, amazingly limber for a sixty-year-old woman, but then, she practiced tai chi on the beach. He'd seen her once. She pulled on a frosted curl of her wig. She simpered. "If it wasn't for you. If I didn't think you were so sweet. From the moment I saw you, really. And this Felix boy's message does feel urgent." She shrugged.

Bayard frowned. "I'm a little worried now. That we can't get it. Could it be I'm somehow being skeptical without meaning to be?"

"Are you?" she asked with a hint of severity.

"I don't know. I don't think so."

"Why don't we try again when we're fresher. That's a delicate instrument you've got there." She pointed to her own head. "The way you feel—it can easily skew things. And maybe, maybe without being skeptical exactly, you're a little bit hesitant to really open up. For this time it's sixty."

Bayard smiled in relief when she smiled. He was increasingly worried, but the instinct to please her was momentarily stronger. He got out three twenties.

With a much younger woman's energy Mitzi sprang from the couch and took her purse from atop the TV. As she was putting Bayard's money in a red leather billfold, her chin drifted up. "Unless . . . Those things might not be the most important." She nodded at the coffee table. "I don't know if that was his regular watch. Maybe the psychic energy is weak."

"That can happen, I've heard. If it's not something they used intimately."

"Very true," Mitzi admitted, but she looked at him as if she didn't like her pupils too bright. "What if we check . . ." she went on. "Come on."

She led him into an unused bedroom she'd set up as an office. "It's not something I really wanted to get into. Too intense, maybe." She had him move several boxes stacked along a wall. "I think this one." She tapped one of the lower boxes. He opened it. "That. Mm-hm." She indicated a shoebox inside, and he took it out. "His things were all sent to me by the mother. See if I couldn't reach him. Understand. Poor woman didn't know what to make of this. Not everyone from my generation is as open-minded as I am." Bayard was kneeling. Mitzi extended a finger toward his face and stared emphatically. "And I'm very, very open-minded." Ever so lightly she scratched the tip of his nose. She folded her arms and nodded for Bayard to raise the shoebox cover. Inside was what looked like a dried black fish. "Take a look at that, Bear."

"Bayard," he corrected her in passing. When he lifted it, the object fell open. It was a full-head leather mask of the kind sold in the more serious sex shops.

"Oh, I know what it's for," Mitzi said, though Bayard had said nothing.

"It's just a game for people," Bayard defended the dead boy weakly. He didn't know why.

"Oh, I know. I know," Mitzi sounded immensely satisfied with herself, but Bayard couldn't help thinking that she really didn't know at all—an old woman like her—or if she once did, she couldn't remember. "I'm thinking if you took that you might get some vibrations," she finished with a practical nod.

"I couldn't take it." This response was involuntary, almost a spasm.

"You don't understand, honey. I don't think he was a bad guy because of this. I figure people's business is their business. I wonder, for instance, is this ringing any bells for you? You and your Rob ever . . . ?" Bayard made an indefinite sound. She rubbed his bulging deltoid with a nervous, bony hand. "It's like we said, sweetheart, the one asking questions has to make an effort, too. Believe me, I'm not interested in the details. I just need to know who you are, so we can get a handle on this message."

Bayard laughed randomly. Sex and death and young gentleman politeness bumped together garishly in his mind like gumballs when the crank turns. But he was chiefly appalled at himself, because the dead boy's mask excited him—right here in front of Mitzi. Just in case, his hips made a maidenly half turn. His pants were thin cotton, and he wasn't the most self-controlled guy in the world. "I can't take it. I wouldn't feel right, but maybe next time we could use it. See if I get anything from it."

Outside he happened to glance directly into the Florida sun, so he saw a neat, dark blot over Mitzi's face when she called after him, "Next Tuesday, Bear. We'll get to the bottom of this, honey." He was thinking about the mask. He made the blot shift from Mitzi's face. When he tried to look at her, it swooped back.

They lived on Jasper Key, Bayard in the town of Jasper, along with most of the small gay community, and Mitzi at the far end of what was called "retirement road." Sometimes in town you'd see elderly couples go a little tight-lipped and look down as they negotiated some gay bar's spillover crowd, but for the most part everybody got along. Life had the pensive quality it does in a resort. People biding their time at the fringes of the world. The he-deserved-it flyer was a fluke, the work of some crank, most people imagined. When an activist in exile organized a town meeting at the community center to discuss the incident, people were heartened that a handful of the elderly residents came to show support. It was there that Mitzi turned in her folding chair and, with an uncanny air of foreknowledge, looked straight at Bayard, who slouched against the back wall. She formed a pinched, peach smile and waved with a forefinger. After the meeting she came up to him and said without introduction, "We have to talk."

Before Jasper, Bayard had done time in a community college, then as a customer service rep for a phone company. He hated the tension, the disembodied loathing, the bizarre arguments with people who refused to talk to him because he was a recording and not a human being. He'd come home from work and read the children's books he'd loved as a kid. In South Beach (a short-lived boyfriend and a job at a gay travel agency) it was worse. An endless round of catty drunkenness, great sex, then maybe the *Chronicles of Narnia* or *Winnie-the-Pooh*. Jasper was perfect. People were more laid back. They didn't sneer if he said he liked kids' books. He had one or two older friends. Nurturers like Alec. And there were always the sexual wanderers, good for an evening or a season. Rob, for example. Rob treated his stint as a waiter with some contempt. Soon he'd go off who knew where. So Bayard could call Alec, a retired caterer with rental property in Mobile ("a foot in both camps," he said), and fret about the guys like Rob. "Ah." Alec drew the syllable out and ended with a triple tsking. "When you say 'I don't know if we even like each other,' I know you're falling in love."

"Oh, please." Bayard shifted the phone to his other ear and dug his feet in the sand. "No, it's just we don't know each other. So far as I can tell it's only a sexual thing. But he's taking up all this space in my mind. The problem is, I was really enjoying how it was—you know—a tiny bit spooky. But now Mitzi's got me all worried about it."

"She's the one who claims coconut boy has a message for you from the beyond?"

"Alec!" Bayard admonished. "It's Felix. And she's impressive. You were there when she looked at me. You pointed her out to me."

"I suppose there's a client or two of hers in my canasta club. They swear by her."

"See! I'm not the gullible dope you think I am."

"I'll have to ask Rob about that . . . No. Of course you're not. But seriously, I don't like seeing you get wrapped up in these superficial— Being gay shouldn't be what you do, the way it is for the Robs of the world. . . . Sure, enjoy yourself, but . . . where are you? I hear waves."

"I'm at the beach."

"Which one?" Alec demanded suggestively

"Just the beach."

"You're at Homolulu, you slut!" Alec accused, using the local nickname. "Watch out for coconuts! Rob not satisfying you?"

"I'm not looking for sex. There's no one out here anyway. It's the middle of the day. I was tired. I'm just sitting under a palm tree. Let's see . . . No coconuts."

"You go out to the end of the island to sit? What are you doing?"

"I was seeing Mitzi Hoyt."

"Oh, she does live out there, doesn't she? So she's trying to scare you about Rob? What was she saying?"

"Asking me these probing questions. And I understand. I mean, I have to be honest with her. But I didn't want to think about Rob that way—like that some dead kid was going to say he was bad news. 'Cause that's what I kept imagining."

"You mean you still didn't get the message?"

"No. It's not clear somehow. We think I may be blocking it. If it's about Rob, I guess I am. But it was awkward. She wanted to talk about sex and all."

"Maybe that's how she gets off."

"No!" Rob whispered.

"You'd be surprised. Like straight guys into lesbians."

"She's sixty. She's an old woman."

"You never know. When you get to be our age, young people start looking like those sex dolls. No personality. Not to me, of course. But I know one old coot who just loves getting the bag boys at market to pick up his cane. He drops it on purpose to watch them bend over. He's toying with them. You should hear my canasta club. They talk about young people like so many eggplants. Pretty eggplants. Something about the distance in time. And, what with Viagra, one or two of the old guys still have it in them."

"It's not that way with Mitzi."

"You're right, I'm sure. That awful wig! She's probably bald and arthritic."

"No, not that, either. She used to be a dancer. She does tai chi or something. I saw her on the beach here one morning."

"After a long night cavorting in the sand."

Bayard laughed. "Just that once. Maybe it wasn't tai chi. But it was some weird dance thing."

"Well, then, why not sex?"

"Just not." Thinking he might be hurting Alec's feelings, he added, "She's not as vibrant as you."

"Well, I think you should tell her whatever she wants. I'm madly curious about this message from coconut boy."

"Felix," Bayard corrected primly.

He thought he heard the name again—Felix—out of the blue the following morning. Bayard lived in a sunny studio above a souvenir and shell shop. A fringe of black flippers hanging under the awning clucked in the wind. He was lying on the floor of his nearly bare room, the *Miami Herald* spread out around him. The radio jabbered discreetly. His mug of coffee steamed a curlet or two. He'd been admiring himself, visible from the neck down in a full-length mirror that leaned against one wall. The sight, white drawstring pants and nothing else, pleased him, but he had to laugh. It wasn't him, really, this anonymous statue he was trying to become.

He thought he heard the name Felix. He puzzled about it a minute. Thinking of the mask. Then he heard it again, for real—it was on the radio—and the eerie feeling it had caused dissipated. On the radio they murmured earnestly about a tropical storm named Felix.

He turned a page of the newspaper, and found himself staring at a huge photograph of a naked boy wearing the mask. Underwear. Incredibly enough, it was an underwear ad. Bayard knew how daring ad agencies had become. But S and M? He looked more closely and noticed the mask was in fact a blot of ink. It obscured the head of the usual underwear Adonis. His unease didn't vanish. Because the image was uncanny. The spilled ink exactly covered the boy's face. What on earth had caused the printing accident to happen just so, just today? In his own copy of the *Herald?*

Now that he thought of it, he'd been nervous since yesterday. He remembered looking into the sun and seeing a blot on Mitzi's face, too. Then there had been his fatigue after the visit. He was certain some psychic electricity linked him and the mask. He reasoned this was as obvious a supernatural experience as he'd ever had. But it brought him no satisfaction. He touched the dark head in the newspaper, surprised that psychic energy could be strong enough to produce this material trace.

He usually got little mail, so he was startled to get a bulging cardboard express mail envelope the next day. He upended it, and the leather mask itself slid out. He had to fish in the envelope for the tiny pink note from Mitzi. "Please don't think I'm pushy. I'm concerned. Think I've been getting negative vibrations. Do see if anything comes through with this. Big hug, M. Seeya Tuesday." He noticed Mitzi had written his name as Bayer on the outside and Baird on the note— "Dearheart Baird."

Bayard's first thought was to return the mask at once. But if he took it back the moment he received it, he'd look too fussy, too inflexible. Mitzi might be hurt or embarrassed. On the other hand, he didn't want to wait until Tuesday. He decided he'd drive by and drop it off tomorrow. Try to seem casual about it. He'd say he didn't want the responsibility of guarding Felix's relic.

He tried to laugh at himself when he found he didn't want to touch the thing. He made an effort to scoop it back into the envelope but only nudged it across the floor. He got a ballpoint pen and carefully prodded the mask inside. With a little finesse he managed not to touch it. He tried to laugh at himself, about his delicacy, but somehow it didn't seem that silly. He leaned the envelope against the jamb of his door—the outside jamb—so he wouldn't forget to take it down to the car.

He thought he'd gotten over all his hang-ups about being gay. But he couldn't help wondering if this wasn't some twisted guilt reaction. The gay boy Felix's death had been a shock. The otherworldly message was still hanging over him. He he-deserved-it flyer had caused him a passing irritation. He was deep in this thing with Rob, just the kind of affair the world frowned on. And though he couldn't bring himself to touch the mask, he couldn't stop imagining, with this out-of-nowhere sexual longing, wearing it—it and nothing else.

On Saturdays starting at four the biggest bar in Jasper had one of those parties archly called a tea dance. Everybody showed up, and the sun usually went down with obliging splendor. Out back people congregated on a huge patio overlooking the beach and watched a show-offs' game of volleyball. In bathing suits and fanny packs, the men leaned over the railing, sometimes lifting their faces, in pure pleasure, into the golden light. The vodka tonics aglitter in their hands rapidly disappeared. Sunburned cheeks got redder and the gleaming whites of eyes blurred.

Bayard waited for Rob at the long white-painted bamboo bar outside. This was to be their first meeting before sunset. "Do you think we're stupid?" the bartender, a sort of friend, asked him. The slack sensuality of the boy's lips invited one answer.

"No," Bayard said. He was nervous, distracted.

"I'm too polite. I wish I could just say 'Fuck you' when these guys—I mean really old guys—try to pick me up. 'Cause they're treating me in this weird . . . like they're trying to fool me, acting sort of sneaky, as though, you know, they think I can't tell what they're up to. Like I'm stupid. It's weird."

Bayard was having trouble concentrating. Thoughts of the envelope on the passenger seat of his car made him feel vulnerable, as if at any moment he might have another unpleasant psychic experience. Talk of stupidity made it worse. If he were smart at all, that would be a shield against what he felt was happening to him. Into the skittish disarray of his thoughts a memory came with a humiliating erotic charge: his smug old boyfriend whispering to him as they were having sex, "You're such an idiot, you're such an idiot"—as if that were an endearment! But this is who I am, he thought defiantly. At least for that moment he believed his true personality resided in a characterless ache of arousal. "Being smart isn't the most important thing," he said aloud.

"But I keep thinking about that kid with the coconuts," the bartender went on desultorily. "I mean, that was stupid, wasn't it? He couldn't look up?" There was wind tonight. Cocktail napkins fluttered. A cigarette ash danced like an angry bee in the bar's huge amber ashtray. The bartender moved away, obedient to a lifted finger. Bayard waited.

After about an hour and a half, a pixie in spandex shorts came with a message. Rob had taken ecstasy with some waiter friends. He was dancing at another club. Bayard could join them if he felt like it, but they weren't sure how long they'd be there. The pixie delivered the message with a rather mean-spirited look of condolence, sweetly, *"If you feel like it.*" Then he raised his eyebrows and waited in hopes, it seemed, of a response worth repeating.

"Oh. Thanks a lot," was all he got.

He shrugged pertly and minced off with floating heels.

Bayard woke in the middle of the night. He seemed to faint awake as you do sometimes when you've had too much to drink. After a depressed meal of fast food, he'd gotten drunk and gone home early. *If he felt like it!* He could still faintly hear the Saturday night music across town. His TV was also on at a low volume. Parched, he went to the refrigerator and polished off a carton of orange juice. He squinted against the bright refrigerator light. The sense of the muttering TV eked through amazingly gloomy thoughts: more about tropical storm Felix, which was soberly predicted to hit the coast now.

He hadn't left the TV on. He hadn't watched TV that night. He was sure of it, and the thought woke him up. His sudden alertness made it plain how groggy he really was, perhaps still a bit drunk. It made his usual nakedness feel more naked.

With a sidling motion he came around to the front of the TV and eyed the blue screen. The weatherman, in front of a map of south Florida, was wearing the black mask. Bayard averted his eyes, checking whether this was an effect of the refrigerator light. But he knew it wasn't. This time it was no blot, but the mask itself, gleaming three-dimensionally under the studio lights. Otherwise the man wore the usual awful tie and a yellow sport coat. The masked head moved fractionally as it spoke. The grim phrases somehow weren't muffled by the gag. "Tropical storm Felix moved a little closer this evening. People on the coast will have to keep an eye on this one. It does appear to be getting stronger." He repeated these phrases over and over again.

Bayard forced himself to press the remote's on/off button. First the movie *Flashdance* came on. Only when he pressed the button a second time did the screen go dark. As if the TV had been off during the masked weather report.

Weak dawn light eased Bayard's jitters just enough for him to doze off. He slept until one-thirty in the afternoon, yet he was still groggy when he woke. His project for the day was simple. Get the mask back to Mitzi.

Except for a fairly strong breeze the weather was fine. There was no sign of the storm yet, nor were people closing up shop as they did when they became concerned. The garland of black flippers clucked under the awning of the store.

Bayard meant to have a quick bite to eat. He kept drinking coffee in an effort to wake up. But it only put him in a buzzed trance. In spite of persistent alarm that he was being haunted by Felix, he was also deeply hurt that Rob had stood him up. He knew he shouldn't be. Making a feeble ping with a teaspoon in his fourth cup of coffee, he was overcome by a doleful sense of obscurity, a conviction that no one in the world was thinking of him. And that this confirmed there was nothing much to be thought of. A body, attractive in a common way, and its anonymous emotions, anxiety, and gloom. When he finally left the diner, two hours had passed.

It took him a while to get through the stop-and-go Sunday traffic in Jasper. By the time he was at the far end of the island, it was almost five o'clock. The sun was low. No band of clouds obscured it, but the car radio was full of warnings about the storm.

Instead of going directly to Mitzi's, Bayard parked at the shelly turnaround where people left their cars on their way to Homolulu. He could walk to Mitzi's from there. Once he'd gotten rid of the mask, he might start feeling better. Less alone. He didn't recognize the bikes on the rack or either of the two other cars.

It took a minute to reach Mitzi's bungalow. No lights were burning. But it was still early. He knocked several times. The longer he stood, the more annoyed he became. He was being shut out. Thwarted, he was unable to think coherently. Should he wait? Come back later? In his stupor, the decision seemed immensely complicated.

Next to the door a window of glass slats offered a tricky view into the dim living room of the bungalow. Bayard bent and peered in. It took him a moment to recognize the form, which he at first thought was a dust ruffle or something shifting in the breeze of the air conditioner fan. But light from somewhere made a dull gleam on an unmistakable rounded shape, a boy's ass. A whole naked body resolved itself, moving in a listless rhythm, a sort of dance. The utter strangeness of the sight put all alarm out of Bayard's mind. He watched as the coffee-colored body, which faced away from him, slowly turned. Even before he saw the face, logic told him this must be Felix, conjured by the objects in Mitzi's possession. His own elbow tightly clutched the envelope containing the mask, and he felt the sweat trickling down to it, as evanescent as alcohol. At last the face did appear, difficult to make out. The expression was lax, as stupid as a human face could be. The lips moved while the figure danced. Barely danced, like a go-go boy when ashtray and drinks crowd his boots. Bayard struggled to read Felix's soundless words.

He didn't feel afraid until the eyes focused on him. Focused with an acknowledgment or recognition so faint it seemed just shy of unconscious. But the lips exaggerated the message. The moment Bayard could make it out—"Dance with me," repeated with stupefying regularity—he turned. Muscles misfiring awkwardly, he walked away. He almost tripped down the steps. He had to think to raise his feet so his sandals didn't drag. And his whole back seethed, like bubbling water, with atavistic fear. Yet he didn't run. The sight was simply too strange. In the narrow book of his experience, Bayard had no reaction to call upon. He walked. He passed his own car in the turnaround. The bikes and other cars were gone. He took the spiny path down to the beach.

After walking quite a distance without encountering anyone, he lay down on the sand in the same golden light that always flooded the bar in Jasper. It was hard to make out, but perhaps the salmon and lavender bands next to the ember-bright sun were forerunners of the storm. The surf was much heavier than usual. But the utter normality of this scene put him in the confounded calm of shock. The rhythmic tremor of the ground under his body was lulling. He closed his eyes.

He woke after nightfall. And he couldn't see. It was pitch black. The single streetlight at the turnaround should have been visible, but he could see nothing. The wind was cold now and strong—obviously a storm wind. He could feel spray carried from the thunderous surf. Unless it was rain already. He didn't remember taking off his clothes. Could he have done it automatically because this was Homolulu? He felt around the sand for his things. The envelope? The mask. His hand went to his face. Nothing.

He knew little about nature, but he knew well enough that if it was this dark, utterly lightless, the sky must have clouded over. No moonlight, no starlight. It occurred to him that he really had no idea whether his eyes were even open. He tried raising and lowering his eyelids with an exaggerated motion. He still couldn't be sure. To make certain, he pulled his eyelids apart with his fingers. He felt the wind on his eyes. They teared. But he could see nothing, except the dim, pointless patterns of light he'd only ever noticed when his eyes were tightly closed. He rubbed his eyes to get rid of the patterns. They stayed. He might as well have been unable to open his eyes. He was on his hands and knees still, feeling for his clothes. He patted out a circle with his hands. Only sand and shells. He stood and drew his foot across the sand in a wider circle.

The fear he'd felt all day was now much worse. On standing he'd noticed his sense of balance was off. Without visual cues it was hard to tell what was up and what was down. For a moment he might have been floating in space. The formless darkness was enclosing the moment he stopped moving, claustrophobic. Walking burial.

The fitful wind now hit his body with the firmness of shoving hands. His sense of balance became even less secure. He couldn't stop thinking how neat this was—his being caught on the beach, blind, naked, when Felix hit. Felix the storm, that is, entirely unlike that slack husk of a soul he'd seen dancing at Mitzi's. Though he'd just touched his face, he had to do so again, roughly, to make certain a second time that he wasn't wearing the mask. He rubbed his eyes more. Still nothing.

He oriented himself by sound. The hollow bass and sizzle of the waves on his left, the higher-pitched fluttering of leaves and palm fronds on his right. He gave up on his clothes and crept forward, feeling with his toes whether the ground in front of him rose or fell. He kept well clear of the palms. Once or twice he heard a bodylike thud through the uproar as clusters of coconuts hit the ground. At the same time, he was more unnerved by the ocean. When he felt a long wave envelop his left foot, the sand dissolving underneath, his knees went as weak as the sand. "Up" was even more difficult to distinguish as the wind grew stronger and rain or spray lashed him. The sand was yielding. "Down" was uncertain, too.

He had to cross a small tidal inlet. The water had been ankle-deep on his way out. Now he could hear from its alto guttering that it was much deeper. Even if he were able to cross it—and his knees buckled when he came to the slope leading down to the water—he had no idea how to find the path to the turnaround on the other side.

Vision is the queen of the senses. All this time, as he groped and listened, he couldn't help staring hard at the moving spots, the particulate nothingness. It seemed his eyes themselves were gone. Something was definitely wrong. From here he should have been able to see the turnaround light.

When his calves were in the water, he felt the wrenching current and wasn't sure he'd be able to stand if the water in the middle were much deeper. The flow ate away at the sand under his feet with each step.

Besides the stones and shells that made him wince and almost lose his balance, other things were in the water. The slick, muscular bodies of fish, or of something, butted against his legs in a frenzy. He had no idea why the water was so alive. Nature seemed convulsed. But he had no understanding of nature. Some of the shells he stepped on had meaty, sluggish life in them. Or was it mud? He began to use his eyes for something—crying, because he was unsure he was even traversing the inlet—he could be wading down the middle in this torrent of flinching bodies, heading out to sea.

Once he did clamber up the far side, he was hardly better off. He was pelted with bits of dried twig and palm leaf. Uprooted dune grass wound itself around his wet legs and his wrists. Even he knew this wasn't natural. He ripped the stinging grass from his body. More invisible bands came out of the wind, stuck to him, twined around his limbs. The more he tore off, the more flew onto him, until he was struggling in place.

The clinging film of darkness couldn't be torn off like the grass. He'd never find the path, so he ran into the brush away from the sound of the ocean. Stubble punctured his feet. He blundered, zigzagging, shredding his legs. After an interminable time of this, crying freely, he came upon packed earth, the turnaround, which he criss-crossed until his knee hit the car's fender. His hands reached out as if to embrace it.

He felt almost no relief, because, now, to see nothing now, within feet of a streetlight, meant something impossible had happened. He got into the car and felt for the keys under the rubber mat. But he couldn't drive blind.

The storm continued, and he sat there bleeding, sometimes crying, and studying the specs of light that appeared among the black on black pinwheels which made up perfect darkness. The only thing he actually saw—so vividly he couldn't be sure he saw it with his mind's eye—was Felix mouthing the mindless invitation, Dance with me. Ir-relevantly, it seemed, he also heard the pixie's voice: *If you feel like it.*

Over the wind, he really heard nothing. The rain must have soaked the packed earth of the turnaround. And certainly the streetlight's concrete footing was too small. The high pole with its one drooping arm leaned in the wind, and a great disc of shelly earth and concrete tipped up at the base. The damp earth opened silently, except for a faint gulping of the puddled ditch. The pole paused in its descent. Then it came down. The car roof yielded with an unresonant bang and a pebbly rustle of broken glass, also dull.

But to an observer, and there was only one, the scene looked en-tirely different. No rain, no storm at all. At her heels the waves un-furled leaf after leaf of placid water. Her back was to the clouds, only a few of them, backlit by predawn blue light. She looked across the sea-grape to the turnaround, hands outspread. As soon as the street-light fell on the car, Mitzi bent and picked up the sandals, the draw-string pants, a flimsy white tank top and the bulging red, white, and blue envelope.

&ν&ν&ν

Sometimes they actually did play canasta, but this evening some-thing better was in the cards. Alec wore a floating white djellabah, which he thought flatteringly disguised his paunchy body. He even managed, with an eager burst of energy, to bound up the steps to the door. When he knocked, a blurred face appeared in the slatted glass "Florida" window next to the door. The door opened.

Inside was a confusion of sound, a croaking voice—"Thick fingers!"—repeating itself over the clattering air conditioner, and a near-subliminal hint of music. The light was low, reflecting off the carpet with a greenish hue. Eight or ten old people were dispersed around the room, none fully dressed. The missing articles of clothing—pants, foulard boxers, golf shirts—were neatly folded in the bedroom. Some of the guests wore bathrobes, which hung open unselfconsciously. One hefty man wore nothing but a studded harness. A skinny, potbellied oldster hunched pantless in a stuffed chair. He diddled his soft, mammoth genitals. Against his spectral thighs they resembled something the sea spits onto the beach at night. You could tell the group was having trouble maintaining an orgy's decorous silence. "Thick fingers, I love that!" "Eh?" "Thick fingers!" Mitzi was perched, legs tightly crossed, on the arm of the couch. Her peach mouth whispered loudly at the pendulous lobe of an ear: "Trick is to harvest them when they don't have the least thought in their head. Docile souls. Easiest to manage." She noticed Alec and patted the ear's liver-spotted head before getting up. Alec and she knocked cheekbones in greeting. At that moment the skinny masturbator quavered loudly, "He deserved it." Alec looked a warning at Mitzi and said, "Mustn't let him get away with the antigay business again." He added almost fondly, his hand twisting eloquently in the air, "The old crank's so confused!"

Mitzi disagreed. "I say intolerant. Don't see why people can't let people be what they want to be . . ." Her gaze shifted to the side of the room where the two boys danced naked, Felix and Bayard.

Coffee-colored and gingerbread-tanned, their feet barely shuffled on the green carpet. What was left of them, their images or their souls, danced or stopped dancing on demand. "Our procuress!" Alec hailed Mitzi. Then his face went slack as he watched. Bayard's hips shifted. The perfect chest twisted back and forth on the spine as if toyed by a breeze. Alec examined the expression and savored a sort of freedom or confidence. He'd never before felt so much himself in the presence of his attractive young friend. "Exquisite," he murmured, unheard over the air conditioner even by Mitzi smiling next to him.

First Cut

Greg Wharton

I cut myself. I was slicing tomatoes for our sandwiches when it happened. One quick slice of the big knife with the ring finger of my right hand hidden underneath and it was over. The blood started flowing freely immediately, before the sensation of the cut actually registered in my brain. It started throbbing and I panicked. There was no pain, but I still yelled, "Shit. Help!" I let the water run over it for a couple minutes before I applied pressure with a paper towel, then gave up on stopping the blood and wrapped a Band-Aid tightly around it. I continued with the preparation of the sandwiches, more careful with each slice of the knife this time.

The next morning the bleeding had stopped. What was left was a very deep cut in a semicircle across my finger about half an inch in from the tip. I played with it, marveling at how deep it was and the fact I could pull it apart and see that far into the inside of my finger. I applied another Band-Aid, and tried to forget it.

Days passed and the wound scabbed, leaving loose skin around its edges. I left it uncovered. No matter what I did during the day, I couldn't help fingering at it, playing with it. The flayed piece of finger had secured itself back down, but it didn't feel quite right. It didn't really hurt, but all sensation in my body was tied directly to it. I trimmed off the excess skin with a nail clipper, leaving a perfect crescent scab that ringed my finger. I couldn't stop myself from picking at it and enjoying the sight of it, amazed at the healing power my body had.

I pulled the last of the scab off. My thumb dug into the crater that was left, soft new pink skin sensitive to the touch, and my nipples hardened. I reclined back on my bed with my hard cock in my other hand and jerked off while sucking on my finger, running my tongue over the healing wound, licking it around the ridge over and over much like a cockhead. I ejaculated hard into the air.

When my lover fucked me that night, I visualized myself with a fresh cut across my chest running through both nipples. I told him to fuck me harder. "Harder!" When he grabbed my nipples, I screamed out in ecstasy. His fingers pulled on the bloody nipples that had been severed in half, and I shot my orgasm with a fury I've seldom known.

The cut is all but healed. All that remains is a slight ridge of pale skin circling the tip of my ring finger, and a memory of the past two weeks. I miss it. I'm making pasta sauce for dinner. My cock is thumping against the front of my jeans as I cut the tomatoes in preparation. I bring the edge of the knife down across the palm of my hand, pressing down hard with the long sharp blade, to carve another cut.

The Disappearing Andersons

Jess Wells

Late in the afternoon on the last day of March, the Andersons' house exploded. A faulty gas line met a pilot light that had been up too high, or so they said. That was the more sensible of the explanations that circulated Loon Lake within minutes of the fireball's ascension into the silent sky.

The entire Anderson family had been gone at the time. Hank Anderson was in his small, paneled office attempting to sell insurance while his wife picked over the jumble sales. His children were in school, his daughter staring out the window, his son running up and down the basketball court without ever being given the ball.

Everyone knew where the Andersons were; it was Loon Lake, after all, and the expanse of the water gave all the residents the opportunity to know one another's whereabouts without actually having to converse. An incident of this magnitude in a standstill place like Loon Lake was certainly cause to pick up the phone, though. No sign of the house, the neighbors said hurriedly into their phones. Absolutely none. The retirees sitting on their glassed-in porches and the anglers in their sheds had seen the enormous red-gold flame, and then had stared, awestruck, at the space that seemed instantly to fill in the area where the Andersons' house had been. On second glance, they whispered into their receivers, it seemed as if there had never been a house there at all.

The Anderson house rained down on Loon Lake and the adjoining marshes. It fell in pieces of wood and pipe no larger than a fist. Enormous pieces of wall, of furniture, of boxes and glass jars were reduced to bits, pummeling what the locals hoped was the last of the winter's snow. Already the ground was visible around the base of the reeds. A brown collar of dirty snow circled the lake, and a few ducks had emerged in the early afternoon, covering their feet with sloppy mud. The snow was nearly transparent, moments from becoming water, and it hung thick and clumsy on the branches and shrubs. It was seductive and dangerous with its hint of spring. It tempted children to barrel into it. The tease of bare ground and the momentary sunshine made them fling themselves, flailing around as an act of revenge against the winter, but it soaked through their mittens in a moment flat, and soon they'd be smelling cold wet wool and the aroma of their own hands going numb. Before they reached their cabins the sky could turn slate gray and freeze their pants and mittens stiff. It was old but not toothless snow.

Hank and Ruth Anderson were the first to reach the spot that had been their home. They got out of the car slowly, gripping the edges of their doors. The anglers who pushed their luck in shacks on ice that was too raggedy for the sane watched them from their windows. They were thankful that the Andersons also seemed to be puzzled over the sudden prominence of trees that had been in the backyard, of parts of the forest that had rushed in and filled up the place where their house had been. Mrs. Anderson began to shriek and throw her arms into the air.

A few of the lake residents drove to the house to see if they could help: poor man shouldn't be left to figure it all out by himself, they thought, but they admitted to themselves that they were curious as hell. Mrs. Anderson paced around each visitor as they relayed as many details as they could muster. The walls were completely gone, and the piping and electrical inside them. The nearest piece of the roof that they could find was halfway across the lake, lying on the ice. There wasn't a single piece of discernible furniture, no personal possessions or clothing. Hank and the men walked around the perimeter of what had been the house, peering into the stubs of the walls, looking at the junction of wire and foundation. It was a complete loss. Mrs. Anderson turned her back on the house.

When the children came home, the daughter stumbled around wringing her long blonde hair, and the son joined the procession of men, who were on their fifteenth lap around the perimeter. The Andersons lived at an isolated bend on the lakefront, and the other residents could only see them from across the water. Everyone was glued to their front porch and the public docks. Mrs. Anderson marshaled her children into their station wagon and admonished her son to leave the other car behind. After much prodding, Hank joined them, and everyone drove away from the site, as if the supernatural had turned their former home into a Bermuda Triangle on the edge of a small Michigan lake. They drove to the nearest town and rented a hotel room.

The late afternoon sun made the snow glow, and the silence of a late winter day descended on the lake. People continued to stand and stare at the former site of the Andersons' home, but now the children were home from school, and the high school boys immediately put on their knee-high rubber boots, packed extra mittens, pulled their dads' plaid hunting hats over their ears, and began to scrounge through the marshland for bits of the Andersons' lives.

Soon the phones were abuzz again, as cracking voices relayed the find of financial papers scattered in bits over the meadow, and pieces of prescription drug bottles discovered near the turtle log. Mothers insisted on being told the stories that they heard in snatches from their kids' conversations, and some men donned their own caps and went outside, ostensibly to find something that would help Hank. Soon the entire lake was in possession of an odd assortment of pieces of the Andersons' lives that had floated into their yard, fallen on their woodpile, lodged in the eaves or bushes around their houses.

That night, lying on the soft and damp mattress of the hotel, Ruth Anderson cried quietly to herself while her husband held her hand. Hank was so stiff his legs were twitching of their own accord. They had moved to Loon Lake two years ago—a mere weekend in lake-time—and no one had ever suspected that there had been a problem back in Detroit. No one in the family ever spoke about the month when Ruth had been unable to get out of bed, unable to cook or clean or even speak to her children, when she lay staring at a ceiling fan that didn't move, turning her head only slightly to see her husband's face twisted up in confusion over her sudden surrender. She hadn't surrendered at Loon Lake, not once. She had gotten out of bed every morning, she had made dinner every evening. She had turned berries into jam with the other women, put little tags on junk for jumble sales. She had pressed her children's clothes, attended bad theater productions in town, stopped to chat with a few women she considered friends when she met them in the supermarket aisles. She had had lunch with these women nearly every month, and even though they just talked about Oprah or their own gasping shock over tidbits from the news—never divulging infidelities or children gone bad—these had been social encounters. The picky little details of life hadn't pinned her to the sheets this time. The Tupperware, the Ziplocs, the dustpans, coupons, carburetors, hair clasps, and the dirty socks—she had conquered them. She was able to juggle them all. She even had a couple of little porcelain figurines with real straw coming out of their baskets perched on the windowsill in front of her kitchen sink, testimony to her ability to tolerate the fussy, pesky, delicate smallness of her life. She barely even trembled anymore.

Ruth squirmed under the sheets in the hotel bed, her husband and children rustling nearby as if trying to keep a kinetic energy circulating around her. She didn't know whether to be relieved that everything had blown to bits, a condition she expected and now didn't have to fight against, or devastated that all her hard work at keeping the buttons buttoned and the snaps snapped would have to be done again. The battle made her roll back and forth like a log against a shoreline.

In the middle of that night, the Big Thaw descended on Loon Lake. Every year there was one particular night that ushered in spring. The nighttime temperature would hover at a midday level, and the ice on the lake would crack with a booming that woke the old folks. Bets would be placed on whether all the fishing sheds would get off the lake successfully, and how many beers would have been drunk by the one guy dumb enough to drive his pickup out there to retrieve them. Tree branches bounced up after a winter of holding great volumes of snow, creeks suddenly came alive with runoff, and rocks and logs that have been held on the edge of the bank by the grip of ice suddenly tumbled into the muddy shore. Nature was lively that night, and animals emerged twitching and chattering.

The thaw only served to exacerbate the Andersons' problems. Papers and scraps of clothing that had lain neat and still on the icy shelf of snow were now sodden and wrapped around the roots of cattails. Parts of Ruth's sofa were now blocking the culvert near the old beaver dam and would pose a problem within a few days.

In the morning, the sheriff arrived at the site, followed by the highest-ranking official in the Bureau of Fish and Game, who took a keen interest in pollution cases. Hank Anderson arrived alone just afterward. The Andersons would have to pick up all the debris, the officials explained, or have the insurance company take care of it, because it posed a threat to wildlife, intruded on other people's property, and was a health hazard. The two men extended their condolences to Hank and wished him luck in dealing with the insurance company, but they held firm. The debris would have to be cleared out.

The Anderson family arrived the next day in new boots and hats, and began gathering their lives into plastic garbage bags. The insurance claim had been filed, but the company was woefully slow, especially in such a rural area, and the water damage that could be inflicted from just a few days' impeded runoff could set the Andersons up for significant damages. Hank Anderson bent to the task as if danger were seconds away. It hadn't mattered that he sold insurance, it hadn't mattered that he had represented the company for years: a policy was a policy and the corporate officials had made it clear that the higher the claim, the higher the premium in the future.

Mrs. Anderson gathered bits of her belongings together as if trying to pull a knit skirt down over her knees. A lone Buick, powder blue, belonging to one of her luncheon friends, pulled up to the site but stopped yards away. Ruth's friend got out carefully, as if afraid the ground contained explosives, straightened the nylon scarf on her head and the raincoat around her sweatpants, and pulled a casserole dish off the front seat.

"My God, it's really gone," Betsy said. Funerals, hospitalizations, bad luck all called for casseroles, but this was too far beyond noodles and aluminum foil. This was black magic. Betsy proffered her casserole reluctantly.

Ruth held the dish in her hand, turned slightly as if looking for a spoon, a microwave, a counter to set it on, then looked back at her luncheon friend as if she had just been presented with a human head on a platter. She took the dish and heaved it into the woods where it smashed into bits on a rock. Betsy backed away, holding her scarf in place, clambered into her car without taking her eyes off Ruth, and backed down the driveway as fast as she could go.

Ruth's daughter sat by the bank of the lake and cried.

After a few days, father and son could be seen hurriedly walking along the county road, bent over like old ragpickers, their hoods up, their clothing dirty and torn.

While they worked, the residents of Loon Lake pondered the little details of the Andersons' lives that had suddenly been revealed. Who was it who took the prescription drugs? And didn't that bottle say Valium? It had a "v" on it, the old women whispered to each other over the phone. And don't forget that casserole. At every luncheon, every ball game, the subject ultimately came up: what bit of debris had fallen into *your* yard, and what did it say about the Andersons? It didn't matter that Hank belonged to the Kiwanis and his wife had volunteered at the blood bank and the medical clinic. Stories began to be created, and soon people stopped inviting the Andersons over because it was just too much fun to decipher their lives from the shards of their belongings. Why, one guy had found Hank and Ruth's bankbook, and it was a sight. Of course most of the pages were gone and the snow had done a number on the writing, but you could sort of make it out. Who would have thought that the Andersons had so much money? Must have inherited it, the stories began, maybe from parents in the East. And them now living in a hotel and wearing those old clothes. Stingy rich people got no pity, the stories continued, soon embellished with stock deals and mergers, property holdings, bond swindles. Some heard they were originally from Philadelphia, blue-blooded family, with madness and infidelity, a couple of abandoned children along the way. The Andersons that trod through the marsh-land picking up paper on the ends of pointed sticks soon bore no re-semblance to the wild-living, moneyed Andersons who had survived wars and immigration, amassed a fortune owning factories, birthed scores of children. Like the forest that had rushed into the spot where the Andersons' home had been, the stories rushed into the place where the actual lives of the Andersons had been. Suddenly their personalities were reinterpreted, their motives for incidences that were years old were suddenly suspect, their virtue was questioned, their backgrounds swallowed up by the ephemeral Andersons, the concocted Andersons, the collective fabrication of an entire lake community suddenly given little bits of fodder for their imagination.

The months wore on and Ruth Anderson became an outcast at the lake. Remember the casserole? the women whispered. Goes to show you don't really know anyone, not really. Besides, why should they give charity to a woman who was slumming it? Hank Anderson's business faltered as the stories continued about shady dealings. He began attracting only riffraff clientele. It took very little to ostracize the high-school Andersons. A few stories about the daughter's virginity, backed up by scraps of what looked like lingerie, and she was eating lunch alone over an algebra book. Girls hurried over the marshlands with love notes in their pockets for the dashing world-traveler Anderson boy, only to pass him unnoticed on the county road as he continued his stoop-shouldered quest for the scraps of his belongings.

A check arrived from the insurance company, but there would be no assistance in the cleanup. With business suddenly going bad, they would have to begin living on the money if Hank didn't do something fast. Ruth Anderson wouldn't allow the family to build again on the same spot, believing that the lake had turned against them, and the family was secretly relieved that they wouldn't have to live among people who were keeping tiny piles of the Andersons' house, clothes, and kitchen in the boat shed or in boxes on the living-room tables. It was just too shameful to have all their dear belongings suddenly categorized as both a public nuisance and a curiosity.

The Andersons made plans to move to Traverse City and begin again. Spring was in full bloom at Loon Lake when the Andersons took one last look at their lot, pounded a For Sale sign into the wet peat, and drove away. The lake residents hardly noticed. Bands of retired ladies, at that same moment, were circling the lake in their new tennis shoes and sweatpants, breathlessly explaining how the Andersons were off to Panama, or was it Caracas? After all, one of them had a scrap of a travel brochure deep in the fleece of her pocket.

Bitch

M. Christian

There was a used condom in the trash, just lying there: slightly yellowed, glistening, full at the tip. Next to the rest of the garbage, the bloated white plastic, the dark-stained brown paper bags, it was brilliant and shocking. Looking down at it, envy was a burning bile in Quinn's throat. Finally the weight of the trash in his arms broke in, and with an unconscious hiss of strain, he lifted it high and slammed it down into the can.

Walking back down the narrow alleyway, retracing his slippered steps to the stairs up to his apartment, he caught sight of one of them, high up on the balcony, leaning flamboyantly back, a half-full glass in his hand glimmering in the dying sunlight. Looking perhaps too long, Quinn summoned him, causing the young man to sip from his glass and look over and down. Eye contact: the lean body, the delicately sculptured hair, perfect porcelain smile, the wicked mocking grin, directed at Quinn. Then a kiss, not blown but rather thrown—like a stone, mocking. At Quinn, at the garbage. Face burning, heart pounding, Quinn walked with heavy steps up to his own place, each tone of his laughter, each bird-chipping sound a cut into his back.

Upstairs (sticky key in gummy lock, stubborn door groaning with age), Mr. Boots was waiting for him. Sometimes, not often, the sight of the skinny little black-and-white cat made Quinn feel that he had, indeed, arrived home. Other times, like evenings discovering the leftovers of someone else's pleasure, the sight of the old, mangy cat just reminded him of Billy. Much had been taken by the Latino hustler—his camera, his stereo, the $2,500 in his bank account—but he'd left at least two things behind. One was a note, the condescending words a bitterness he recalled too often, and the other was the sad little kitten they'd picked out together at the shelter.

"Okay, okay," Quinn said, shuffling inside and dead bolting the back porch door, "I'll feed ya." It was a standard, the closest the older man came to a religion, a litany that held his life together. Again, the dark, smelly kitchen, the piles of magazines, newspapers. The Tom of Finland signed print in the dusty frame that Lorenzo had given him—Lorenzo who had left with not as much money, not as much damage, and so more frequently dropped into Quinn's fantasies.

The living room was as dark, with a bouquet of its own—musty, a lethargic smell. A weight of too-same days. Walking in, Quinn thumbed, first, the set on, and then the machine. The old television crackled menacingly, humming a firm base, then glowed into a news-caster's head and shoulders. The other machine did a much more clean start, showing the familiar ribbed-chest backdrop, the same Mapplethorpe pectorals, the intimate parade of icons down one side. Normally, when the litany of his days was more comfortable, he might have wandered down to the Shamrock, watched some game or other with the cronies there, or sat at the kitchen table with his latest Honcho, Inches, or Torso sipping from an amber bottle until the im-ages seemed to swim in a lazy haze of self-imposed steam.

Condoms in the trash. The anger was too present, too acid. The old desk chair creaked under his ass, the mouse skipped across the screen—a half-conscious reminder to clean it—and with a click Quinn opened a door.

It hadn't always been that way. It was a quicksand of life, a slow de-scent. He hadn't struggled—at least not at first. Birth was in a cool house in Virginia, mother who drank, Chief Petty Officer father, and Benjamin, their "sensitive" son. First memories, painfully recalled as a dull ache when he sat at the kitchen table, of muscle magazines smug-gled up into the attic. Thinking of them, of their strong smiles, their marble muscles, made him long for their innocence: children's desires mixed with ancient dust. One summer, the summer he'd first seen an-other boy's penis at swim camp, he'd stayed there so long the dust had lodged in his throat. Till the day his mother died she expressed con-cerns over the allergies that had so affected him then.

He used to keep some shutters open, the one to the left in the bay window, looking across the narrow alley at the neighbor's mirror Victorian. Sometimes, sitting in front of one glowing screen or other, he would catch sight of them—the boys with the golden hair, the magical eyes, the so-smooth skin. A picture book he'd seen as a boy, that same year as when the "allergies" had made his eyes water, the artist long since forgotten—but the images, naiads flitting through carbonated pools under an azure sky, clouds like white satin had remained: an ideal, an absolute. Mythical sprites, with skin like fresh cream. A favorite fantasy from then on, being something other than the old Quinn, the bowed and balding Quinn. Being one of them, diving through the bubbling waters, hips brushing against theirs, mouths fluttering sweet kisses, eyes full of love and sweet desire.

Once the painting had been across that tiny alley, once he'd looked out the frame of that open window and seen them: blue eyes, wheatfield hair, laughter like the chiming of precious bells, chests like marble—stone carved by swimming, running, fucking. Then one of them had looked, had seen Quinn staring back. The stuff of dreams . . . but then he had laughed, producing the cruel biting caw that had since begun living in his disturbing half-sleeps, his hollow and lonely nightmares.

Are you horny tonight? The bluntness of the newbie, flashing up on his screen. The skies were phosphors, microscopic dots arranged in a grid, illuminated by a tight spray of electrons. No clouds. No water. But the boys could be as lithe and alluring as in that painting. All it took was a polite deception, a sensual lie. It wasn't idyll, wasn't perfection, but maybe someone, somewhere, would think that. For old Quinn, with his threadbare slippers, his old cat, his stacks of yellowing porno magazines, it was still a kind of magic.

Tonight though he didn't feel like being Troy, or Lance, or Julian. Tonight, Quinn was too much . . . Quinn. He didn't answer the message, and instead just lurked, watching the scrolls of chatter, feeling the anger chew and gnaw.

Empty-headed peacocks. A simple, bold font.

You're insulting peacocks, Quinn click/clacked back, his hands dancing on the faded letters of the keyboard. *At least peacocks produce something.*

It hadn't always been this way, which made it so much worse. When you fall, however slowly, you know what is possible, what's being denied, been taken away. He'd never been one of the . . . peacocks, but he hadn't always lurked in the heavy darkness. Some good timing—the death of his father, a heart attack at fifty-five, had left him some real estate. His mother dropping into a sullen old age. The ties cut, severed quick and clean. He'd had money—enough—and a mission. To put flesh to dreams, to make dusty attic fantasies real.

Disgusting. Just disgusting—

Rude, inconsiderate, Quinn typed back, watching the characters appear on his glowing screen. *Parading around, flouncing it up. Rubbing our faces in it. Yeah, fucking disgusting—*

Many years of goodness—a heavenly parade of memories. Boyfriends, money, glitter balls, and beer. Snapshots that flipped through his mind when he didn't want them: the Latin boy, all darkness and smiles, jeans too tight, lips too full. The hot kiss after the parade. Then, there, the world had been wide, open—full of love and potential for more. The blond treasure who'd served him coffee one day— beaming grin, flirting eyes. "Call me, hon," slender fingers grazing Quinn's palm. The seven digits on the check. He'd been too scared to call, too intimidated by perfection. Now, he masturbated in the dark, hating himself for his cowardice.

Hate them. Know how that is. Disgusting peacocks. So pretty, so stupid. Shoving our faces in it.

He felt lied to, the bitterness seeming right, justified. He'd crossed that bridge of knives, lived with the hatred: "Fag! Homo! Fucking Queer!" He'd wanted to be welcomed, embraced, brought into the Muscle Academy, whisked away to the dude ranch where cowboys would use him to his utter enjoyment. He'd wanted . . . to taste it. Now, though . . . now he knew it for what it was, a rainbow lie. It was there, but only if you had the money, the looks, the courage. If you didn't have any of that, then it was all out of reach or—soiled condoms in the trash—just a bitter reminder of failure.

Just disgusting. Hate looking at them, he typed, feeling a little strong in his hatred, his bitchiness. The other, Rollin58991, was an illusion—but one he felt a closeness to. An illusion because so much was unknown—or just unnecessary to share. Quinn imaged him as a mirror, somewhere in the city, somewhere like where he was: seeing the beauty, having the hunger, but knowing the smiles were mocking—not inviting.

They chatted for a few minutes more, till the anger exhausted Quinn. Slippers on his feet, he shuffled off to bed. He thought about masturbating, but the sourness in his throat made their lithe young bodies hard and cruel, distant and vicious. He let sleep take him.

❧ ❧ ❧

A day—or it could have been just a bit longer. He did remember the walk back from the bar. Three beers in his pale belly, legs tired from the hill. Disco, thumping down the tree-lined street. With the first note he knew it was a party, knew it was next door.

It was. Pretty young things, features cut from tanned stone, brilliant smiles flashing desire. Lithe bodies poised on the balcony, sparkling laughter and gruff desire drifting down, mixing with the sexual base of the music.

Quinn got older, fatter. He hadn't noticed his reek before, but now it hit him—booze and cigarettes, the perfume of the pathetic.

Key in the lock, gate swung wide. Down the alley, upstairs, the other balcony. Cheap plastic tumblers in thin, strong hands. So easy . . . so easy he did it without thinking: those hands around his cock, those soft lips on his own. He felt himself stir despite the pain of reality.

One of them turned, looked down. His smile lit up the world, a burst of innocent light. That it could have been pity never entered Quinn's mind—that he had looked and not looked away was enough. It was a kind of touch, a kind of love. Distant, yes; never more than a look, but there was something special in this young statue, this young David's glance: he saw a man, someone like himself. They had something in common—a lust for men's bodies, for men's love.

But then someone took his arm, pulled him back into the tanned and buffed chaos, back into the merciless rhythm of the party. Words, maybe his or maybe someone else's drifted down, lacerated Quinn, poured alcohol into the cuts . . . "fucking troll . . ."

He didn't feel it at first, not as it slipped past his ears and into his mind. But with the first heavy foot on the old wooden steps, it started: the anger, the shame. Upstairs, the dark, smelly apartment, the cat—and the reminder of the acid in the smile, the promises not kept but, rather, taken advantage of. "You just ain't got anything I want," the little Latino had said, almost his last words to Quinn.

Nothing was there—the apartment, as always, was empty. Alone and burning, he walked into the darker front room. He'd left the machine running, a fact that surprised him. A creature of habit, Quinn had rolled his routine around him—a warm blanket, thick armor. The machine had been left on. Unusual.

A screech of mating modems. Chat, at first—pleasantries, but feeling forced, wooden. He was a false Quinn, one following the rules he'd set out for himself.

There was something wrong. "Them" again?

Fingers paused above keys. The anger, the shame, bubbling—making his ears ring, his breath come in ragged gasps.

Fucking hate them, he finally typed, slowly.

I know. I know how they make you feel. I understand.

Disgusting. Stupid, fucking, pretty-boys.

Let it out. All of it. It'll help.

So he did. Fingers, slowly at first, but then faster, spelling out his pain. The hate. Later, looking over his shoulder at that dark room, lit only by bluish technology, he realized just how much hate had dribbled . . . poured out of him. He opened a vein and bled on the keys —frustration, bitterness, resentment. The lies of love and happiness. The lies of Honcho, Torso, and Tom of Finland. The rainbow lie. It could all be yours if you were anyone but Quinn—fat, ugly, and old.

Mostly, he talked about his anger. The disgust he felt for them— they way they paraded around, showing off their shallowness, their petty, whining voices. Peacocks, empty-headed peacocks. Giggling like girls—nauseating.

Finally, he couldn't see any more. Going into the bright yellow bathroom, he pulled off a long streamer of toilet tissue, blew his nose, gagged, then threw up—something that always happened when he cried.

When he went back, the machine was still on, the screen still glowing.

Can you sleep?

Smiling, Quinn typed an affirmative.

Then sleep. It will all be better in the morning.

No alarm clock. Sirens, instead. A short, sharp whoop. The sound of tires scraping a curb, breaking a bottle. Quinn rolled over and felt sleep tug at him again.

But then—another sound. It wasn't something he was used to hearing, so it pulled him back out of his doze. A basic kind of sound. Getting up, he threw on his threadbare yellow robe and fumbled to the window, the one that looked out onto the narrow alley. When he opened the old window, the sound was louder. For a moment, and just that, he thought that it was, perhaps, the cat—trapped and maybe dying somewhere. But a glance over his shoulder showed him the small animal, asleep, curled into a ball on the kitchen table.

Crying. No—sobbing. No—screaming. No . . . a sound he hadn't quite heard before, but still essentially human. It came from within the house next door, in waves.

Quinn went around to the front: blue and red flashes through the thick curtains. Parting them—a police car. No, two. And a white panel van.

Quinn watched, not feeling much of anything, as the stretcher was brought out. Long form in a black plastic bag. One of the men, nothing more than a boy, walking alongside, face haunted, drawn.

After a point, the cars and the van left. The neighborhood, after, was soft and quiet. Quinn didn't think that morning; at least, he tried not to. He was confused, puzzled, and sad. Instead of thinking, he absently watched television, the sound loud, booming. Finally, as the sun started to set and the night grew cool, he went to his living room, and his computer.

A piece of mail was waiting for him. The words, at first, didn't make any sense. So he read them again and again.

Disgusting fags, the message said. Then, I hope that will make you feel better.

When he did believe it, the tears started again—but not for himself.

The Abdominal Snowman

Lawrence Schimel

It was my cousin Julie who found the footprints first.

I know, because when Julie screams it makes my teeth hurt. I rubbed my hand across my jaw, waiting for the aching to stop, then picked up the left wing of the model airplane I was working on and began fitting pieces together again.

A moment later there was another scream, higher than the first one, that left my ears buzzing even after she'd run out of air. "Jessica," I muttered to myself. I could hardly work with such loud distractions and put down the wing, knowing there was still one scream yet to come. I put the cap on the glue and turned off the lamp.

"Might as well go see what trouble they've found now," I sighed.

A new scream pierced the air, so high it made the bones in my toes tingle painfully, as if they'd fallen asleep. Melanie.

I stood up and began walking slowly toward the stairs.

All three of them screamed together.

It's a real pain having three younger cousins, and I mean that literally. I felt a headache coming on, which always happened when they all screamed together, and my jaw, ears, and toes were still hurting.

What made it worse was the fact that my cousins would scream at anything. I wondered what it was this time, but felt little need to hurry. Yesterday it was a silverfish they'd found in Aunt Ellen's bathroom.

We were all visiting Dad's sister, Aunt Ellen, for Christmas vacation. We hardly ever see Aunt Ellen, because she lives so far away, in the uppermost part of Maine, while Dad and I live down in Maryland with Dad's boyfriend, Eric, who's a computer programmer. Aunt Ellen's real nice, not like Dad's brother, Richard, who's a lawyer in

Washington, DC, so we have to see him all the time. He's a real grouch. And his three daughters are always causing trouble.

Aunt Ellen, on the other hand, is as sweet as toffee—especially since she made us all sorts of cakes and brownies and cookies. Eric is a real health nut who is always watching aerobics tapes—Richard Simmons, Jane Fonda, and all the rest of them. He has more workout tapes than the model Aunt Ellen gave me for Christmas has pieces! He makes us eat only 100 percent organic foods with no added sugars or salt or anything. If we want to add spice to something, he makes us use ginger-sesame seasoning instead of salt or pepper. It tastes like powdered cardboard. Whenever Eric has to stay late at the office, Dad and I get very excited and go out for pizza or triple cheeseburgers or any of the things Eric won't let us eat when he's with us, reminding us to watch our health.

But because we were on vacation, and to be polite to our hostess, Eric let Dad and me eat anything Aunt Ellen made for us, which was fortunate since Aunt Ellen had made mountains of food for us to eat and she'd have been insulted if we didn't at least try and finish it all. I felt like a camel sometimes, eating as many sweets as I could to store away sugars for the long desertlike stretch of time when we returned home and weren't allowed to eat desserts anymore. Aunt Ellen was such a great cook that even the healthy foods she made, like brussels sprouts and cauliflower with dinner, tasted good. I wasn't looking forward to going back to Maryland at all.

When I got downstairs, I didn't see my cousins anywhere, so I put my coat on and went outside. I walked around the house, searching for them, and almost wished they'd give one more scream to lead me to them, but my head began to throb at the mere thought and I decided it was just as well that they didn't.

I found them anyway, in the backyard, just outside the living-room window. They were all huddled around something on the ground. I couldn't see what it was as I approached, but I was afraid it was going to be the body of a bird that had flown into the window by mistake, unable to see the glass or realize what it was. My friend Michael's mother kept a canary, and wild birds were always attracted by the canary's song. They would try to fly into the room, and wind up breaking their poor little heads against the glass window. The neighbor's cat usually took care of removing the bodies before anyone even realized they were there, although the cat sometimes left the feet and beak behind to show that it had been there.

The girls hadn't heard me approaching, and since I was still mad at them for giving me a headache I decided to give them a fright. I snuck up to Jessica, who's the middle of the girls, and let out a roar as I grabbed her.

All three girls let out a high-pitched scream and scattered to the wind.

I clutched my poor head, which had now developed a full-blown headache. I hadn't thought through the consequences of my actions, and had forgotten that this would happen if I scared them. I sighed, vowing to learn from this mistake, and bent down to look at what they'd been staring at in the snow.

Then I screamed.

It wasn't a bird at all. It was an enormous footprint, nearly as long as one of my arms. And I knew who it must belong to, too. No wonder I had terrified my cousins a moment ago. They must have thought I was Bigfoot come back to finish them off.

That was when I nearly screamed again, but I swallowed it so only a gurgle of sound escaped. No sense in alarming everyone unless it was really an emergency. Because I had a feeling that pretty soon we really would have an emergency. Because the footprints my cousins had found showed that Bigfoot hadn't just been wandering nearby; he had walked right up to the window and been looking inside the house. Watching us. Probably picking out which of us to eat first.

I felt a chill rush down my spine, and I was so scared I forgot I had a headache, which was fortunate since I had to think. Fast. Hard.

Bigfoot. The Abominable Snowman. The Yeti.

What were we going to do?

I didn't tell the adults because I wasn't sure they would believe me. Actually, I was more afraid that they'd do something foolish, like try and prove that there was no such thing as Bigfoot, walk out into the woods, and get eaten. Earlier today I might've been the one to do something like that, but then I'd seen the footprints. There was no way they could be anything but real. Now, my every instinct was telling me to PANIC!, but I ignored them as best I could and tried to plan what to do.

I resolved to keep a vigilant watch on everyone and make sure no one was ever alone. I'd even watch over my cousins.

But I had no idea what I would do if the monster came back. Correction: *when* the monster came back, for there seemed no doubt in my mind that he wanted one of us. Why else would he have been staring through the window, as if it was the glass counter at the butcher shop?

The girls had come inside and were upstairs in Aunt Ellen's bedroom, playing in her closet. Their mother, my Aunt Veronica, was helping Aunt Ellen make stuffing. Dad was in the basement with Uncle Richard, helping him fix some wooden doors that went in Aunt Ellen's attic. Eric was downstairs in the living room, doing aerobics to the new video he'd gotten for Christmas from Aunt Ellen, who was very thoughtful and always gave everyone exactly what they wanted. I was uncomfortable with his being in there, since that's the room the monster had been looking into, but it was the only room with a TV in it, and I knew that Eric would become even more of a monster than Bigfoot, probably, if anyone got between him and his exercise program. So I decided to go upstairs and keep a careful watch out the window of my room, which was the guest bedroom directly above the living room. If the monster came back, I would see it the moment it left the woods, and have time enough to get Eric to safety.

Everything looked placid and calm from the window. It was hard to believe we were in imminent danger. But I wasn't fooled. I knew the footprints were down there, right below me. I opened my window, despite the cold wind that blew in, and stuck my head outside to look down at the footsprints.

But I couldn't see the footprints. Instead, I saw a huge, hairy, gray shape leaning up against the building.

I started to scream, but banged my head against the window as I jerked backward, and I bit my tongue. The pain made me want to scream again. But I was afraid it would alert the monster.

I ran for the stairs. What would I do? One eight-year-old against a fearsome creature. I didn't know, but I knew I had to hurry.

"Eric," I cried, rushing into the living room, "are you all right?"

I ran straight to the window and looked out. What if the creature reached through and grabbed me? I worried. But I couldn't just let him get Eric. I stared out into the backyard. Bigfoot was gone.

Had he really been there? I wondered. I looked at the snow and saw it was freshly trampled, with a new path leading out of the woods and up to the window. He was real, all right. I'd scared him away— this time. But he'd be back, I was certain.

Some vacation this was turning out to be. I was going to have to spend every moment protecting my family's lives.

I couldn't wait until we went home.

But what about Aunt Ellen? She'd still be here after Dad and Eric and I went home to Maryland, and Uncle Richard and Aunt Veronica and the girls all went back to DC. No, something had to be done about Bigfoot, once and for all. Before it was too late.

I turned back to Eric, who was glued to the TV set, doing squats. When he answered my question, he squatted between each word.

"Of" squat, "course," squat, "dear," squat, "why?" squat.

He was oblivious, as usual when he was working out. He didn't even know what danger he'd just been in.

I still didn't want to alarm him. Not that he'd notice anything while he was working out. "It's nothing, I guess. I just thought I heard something. Must've been a deer."

Eric was doing stretches now. "How" stretch, "sweet" stretch, "of" stretch, "you" stretch, "to" stretch, "worry."

I'd have to be especially vigilant now, I realized, because Eric wouldn't notice a thing if the monster tried to get him while he ws working out. I wondered if it knew that, instinctively, the way lions or wolves will cull the weakest animals from the herd. Or maybe it had singled Eric out because he was so much healthier than the rest of us . . .

Whatever the reason, I wasn't going to let it get him.

Now, if only I could figure out how I was going to stop Bigfoot!

❧ ❧ ❧

"Is everything all right with you, David?" Dad asked at dinner.

I had hardly touched my food. How could we so calmly eat, when it was just fattening us up for Bigfoot to come and eat us? I knew Aunt Ellen was disappointed, and I was sorry to make her feel bad, but I just had no appetite. I'd spent all afternoon on edge, trying to figure out a plan, and I hadn't been able to come up with anything.

I'd wished I were a fighter pilot for real when I got upstairs again and looked at my model airplane. I could then fly over the woods and shoot the monster down before he got one of us.

But instead we just had to sit here and let him come pick us off, like shooting fish in a barrel.

And Dad wondered why I couldn't eat!

Why couldn't he bother one of the girls? I wondered. "I think I ate too many of Aunt Ellen's brownies when she wasn't looking," I said. I could feel myself blushing because of the lie, but I hoped none of them noticed, or perhaps they'd think I had a fever. "Can I go upstairs and lie down?"

"Okay," Dad said, after getting a concerned I-told-you-so look from Eric. As I got up from the table I knew I should've said something else; now I'd never be allowed to eat another brownie until I was eighteen and moved out on my own. But if I didn't think of something to do about Bigfoot, I wasn't going to live to be eighteen, so it was a fair compromise, I thought.

First thing I did when I got upstairs was check the backyard. But Bigfoot wasn't in sight, not even when I opened the window and looked directly down. I tried to drag the desk closer to the window, so I could work on my model and still keep an eye out for the creature, but as it got darker I realized I wouldn't be able to see anything because of the glare from the lamp.

I was too nervous to work on the model, anyway. My stomach kept doing little flip-flops, and it wasn't because I hadn't eaten anything for dinner. At least, it wasn't entirely because my stomach was empty. I was frantic.

My mind was racing something awful. It wasn't doing much good, for all that I was thinking so fast. I spent hours worriedly staring out the window, but I couldn't think of anything to save us. I could hardly make one thought follow the other.

My cousins came upstairs and went into the room they were all sharing. I could hear Aunt Veronica putting them to bed. Soon Eric and Dad would be standing at my door, telling me the same things. I resolved to tell them about the Abominable Snowman that was waiting outside. We couldn't go to sleep unprotected; what if it came during the night and killed us all?

But when Eric came by to tell me it was time to go to bed, I couldn't speak. It was up to me, then, I told myself, and I rushed through getting ready for bed, in case the monster came back when I wasn't looking. But when I got back to my room it still wasn't there. Eric tucked me into bed as if I were still as little as Melanie or Jessica. "I love you," he whispered into my hair, then turned out the lights. I knew I would do anything to save him. I could hear him walking down the hallway, then the stairs. A moment later I heard the television go on.

I sat bolt upright in bed. What was he thinking? I could imagine the light shining out of the living room window, calling to the Abominable Snowman like a beacon. I heard Richard Simmons shouting "Come on, ladies, one and two and one and—" and knew Eric would be dead to the world while he did another workout. It was therefore up to me to make sure he didn't wind up dead for real.

I slipped from bed and crept to the window. I could see the glow of the living room stretch across the snow before me. And the light from the television made the shadows flicker. Eric sure casts an enormous shadow when he does jumping jacks, I thought—and then I saw how big the shadow's feet were as they flew up into the air, and I knew it wasn't Eric.

Bigfoot!

I threw the window open and stared down. He was there: enormous, hairy like a yak, and doing jumping jacks.

Jumping jacks?

This was certainly unusual behavior, I thought, even for a monster. Especially for a monster. He should be roaring and shaking his arms and trying to tear us limb from limb.

Could it be that he didn't want to eat us? That he wasn't staring in at Eric when he was working out, waiting for the proper moment to strike?

Bigfoot began doing squats.

I guess maybe even monsters could be health nuts.

Maybe Bigfoot was a vegetarian. Most of the health nuts I knew— and I knew plenty, since most of Eric's friends were some variety of nutrition freak—wouldn't eat red meat. Dad still had a few friends from before he and Eric moved in, and sometimes we'd get to go over to their house for a barbecue in the summer. But mostly when we visited someone, or they came to eat at our house, it was stir-frys and tofu and vegetarian stuff like that.

So Bigfoot's a health nut, too, I thought. And suddenly I had a plan for what to do.

I just hoped I wasn't wrong about Bigfoot being a vegetarian!

I slipped from my room and down the hall. I peeked in the door at the room where Dad and Eric were staying. Dad had already gone to bed. He'd worked hard with Uncle Richard, carrying doors from the attic down to the basement and back upstairs again.

My heart froze when I suddenly heard Uncle Richard's voice, as if my thinking about him had called him to me. I was afraid he'd send me back to bed before I'd had a chance to save Eric. But then I realized I was standing outside his door, and he was just talking to Aunt Veronica in their room.

I slipped over to the stairs. Eric was down there, but I wasn't worried about him hearing me. I could come through with a huge parade now, and Eric wouldn't notice a thing. Not even if I gave away his own Christmas present.

I was pretty sure he wouldn't mind, since he already had a copy of the book at home. Aunt Veronica and Uncle Henry hadn't known; they just knew he was addicted to exercise programs, and so had bought him a copy of *The Big Book of Abs*.

As I picked the book up from under the tree and brought it to the backyard, I was suddenly afraid that Bigfoot might not know how to read. I flipped through the book. There were more pictures than text, anyway. Surely he would figure out what to do . . .

I opened the back door.

Bigfoot froze, mid-squat.

Even crouched down like that, the monster was humongous.

What am I doing? I shouted at myself. But I didn't say anything. I swallowed, and realized I wasn't breathing. I tried to stay calm, but I couldn't help thinking that I'd just opened the door for the Abominable Snowman to come and eat me and the rest of my family.

Its eyes glinted in the flickering light from the television.

Before I could run away screaming, I forced myself to thrust the book out to him. I'm like that. Once I've made up my mind to do something, I won't stop until it's done.

Bigfoot growled. I flinched, but didn't pull my hands back. I think they'd frozen that way. From fear, if not the cold weather. Why hadn't I put on a jacket before I decided to do this? I knew Aunt Ellen would yell at me for standing in the open doorway if she saw me letting the house fill up with cold air. My mind kept thinking about the warm house behind me, and how foolish it was for me to be standing here trying to give a Christmas present to a monster. As the creature rose to its full height, I couldn't help feeling awful about all the times I'd scared my little cousins, and then thinking that this must be what it felt like when they said your life flashed before your eyes, since that's what was happening—I was remembering every happy moment, from my fourth birthday party, which as the first one I remembered, to playing computer games with Eric last Sunday while Dad lay on the couch doing his crossword puzzles.

The beast lunged a huge paw at me. I knew I was done for then, that I was going to be rended limb from limb and eaten up in two or three big gulps.

But the creature merely snatched the book away from me. It held the book close to its face, squinting at it in the moonlight. Maybe it was nearsighted, I thought, feeling my knees go weak with relief that it hadn't eaten me yet.

Suddenly the beast looked up at me again and opened its mouth. There were fangs everywhere!

So much for escaping disembowelment; the creature meant to eat me whole!

I squeezed my eyes shut.

When, after a few moments, I didn't feel like I'd been eaten, I opened them again.

Bigfoot was still there, mouth wide open, fangs shining in the moonlight.

He's smiling, I realized at last.

I smiled back.

"Merry Christmas," I said.

Still smiling, the creature turned and lumbered back into the forest. It was growling softly to itself and flipping through the book as it walked.

"And they always said it was music that soothes the wild beast," I muttered to myself. Then I smiled, because I'd thought of a wicked pun. "I just hope that abs make the heart grow fonder," I said to the woods, knowing that in this case they would. Bigfoot, if he came back, wouldn't be trying to hurt us.

I went inside and watched Eric doing calisthenics for a few minutes, before climbing the stairs. I was utterly exhausted as I climbed back into bed, but as I drifted off to sleep it was with a smile on my face. We were safe.

A Ghost of a Chance

J. M. Redmann

So there I was, dead.

This is New Orleans. Dead happens a lot, but it had never happened to me before. Dead drunk, dead tired, bored to death, but never dead dead. Until now. I knew I was dead because I was hanging somewhere up in the air, feeling no pain and looking at the body I used to live in sprawling across the ground, a mess of blood and bullet wounds.

Elmo had ceased to be a gentleman when the bullets started to fly. He always made a point of it (back when I had been living, that is), to open doors for me, help me with my coat, offer to clean my gun—"Denise, a lady like you shouldn't be carrying such a big piece." Even after I told him that people with penises held no interest for me in the romantic arena, he still liked to play gentleman. I guess to prove that he was a liberal boy who held doors for women who weren't impressed with the male equipment.

He had called me this morning, saying he had a routine skip trace for me to do. I had no interest in his penis, but his money was the perfect shade of green, so I agreed to meet him on the corner of Rampart and Dumaine on the seedy edge of the French Quarter.

And now I was dead and it wasn't even noon yet.

Elmo had set me up. When the black car had turned the corner, he had dived into the gutter, rolling under a parked car, as if he knew the window was rolling down and a gun was about to fire.

Why the hell did Elmo want me dead? I've always more than earned the money he paid me. I'm clean, keep my nose out of numbers and drugs. And I only ask enough questions to make sure I stay clean. I'm a private investigator who mainly does missing persons. Make that I *was* a private investigator.

He was brushing off his suit; he favored sedate, smartly tailored ones. I hated him then because I realized that he didn't hate me. He had set me up to be killed for convenience. I was in the way of something and now I was out of the way.

Way out. My incorporeal self again looked at my former body.

"Ready to go?"

"Go?" I spun around to the voice. It was . . . well, what was it? A man? Not quite—a transparent, floating thing in sort of manlike form.

"Blow this popsicle planet," he, she, it, whatever, replied.

"I just got murdered and you want me to leave the scene of the crime?" I retorted. Being dead didn't seem to much affect my argumentative streak. Then it occurred to me that perhaps I was arguing with an angel. "Do I have to go?" I asked in a more reverent tone.

"You want revenge, retribution, whatever?"

"Maybe, maybe just to know why I had to die."

"A curious ghost. Okay, no problem. This is New Orleans, crawling with ghosts. I'll come fetch you in a bit."

"Fetch me? When?"

"When you're done."

"But how will you know when I'm done?"

"Hey, kiddo, you're dead now; the old rules don't apply. I'll know." With those sage words of advice, my spiritual advisor left me.

Elmo was doing his best 'I'm shocked, truly shocked' imitation. Like he hadn't wanted me dead.

Somehow I knew the rules wouldn't let me punch a guy after I was dead, but I thought that taking a swing anyway might be good for my soul . . . well, good for something.

If I'd been alive, Elmo would have been flat out on the street. It was a perfect swing, a more perfect punch than I'd ever delivered before. But with no bones to back it up, my late, lamented fist just passed right through him.

The look on his face told me that something had landed. He turned as white as . . . a tub of lard. There, much better metaphor.

"Ooooh, baby, I'm going to haunt you like you've never been haunted before," I crooned to him.

He shook himself, then wiped his hands across his face as if trying to rid himself of something. Having given his lying statement to the police, he was free to go. Go, he went. I followed him, since the choice seemed to be either go in his direction or follow my body. I knew as much as I ever wanted to know about what the coroner did to dead bodies; I didn't want to learn the details from my dismemberment.

Elmo kept a quick pace. I discovered something else about being a ghost. We got tired. Movement, listening to what Elmo was saying, being in the world that I should be leaving was wearing. How do ghosts rest, I wondered? Can you sleep if you're dead?

He passed three phones before he found one he liked. I had told him to get a cell phone, but Elmo worried about things like microwaves eating his brain.

"It's done," he muttered into the receiver. "I'm on my way."

Well, that was certainly enlightening. I knew it was done and that he was on his way to somewhere. He walked another two blocks, which took him to his car.

Locked doors don't stop ghosts, so I floated into the passenger seat. Didn't worry about buckling my seat belt either.

Elmo went to Lloyd's house. The pieces were starting to fit. Lloyd was Mr. Scheme, always a new plan to make money. Some of them were even barely legal.

"It's done," Elmo said. "We're on our way." I punched him again, my airy fist passing through his blubbery face, for being so boring.

"What's the matter?" Lloyd asked. "You not gettin' a conscience, are you?"

"No, I'm fine, just a bit tired. You sure this'll work?"

"It'll work fine. Who's gonna notice if an old widow lady has a heart attack?"

"Yeah, guess you're right. Hey, I'm tired. Okay if I take a nap?"

"Sure, fine. Whatever. Just don't snore loud enough to bother my afternoon shows."

I guess that killing friends is such hard work. Elmo lay down. Lloyd turned the TV onto the sports channel until Elmo started snoring, then he switched it to one of the afternoon soaps. This was too exciting for me, watching Lloyd surreptitiously watching soap operas and Elmo's openmouthed snoring.

My cat. I'm dead and who's going to feed my cat? I've been murdered and I'm worrying about things like that? But it did worry me. I doubted that Lloyd was going to go anywhere until his soap was done.

Not moving had restored me. Just hovering and floating seemed to be the ghost version of at rest. I floated out the door, with a ghostly spit into Lloyd's beer on my way past him. He coughed, choked for a moment, then turned white as . . . a snowball in hell.

I headed for my place by sitting on the roof of a car that was headed in the right direction. When it turned off, I floated onto another car going my way. Three cars and one truck later, I was at my doorstep.

For a brief moment, I fumbled for my keys. Then I remembered that I was dead. I would never have to worry about forgetting my keys again. I floated into the apartment, wondering how the hell I was going to feed my cat given that I couldn't really touch or move anything.

Molly was there. Of course, Molly would be there. Molly had always been there for me. She was in the kitchen opening a can of cat food. Molly was my best friend, the one whose shoulder I always cried on when yet again another love affair didn't work out, the one friend who could beat me at pool and not brag about it, and the one friend I could always count on to feed my cat when I wasn't around.

Sylvester, my black-and-white cat, turned to look at me as I drifted into the kitchen. Uh-oh, I realized, cats do know all the things we were afraid that they did know. She meowed at me. I understood what she was saying. "You had to go and get yourself killed. That's life. Molly fed me more than you did anyway and she's already promised to take me in."

"Too bad I died before I taught her the catnip trick," I replied.

"Guess there are some things I will miss about you," Sylvester sighed at me. "But don't worry, cats go to heaven. We'll meet again." With that, she turned (I didn't know she was a she when I named her Sylvester, okay?) to more important things, namely the food bowl Molly was placing in front of her.

As Molly turned from the kitchen counter, I saw her face. She had been crying, her eyes red and swollen.

Please don't cry, I wanted to tell her. I'm okay. Death isn't so bad, though it does take some getting used to.

I watched Molly as she wandered like a lost little girl through my apartment. Finally, she lay down on my bed, embracing my pillow, resting her face against it. Oh, hell, I had meant to change those sheets yesterday. . . . Sylvester, having stuffed her face, jumped up in the bed beside Molly, snuggling in with her. My aloof cat offered her more comfort than I could.

She loves me, I suddenly realized.

"She loved you. You're gone now, toots." My spiritual guide was back.

"Why the hell didn't I realize it when I was alive? What the hell are you doing here?"

"Transitions are hard, and death is a pretty hard transition. Only here to help."

"Hell, I have to die to see that the love of my life was my best friend and was sitting there in front of my face the whole time I was out there looking for her. Bad timing, I have to say."

"Too bad you were hung up on that physical thing for leggy blondes. Guess you got to die to learn a few lessons."

"Would I ever have figured it out?" It was a rhetorical question, but he/she/it/whatever answered.

"When you were eighty-two, you would have. Unless you survived the bullet and ended up in a wheelchair, needing your urine bag changed. Molly would have stuck by you even through that. Even you wouldn't have been blind enough not to have noticed it then."

"I was a fool."

"Yep, you sure were. You ever heard the expression Live and Learn? We say Die and Learn. But don't get too upset, with you dead, Molly will have no reason to stay here in this swamp. She'll go to law school, and with your death to motivate her, she will be instrumental in arguing the case that gets real gun control going in this country. If you hadn't died, she never would have done that. And, one of the Justices will fall in love with her and resign from the Court to be with her. So cheer up; your death will be good for her."

I turned from him/her/it/whatever to gaze at Molly sobbing in my bed, with Sylvester, my aloof cat, licking her face to try to comfort her.

"It'll be good for her in the long run, that is," he/she/it/whatever amended softly. "Come on; Lloyd's soap is almost over. I'll give you a lift back there."

I started to go with him/her/it/whatever, but stopped. I wasn't quite finished here. Instead I lay down beside Molly, wishing I had held her in life, and embraced her as best I could. "It will be okay," I told her, wondering if my ghostly words could give her even the barest touch of comfort. "It will be okay."

Sylvester answered, "I'll take care of her. I'll do my best for her. We'll miss you, Mom."

Molly's sobbing slowed, and she curled around my cat and my pillow. A shadow passed from her face, as if she knew that I was okay and that someday she would be, too.

I let her go, and turned again to my ghostly companion. "I'm ready to go."

"Grab a shoulder, toots. We're on our way." I did and he/she/it/whatever glided us through the door, then rapidly up over the trees and houses.

I was relieved to notice that I wasn't getting airsick. There are some advantages to being dead.

"Who are you? How did you get stuck with this duty?" I asked.

"Oh, I volunteered. Got murdered, let's see . . . about thirty years ago, earth time. So I specialize in murders. Been there, done that, hated it, as they say."

"Why were you murdered?"

"Bystander. Just standing there at the bar, sucking down a Dixie, when these two guys started a fight. Argued about how tough they were, but it turned out that they couldn't shoot straight. Bingo, my time to go."

We swooped back down again, and he/she/it/whatever deposited me in front of Lloyd's place.

"So you're a man?" I was determined to figure that out so I could stop thinking of him/her/it/whatever as he/she/it/whatever.

"Was back there. Once you're dead little things like sex and race and who you slept with and money don't much matter."

"What does matter?"

"You know, the usual. Good, evil. That kind of thing. Did you struggle to do the right thing? Or did you worry only about yourself, your new car, your smart clothes?"

"Wake up, Elmo," I heard Lloyd say from inside the house.

"Catch you later," he (still not sure, but it'll do for now) said. And he was gone.

I floated back into Lloyd's run-down apartment. The TV was changed back to the sports channel. Elmo was in the bathroom, with the seat down, and not doing a good job of aiming. Given the state of cleanliness of the rest of the place, I doubted that Lloyd would notice.

"C'mon, you gotta make the phone call. She said call by five," Lloyd hollered at him.

"Coming, coming," Elmo answered. He didn't wash his hands and he didn't wipe off the seat.

He first went to the refrigerator to get a beer. Cheap beer, of course. Then he picked up the phone. Elmo, who wouldn't use a cell phone because of radiation, wouldn't wash his hands after using Lloyd's bathroom and guzzled cheap beer. There are worst things than being dead, I concluded.

"Hello, Mrs. Lee?" he said. "This is Morgan Whitman. Remember me? I'm calling you about the investment in Federal Fidelity Mutual Trust Guarantee."

That was why I had to be dead! Mrs. Georgia Lee was an elderly neighbor of mine. She had called me the other day about this Federal Fidelity Mutual Trust Guarantee fund. Said it sounded interesting, but she wanted someone to check it out. I had done a number of favors for her throughout the years, from mowing her lawn to shooing away scam artists that preyed on the elderly, and she had been sort of a substitute grandmother figure to me, cookies and Thanksgiving dinner and knitted sweaters. Her husband had been a ship captain, and when he had died, his insurance had left her well off. A few decades of prudent investments and conservative living had left her very, very well off. She told me that what she wanted was a comfortable old age and not to be a burden to any of her children. Anything left after that would go to charity.

And, of course, I would have spied something as pretentious as Federal Fidelity Mutual Trust Guarantee as phony from the get-go. Mrs. Lee's ample piles of money were enough to get me bumped off.

"As I've said," Elmo continued, putting on a bad fake British accent—it went from cockney to Oxford; he probably crammed for this by watching a few hours of *Masterpiece Theatre*—"it's very important that you invest now, as the window of opportunity is closing fast. I'm sure that the private investigator Denise Smith [hey, my mother was a Boudreaux. Can't help that my dad had a boring name] has told you. . . . You haven't heard from her? Well, I'm sure that means that she found nothing amiss. You know she would have called you if she spotted any trouble. . . . Okay, I can be there in half an hour."

Half an hour. I didn't have a ghost of a chance to stop them. I swung another punch at Elmo as he hung up the phone.

"Hey, you're not feeling guilty, are you?" Lloyd called to him. "You look white as a ghost."

White as nothing in this house will ever be again, I amended, taking umbrage at having Elmo compared to ghosts.

"Nope, not a problem. Let's get going. The sooner we get her to sign the documents, the sooner we get the money."

Elmo left his cheap, half-finished beer just sitting on the table, so they would have drunken roaches when they returned, and he and Lloyd headed for their car.

I followed them. I didn't know what I could do, but somehow I couldn't just walk . . . uh . . . float away.

I wafted into the back. Good thing about being a ghost, I didn't actually have to rest on the jumble of fast-food bags and empty cigarette packs that covered the seat.

Mrs. Lee lived in one of the beautiful old homes in Algiers Point, on the west bank of the river. As we crossed the bridge, caught in afternoon rush-hour traffic, I viewed the city as it stretched off into the fog of evening, the tall buildings of the Central Business District stopping at Canal Street, the transition line between the new modern city and the old streets of the French Quarter. I could see Jackson Square, the heart of the Quarter, the lights of St. Louis Cathedral shrouded by the mist. I wouldn't walk those streets again, and these were the men responsible.

Elmo got a bit lost, so the promised half hour turned into almost an hour before he pulled up to Mrs. Lee's front door.

I wanted to scream, "Don't open the door," but of course, only the cats would hear me.

She let them in, even offered them coffee or tea.

Elmo put his pinkie out, like he knew it was sophisticated. I spit in his tea. He choked on a lemon seed that he wasn't paying attention to.

Robert E. I had to find him. No, not the general, but Mrs. Lee's cat. He was an orange cat and favored sitting amid the plants on Mrs. Lee's screened-in porch. That was where he was.

"Hey, wake up," I called to him.

He opened a lazy eye, like ghosts were a common occurrence to him. "Oh, hello, Denise," he said sleepily. "When did you pass over?"

"No time for small talk about my death," I told him. "The two men in the parlor with Mrs. Lee want to swindle her and then murder her."

"Oh, dear," Robert E. said. "That would interfere with dinner."

"Don't let her sign the papers," I instructed him.

Robert E. jumped up, then trotted back to the parlor.

Mrs. Lee was poised with pen, ready to sign. Lloyd was standing behind her, ready to strangle her.

Robert E. took a flying leap, landing on top of the papers under Mrs. Lee's poised pen, sending them scattering across the room. He then bumped his head against her pen, knocking it out of her hand.

"Hey, stop that cat," Elmo yelled, his fake Brit accent lost in the annoyance at Robert E.'s antics.

I sidled up next to Mrs. Lee. "Don't sign those papers. You're dead if you sign them." I wondered if my ghostly whisper could have any effect on her.

"Perhaps we should wait until the morning," she said. "I would really like some time to look these over."

"But it has to be in by noon tomorrow," Elmo cajoled. "Better to sign it now and not have to worry in the morning."

"We can do it first thing in the morning," she said. "I would like to talk to Denise and I would like to read everything over again, if you don't mind."

I knew her tone of voice, and knew that she wouldn't sign until the morning.

"See, she listens to me," Robert E. informed me. At least she took the hint.

Elmo wheedled and entreated, but all for naught. Lloyd glowered. Finally, they left with promises to be back in the morning. First thing in the morning.

Once they were outside her house, Elmo turned to Lloyd and said, "You've got to get here and steal her paper."

Of course, Mrs. Lee didn't watch TV, so she wouldn't know I had been murdered until tomorrow's paper.

"Why don't you do it? That's too friggin' early in the morning for me," Lloyd retorted.

They argued back and forth, but it was clear that one of them would steal the paper, so Mrs. Lee wouldn't have a chance to wonder about my being murdered just before I got back to her about this phony investment.

"You drive; I gotta think," Elmo informed Lloyd.

If Elmo was the brains of this gang, there had to be a way even for a ghost with no body and no voice to be able to stop them.

I again hovered in the back seat of the car.

"Hey, where you going?" Elmo suddenly asked Lloyd.

"Hey, what's it to you? I'm driving. Don't want to pay the toll. What's the matter, don't like the Huey P.?"

Lloyd was heading over the Huey P. Long Bridge, a much older bridge than the Crescent City Connection that had led us to this side of the river. The lanes are narrow on the Huey P., and in the center of the bridge is a railroad track. Being sandwiched between an eighteen-wheeler on one side and a rumbling train on the other can be an unnerving experience for even the calm and collected.

Elmo didn't appear to be in that category. Lloyd also didn't belong in the c/c category, but the beer in his hand explained where his courage came from.

The fog was rolling in, making the Huey P. an even more nerve-wracking experience. Almost made me glad that I was dead, so I couldn't get killed.

"Hey, if I kill them, does that send me straight to hell?" I asked the cosmos.

"Listen, toots, you got to do what you think is right." My guide appeared. Somehow I was not surprised. "Just be aware that things like manifesting and haunting take energy. Use too much and you get scrambled into pieces. Your hand will wander for a few millennia looking for a friendly foot."

"You're no help," I grumbled at him. "But I can't just let them return tomorrow and kill Mrs. Lee."

"No one lives forever." And with that he was gone.

No one lives forever. Not me, not Mrs. Lee. And not Elmo and not Lloyd.

I spit in Lloyd's beer. But he barely noticed, just a half cough before he guzzled it down.

Elmo was the key. I put my ghostly hands around his throat and squeezed.

"Christ! Open the window, I can't breathe," he let out.

"Sure, whatever," the beer-mellowed Lloyd answered.

But the open window let in a blast of diesel fumes, and Elmo quickly closed it again.

"You're going to die, Elmo. You're a murderer and a coward," I told him. He turned as white as . . . the headlights of a passing truck.

"I hate this stupid bridge," he said. "Lanes are too narrow; it's dangerous."

"Hey, I'm driving. Perfectly safe," Lloyd, with another swig of beer, reassured him.

"Yeah, you're drunk. This rickety old bridge. Perfectly safe."

"You're a coward, killing old ladies for a few dollars," I whispered at Elmo.

"What'd you say?" he demanded of Lloyd.

"Say? Didn't say nothin'. You hearing ghosts or somethin'?" Lloyd answered.

Or seeing ghosts. I concentrated my energy, focusing it into giving myself a ghostly shape. I suddenly felt heavy, burdened by remembering the body I had left behind.

I wanted to speak, but the energy required to appear drained me. I hovered in front of Elmo, a bare wisp of shape.

"What the . . . ?! Denise???!" he bellowed.

I faded. I couldn't hold the shape any longer.

"Hey," Lloyd said, "you losin' it?"

"I saw Denise. She was here." Elmo said.

"You saw some fog. Get a grip, you wussy."

"Yeah, fog. Yeah, that was it." But Elmo was as white as . . . bleached bone.

I hovered on the dashboard, trying to regain my strength. I didn't want to be chasing my left foot for eternity.

Then I had an idea. I concentrated my energy on my hands, balling them into fists, forcing them into a glowing life. Headlights in the fog. I slowly moved my hands toward Elmo.

"Look out!" he screamed.

"What?" Lloyd asked.

"Those lights! There're coming at us!"

"What the hell you talkin' about?" Lloyd couldn't see any lights in front of us.

"Swerve, you idiot. They're coming at us!"

My energy was fading, but I had to keep my hands glowing, make them brighter, like headlights coming closer and closer.

"You're crazy. There's nothin' there."

"You're crazy and drunk! We'll be killed!" With that Elmo grabbed the wheel. He jerked it hard.

Lloyd, his reflexes slowed by the beer, tried to control the wheel, but Elmo's panic won out. Suddenly the car careened into the railing, bounced off slightly, then angled back into it and, finally, through it.

It fell into the black night, into the black river.

I hovered above it, watching its descent into the waters. The Mississippi is not a kind river, not here with its strong current and the tight twists and bends that make up New Orleans.

"Ready to go?" my guide asked.

"Can't I watch for a bit? Curse them out as they pass by."

"They're not coming this direction. Those boys are going down, straight down."

"And where am I going? Didn't I just murder them?"

"Can a ghost murder a living person? Mrs. Lee gets to feed her cat tomorrow and the next day. That's not a bad outcome. Come on, follow me. It's a great night to ride past the stars."

So I left behind the mist-covered City That Care Forgot, and followed him to the stars.

The Troll in the Basement

Quentin Harrington

He can hear him down there, moving around.

He can feel the coffee in his stomach turning to acid, rapidly dissolving the fat-free blueberry muffin he picked up on his way into the office. He tries to focus on the computer screen in front of him. The design image begins to swim; a muscled hairless torso, lips pursed at the camera, perky nipples erect, bright yellow Lycra stretched over the unmistakable bulge of an erection, blurring, becoming indistinct. He reaches for his cup of coffee, the scent of French roast mingling with French vanilla flavoring, assailing his nostrils, turning acrid, nauseating rather than enticing. He puts the cup down and rubs his eyes. He eyes the telephone.

How long before the intercom buzzes?

He sighs and saves the document. The computer would probably freeze up soon anyway, losing an hour's worth of work for the umpteenth time. He hears the voice inside his head, searing through him like a lightning bolt of pain, causing his fists to clench. "You should always save the document every time you make any change to it because the network will crash." That smug, know-it-all tone, driving him insane, pushing him to the limits of his tolerance. The knowing smirk broadcasting I-told-you-so, the lips not curled back enough to reveal the sharp points of the teeth, the out-of-control eyebrows that looked more like a cat's whiskers lifting over the watery blue eyes. He opens his right-hand top desk drawer and dry swallows two more Extra Strength Tylenol. The headache was coming on; he can feel it behind his temples, the heart beating through the veins throbbing.

He switches over to his e-mail program. Three new messages, none of them he wants to read or respond to.

The first from a writer: *"I still haven't gotten my check for the feature I did in the September issue; has there been some kind of mix-up? I could really use the money right now; is there someone else I could follow up with?"*

Knowing it was pointless, useless, an exercise in futility, he forwards it to the troll in the basement with the message, *"Can you please take care of this?"*

The second from the photographer who did the September cover: *"I still haven't gotten paid for my work. This is getting a little ridiculous. It's been over two months and you promised me when I did the shoot I would get paid when the issue hit the stands, and this is about the tenth message I've sent you. Am I going to need to retain an attorney? Please respond as soon as you can."*

Oh God oh God oh God. Forward. Mark urgent. Hit send.

The computer makes that annoying sound that means new mail. He refreshes the page. Response to the writer's request for payment. His stomach churns a little faster. *"No checks came in the mail today, and we are probably not going to make payroll on Friday as it is unless we get some money by Friday. No money means no money. How many times do I have to tell you that?"*

No money means no money.

He thinks of the credit-card bills piling up on his desk at home, the messages from collections departments of assorted Visas and Master-Cards saved on his voice mail, calls that he can't return.

. . . we are probably not going to make payroll on Friday . . .

Thirty-five dollars in his checking account. Fifty dollars in savings. Three dollars in his wallet. No food in his pantry.

He doesn't respond to the e-mail. There's no point. He switches back over to the design program. The computer freezes, the cursor not moving. As he has already done three times that morning, he reaches under his desk and flicks the switch on the surge protector, killing the power to his computer, thinks yet again that this can't be good for the hard drive, and turns it back on again. While it loads he walks to the bathroom and dumps the remains of the coffee into the sink, splashes cold water on his face. The headache seems to be receding; maybe it was just a false alarm. He hears his assistant typing away on his computer in the back office. He sticks his head in, says hello.

His assistant doesn't look up, just nods in acknowledgment and keeps typing away. He walks in farther to see what he's doing (not to check up, he tells himself, just out of curiosity) and sees that he's working on the Web site, loading images of bare torsos, bulging pouches, come-hither looks.

He walks back into his own office and starts working again. He loses himself in the work, laying out the pages, pulling in text, loading images, making it all look nice, neat, orderly, even though it makes no difference. It won't come back from the printer looking like that, because the troll will change everything he has done and won't pay attention to italicized text or margins but will point out gleefully every mistake that he has made, saying things like, "You don't pay enough attention to detail. It's all in the detail," but won't ever acknowledge his own mistakes except with a "Oops!" and a shrug.

He hears the unmistakable sound of the cloven hoofs on the steps, shuffling, on his way up the stairs. Staff meeting. He realizes that he's forgotten the staff meeting and the headache begins to gain strength again. A wave of nausea sweeps over him. He coughs, once, twice, the second hard enough to bring bilious burning sour coffee up into his throat, but he forces it back down. There are some days he can make it through without seeing the troll, but today is not to be one of those days.

The door to the basement swings open and he comes into sight, wearing shorts and a sweaty T-shirt. Gray wisps of hair stick up from his legs in bizarre angles, as though held in place by static electricity. The beady watery eyes move back and forth. "Oh, you're here," he says, as though the forwarded e-mail had never been sent. "Staff meeting."

He sticks his index finger in his mouth and starts chewing on a cuticle until it tears away from the skin, sending a small jolt of pain through his body. He looks down at it and sees the blood welling up, spreading around the outline of the nail. He sticks it back in his mouth and sucks on it, closing his eyes, willing the nausea down, willing the headache to go away. He smiles, nods, grabs a notebook, and follows the troll into the conference room.

The meeting is like any other, boring, pronouncements about the magazine's financial sickness, the desperate need for more advertisers, the desperate need for advertisers to pay their bills, where do we stand on the next issue. He answers when necessary, short answers that convey just enough information but not too much, for he has learned that lesson the hard way. The more information that is shared the more his decisions will be called into question, picked apart, ripped to shreds until any work that is already completed will have to be redone, the time and energy and effort wasted.

His assistant is giving an update on his progress on the Web site when it happens again. It has only happened twice before, the human mask slipping down and the true creature he works for displaying his face, his demonic yellow eyes, the pointed teeth behind the lips, the pointed ears usually so carefully hidden. The other times it happened the mask quickly slipped back into place, but this time it stays down, as if daring him to say something, anything, taunting him.

He looks at his assistant, who is looking right at it. Can't you see? he wants to scream. Can't you see what he really is?

He looks at the circulation manager, idly doodling with his pencil. No reaction, no nothing.

Why can't they see?

His throat closes and he manages to say "excuse me" before leaving the room, the acrid sour acidic coffee churning, fighting its way back up the digestive tract, sweat streaming from his forehead. He makes it to the bathroom before it reaches his mouth, and it expels from his mouth which he points in the general direction of the toilet and manages to get the majority of the stream into the clear water. He coughs, once, twice, and on the third cough another stream comes up, his stomach clenching and revolting, rejecting the coffee and its artificial sweetener and its artificial flavoring. His mouth tastes sour; his teeth feel raw. He takes several deep breaths, splashes more cold water on his hot face, gathers some paper towels and wipes up what missed the toilet, dries his face with another paper towel. He reaches into the medicine cabinet, squirts toothpaste onto his toothbrush, and grimly tries to scrub the taste out of his mouth.

He goes back into the meeting, which is pretty much over. No one says anything to him. There is nothing to say. They are used to his throwing up in the mornings. He blames it on his sinuses; they pity him and say nothing.

"Back to work," says the troll. The mask is back in place, covering up his evil visage. He shuffles back to the stairs but stops and looks back. "Are you all right?" he asks, but as he says it the mask slips again, to show that he really doesn't care if he is actually all right or not.

"Fine." He forces a smile onto his lips.

The shuffling walk begins down the stairs, the sound of the hooves smacking against the wood. Why don't the others notice his footsteps don't sound right? he wonders again. Why can't they see the mask slip? Why don't they understand? Why does he only allow me to see?

Because I came for you.

The words dance across his computer screen, streaming across. He gasps and pushes his chair back.

Because I came for you because I came for you because I came for you because I came for

He throws the switch again and the computer screen goes blank. He takes deep breaths. His head is pounding out of control. He turns it on again. It boots up like any other time, nothing out of the ordinary. No words streaming across the center of the screen.

I'm going crazy; is that what this is?

But I know what I've seen.

The intercom buzzes.

"Can you come down here?" the troll asks.

He gets up and walks down the stairs. The sound of a Strauss waltz comes to him. The troll likes Strauss and often plays it; or the soundtrack to *The Sound of Music;* or *Liza with a Z,* or something horribly stereotypical.

He catches a glimpse of himself in the mirror at the bottom of the stairs and recoils. His eyes are bloodshot and wild, his clothes disheveled and coffee stained, the roll around his middle bulging out of control. I have gained thirty pounds since I started working here, he thinks as he pinches the roll of fat. I don't go to the gym anymore. I eat at Mc-Donald's three or four times a week. Why have I let myself go?

And then he remembers the leering voice, the stares, the comments about his legs, his arms, his butt.

That all stopped when he started gaining weight.

I gained weight on purpose, he thinks as he walks into the troll's office, so that he would leave me alone, stop putting his hand on my shoulder or on my back while he stood at my desk.

The troll looks up at him from his computer screen. The mask is gone.

He takes in breath quickly. He struggles to get control. He sits down, grabbing the arms of the chair to keep his hands from shaking. He forces his voice out: "Yes?"

The troll's yellow eyes gleam. Spittle drips from his fangs. "I don't like the cover images you've come up with. Can't you ask your friend Michael for some of his shots? He's such a great photographer."

"We haven't paid Michael yet for September." His throat and mouth are dry; his lips feel swollen. He can't take his eyes off of the glowing yellow eyes. "And even if we do right now I doubt that he'd want to work with us again."

"Call him anyway." The troll's lips curl back in what is most likely supposed to be a smile. "Money's money, even if it is late in coming."

"Why are you doing this to me?" he asks in a quiet voice, not meaning to say it out loud, but the words have spilled out.

The head goes back and laughs, a high-pitched whining sound that pierces his eardrums, bringing the headache to a crescendo of pain, throbbing, pounding pain, as though someone is driving a nail into each temple with a hammer. "Because I can," the voice booms, lowering several octaves, slowing down like an old 45 record slowed down to 33 1/3.

The pain. Oh God, the pain.

He gets to his feet, the pain in his head squeezing everything else out, all senses gone, his eyes swimming in red, as though blood vessels have popped and blood is leaking out through the whites of his eyes, bloody tears flowing down his cheeks and dribbling off his chin. He picks up a letter opener off the corner of the desk and clutches it hard until the metal handle is piercing his skin, blood flowing out of his hands as he brings it up in the air and down into the troll's left eye, and it isn't blood that's coming out but a greenish goo, splattering his face his hands his shirt and he brings the letter opener down again and he can hear in the distance something screaming, and he yanks the letter opener downward and feels it hit bony resistance and he summons strength, he doesn't know from where, perhaps from the pounding in his brain and he feels the bone start to give but then the letter opener snaps in half and the troll is screaming, screaming, as his hands close around the throat and squeeze, feeling the Adam's apple crush beneath his thumbs as he chokes it to death, the troll is screaming as he sends it back to hell where it came from, and when it goes limp in his hands he steps back.

He looks over at the foot of the stairs and sees his assistant and the circulation manager, all color drained from their faces.

"I've killed it," he says calmly. "It won't bother us anymore."

And he looks down at his hands and doesn't see the greenish guck, the goo, but sticky red blood.

And he looks at the troll's shattered head, and the ears aren't pointed, the teeth in the open mouth aren't pointed anymore, in death . . .

In death the mask returned.

And he starts to scream.

Waiting for the Vampire

William J. Mann

"There is a very good reason I have not allowed myself to die, not for nearly one hundred years," said old Mr. Samuel Horowitz, the oldest man at the Hebrew Home.

"And what's that, Mr. Horowitz?"

"It's because when I was a young boy in Russia, back in the days of the tsars, I was bitten by a vampire, and now I am afraid to die." He opened his eyes wide. "I am afraid that when I die, I will rise from my grave as one of the undead."

Ogden Smith, twenty-five and new to his job at the Hebrew Home, certainly hadn't been expecting such talk. He knew Mr. Horowitz was a strange old man who had been known to grope the male aides in places he might never touch the females, but Ogden Smith was not expecting talk of vampires. He was sitting next to the old man, who was one hundred and six, and he had just finished pouring him a cup of tea.

"Oh, Mr. Horowitz," Ogden said at last, not knowing what else to say.

"You don't believe me." The old man shifted in his chair, as easily as a hundred-and-six-year-old man could, and looked out the window. It was a cold January day, and the snow had drifted high, covering the bottoms of the dusty panes of glass. It was very white outside, and Samuel Horowitz's old brown eyes blinked against the brightness.

"The light hurts my eyes, you know," he said finally. "Has ever since." He sighed. "No one has ever believed me," he lamented in that odd guttural Russian accent of his.

Ogden offered a small, timid laugh. "There aren't such things as vampires," he said. "Here, drink your tea."

"You think not?" the old man said, turning on him with all the ferocity of a child denied. "You are wrong. In Russia, there were vampires. And one of them came to my home. Invited by my father, in fact. They must be invited, you know. They cannot enter a place unbidden. His name was Count Alexei Petrovich Guchkov. He was a most charming man. Tall and handsome and dark. I was just sixteen. My father had money. They all hated my father because he was a Jew, but he had money, so they tolerated him. At least for a little while. Count Guchkov would come to our house and my mother would offer him wine, but he would always refuse. I found him mesmerizing. I could not take my eyes off him."

"Mr. Horowitz . . ." Ogden was growing uncomfortable with such talk of mesmerizing men.

"What? Will you tell me it was merely a schoolboy fancy? That he forced himself upon me, or that perhaps somehow I wanted it? Well, I did. One night, on our terrace, on a cold black winter night, with the moon in the sky and the snow anxious to fall, he put his warm lips on mine and kissed me, deep and hard, with my parents just a few feet away, not knowing . . ."

"Oh, please, Mr. Horowitz . . ."

"He kissed me, Mr. Smith, and I liked it. He awoke in me passions I had forgotten from another life, passions that I have never felt since. His lips were warm but his hands were cold, but that was all right by me, especially when he moved his hands down my neck and over my shoulders, down between my legs . . ."

"Oh . . ."

"And then he pulled me into him, his strong arms wrapped around me, and I surrendered, willingly, eagerly, as he sunk his teeth into my throat and drank my young virgin blood."

Mr. Horowitz was quiet. He let out a deep, long, labored breath and resumed looking out the window. Ogden Smith said nothing. He just sat there, breathing. Finally, with trembling fingers, he lifted Mr. Horowitz's cup of tea to his own lips, and drank.

❧ ❧ ❧

"I want to have my hair cut short, like Elizabeth Taylor's," Bernadette Smith told her brother.

"That would be attractive," Ogden agreed.

"Chase just *adores* Elizabeth Taylor. More than Kim Novak now. Remember all he could talk about was Kim Novak?"

"Yes," Ogden said.

"We're going away, you know," Bernadette said, still looking at herself in the mirror. Her brother sat behind her, at the foot of her bed.

"You are? Oh, Bernie, when?" There was some degree of panic in his voice.

"On Tuesday. Just for three days." She looked at her brother in the mirror. "Now, don't start. I'm twenty-six years old, Og. I've wasted enough time."

Ogden knew better than to debate his sister. He waited a few minutes, until Bernie had moved away from the mirror and stood in front of the window, pulling on her stockings.

"So where are you going?" he asked.

"We are going on an *airplane!*" Bernadette said, wide-eyed and big-mouthed, and for a moment Ogden wanted to slap her, but then pushed the thought away.

"An airplane?"

"Yes. To get away from all this cold and snow. We're going to St. Croix! It's in the Virgin Islands. We own it. The United States, I mean."

"Yes, I've heard of it."

"Can you just imagine, Og? White sandy beaches and a big sun overhead. And the water's so crystal blue and clear you can see the brightly colored tropical fish." She paused, as if expecting her brother to voice disbelief. "It says so in the brochure."

Ogden smiled.

"Isn't it just too divine? It was Chase's idea. He's paying for the whole thing! He got a deal, a special midweek deal, through the travel agency he works for." Bernie flopped down on the bed next to her brother, clutching the pillow to her chest and squeezing it. "Wasn't I lucky to find him?"

"Yes," Ogden said, standing up and going to the mirror himself.

He discovered her eyes. They stared back at him like big black balls, like the eight balls Papa used to shoot down at the pool hall.

"Bernie," he asked, not turning around. "Do you believe in vampires?"

But his sister had left the room. To start packing, no doubt.

❧   ❧   ❧

"It was the year 1868," Mr. Horowitz told him the next day when he again brought him some tea. "Ever since then, I have been determined to stay alive."

"That is a good thing," Ogden told him. "You have lived a long and eventful life."

"A good thing? My young friend, would you want to live a life of such fear? The fear every night that grips you, the fear that when you go to sleep, you will not wake, until one cold night you awake in your coffin, the lust for blood overpowering you?"

"Please, Mr. Horowitz, please don't start talking that way again . . ."

"When I saw you the first day you were here, I thought maybe you might believe me, that you weren't like the others."

Ogden Smith, standing over the old man's bed, looked down at him with his eyes, not moving his chin.

"I thought there was a chance you might believe." Mr. Horowitz pouted.

"Vampires aren't real," Ogden said firmly.

"Count Guchkov was. I can still feel the warmth of his mouth and the coldness of his hands, here," he said, placing his right hand over his crotch, beneath the flimsy white sheet.

Ogden Smith turned away. "Do you want some honey for your tea?"

"Are you Christian, Mr. Smith?"

Ogden turned back to face him. "Yes."

"And you work here, as an aide in the Hebrew Home?"

"Yes."

"That is why I noticed the difference. The Jews have stopped believing in such things. We have seen too much horror at the hands of men to believe in such things as vampires anymore. But we believed once. Have you ever heard the story of the Golem, Mr. Smith?"

"No, Mr. Horowitz, and please, don't tell me. You frighten me."

The old man moved his head against his pillow. He still had thick white hair, loose around his face, a face of old bark, of a thousand crevices, of years of pain and anguish and scattered moments of joy, but mostly of fear.

"Frighten you?" he sighed. "I do not mean to. Yet fear is the great equalizer, my friend. What kind of Christian are you?"

"What kind?"

"Yes. Are you Anglican? Catholic?"

"Lutheran."

"Ah. The German Protestant." Mr. Horowitz closed his eyes. "They hunted us down, but that was many years later. I was living with my sister and her husband then. I had never married, of course. Who would want me? I had been defiled. We had been driven from Russia by the Communists, but Germany wasn't far enough away to save me from a vampire. He still haunted my dreams. He could have found me, come to me, drunk my blood again, if he had so chosen."

"Mr. Horowitz . . ."

"So leave if you don't want to hear! Why do you stand there, if what I tell you so disturbs you?"

"I'm concerned that you may be upsetting yourself."

"Upsetting myself!" The old man turned his head away from Ogden Smith. "I have felt this way for ninety years, as I hid not only from the Russians and the Germans but also from a creature of the night who was even more loathsome. I have feared death because of what it could mean to me. When the Germans forced us out, when in the black of night my brother-in-law huddled us under blankets and drove us to a waiting train so we could escape to America, I rejoiced. For so long I had wanted to come here, for only here, across the ocean, across the moving waters, would I be safe." He paused and looked hard at Ogden. "You see, a vampire cannot cross moving water."

Ogden had sat down in the chair beside the old man's bed. "But yet you are still afraid," he said.

The old man closed his eyes. "Yes. There is no escape. He could not get to me here, but in my blood his taint remains. That has never left me. And when I die . . ."

"Mr. Horowitz, please don't say it . . ."

"I can't go on living forever! It has been an act of sheer will to live this long. I have kept death at arm's length for nearly a century. I have refused to open the door when he came courting, and he has come many times, Mr. Smith, many times. But I grow tired. I cannot continue much longer. And when I die, Mr. Smith . . ."

"Yes? What will happen when you die?"

". . . on the night of the third day, I will arise, out of my grave, a vampire myself, returned to feast on the blood of the living, one of the undead."

Ogden Smith had put his hands to his mouth. He could not speak.

"Hey, stop that!"

Bernadette was standing in front of the mirror again, wearing nothing but her black bra and red panties. Chase, her rich young boyfriend, was on his hands and knees on the bed behind her. He had snapped the back of her bra strap so that it made a sharp sound, slapping against her flesh.

Ogden had been passing in the hall, and now paused in the doorway.

"Are you all right, Bernie?" he asked.

"Sure. Hey, Og," Bernie called.

"Yes?"

"You will be all right here by yourself while we're gone, won't you?"

Chase laughed. "'Course he will. Og's a big boy, honey. Ain't ya now, Og?"

Ogden looked at him. "I'll be fine," he said.

"Sure you will, Oggie kid," Chase said, pouncing off the bed and coming at him. He put his hands on Ogden's hips and gave him a quick kiss on the nose. Ogden hated it when Chase did things like that, but he didn't pull away.

"You just need to remember a few things," Bernadette was saying, pulling on her lacy white blouse and buttoning it down the front, the black bra showing through. "Freddie, the paper boy, needs to get paid on Thursday. I've left the money in an envelope. And Mr. Otfinowski, the milkman, he gets paid on Friday morning. Make sure you leave his money in the crate Thursday night because he comes so early, otherwise you'll never catch him. We'll be coming back Friday afternoon, but by the time Chase's brother picks us up at the airport and we grab some dinner, it might be late."

"That's fine," Ogden said.

Chase was still in his face. "Gosh, you've got pretty eyes," he said suddenly.

He yanked away and hurried down the hall to his room. He could hear his sister shushing Chase, saying he shouldn't have said that. "But I never noticed," he said, "till just then. They're so *green*." That's when Ogden turned the radio on very loud, singing along in his head with Bobby Darin to "Mack the Knife."

❧ ❧ ❧

The Smith siblings lived in an old flat in an old building on Pleasant Street, just off Main, one of the grand old buildings in town, with the elegant moldings of the nineteenth century. Despite its years, it was a clean building, and good, decent families still lived there: families with names like Wright, and Russell, and Williams. Only one immigrant family lived there, and they on the topmost floor: the Trykowskis, a Polish man and his second wife and their three teenaged daughters.

Mr. Otfinowski, the milkman, was Polish too, but he lived down by the great bend of the river with the other Polish and Italian families. Ogden liked Mr. Otfinowski a great deal. "Top o' the morning to you," he'd say like an Irishman. It always made Ogden laugh.

From his window he could see the top of the next building, and the next, and just beyond that the steeple of St. John the Baptist, the Catholic church on Main Street. Sometimes, atop one of the buildings, he'd spy some kids in the summertime, sunbathing, the girls seemingly always on one side of the steeple, the boys on the other. Of course, it was too cold for sunbathing now, so Ogden didn't even bother to look. Sometimes, instead, he'd look out the window in the other direction, up the hill toward the orchard, where the great houses stood. That's where his father had been born, in one of those houses; he'd pointed it out to him when he was about ten. But Papa had married a Catholic girl, and Grandfather had been very angry, and booted poor Papa all the way down that great hill. That's why they ended up here.

Tonight Ogden was thinking about vampires, and wondered if he'd ever been frightened of such things before. No, he didn't think so, but he couldn't be sure. He had seen a vampire movie years ago— with Papa, he thought, and surely he would have reassured him that such things were not real. There was another vampire movie now, playing at the Palace on Main Street, something with a man named Lee. Ogden had seen the ads for it in the paper. But he certainly had no plans to see it. *How silly,* he chided himself, pulling his blankets up to his chin as he lay there in the dark. *How silly I'm being.*

He heard his sister moan. Tomorrow she would be gone: for four whole days and three nights. And Chase with her.

"Oh, God!" Bernie shouted in ecstasy suddenly from her room, and Ogden turned his face to the wall.

"Yeah, that's it, baby," Chase said, and Ogden wasn't sure if he actually heard him, or if the words were merely inside his head, a memory from other times like this.

He flung back the covers and placed his bare feet against the cold hardwood floor.

"Ohhhh," his sister groaned through the wall.

The flat was utterly dark. In the winter, with the windows closed, the rooms were as quiet as they were dark. Ogden could lie in bed and listen to Mr. Trykowski's old pendulum clock strike the hour from two floors above. Then their own clock would chime: one o'clock, two o'clock, three o'clock, all through the night.

He knew the blueprint of the flat; scuffing in the darkness was easy. He padded into the hallway, and a small flickering light shone from the crack of his sister's door. That tiny little sliver of light, cast from a candle by the side of the bed, was enough to let Ogden see just a little: the heaving of Chase's strong muscular bare back, the red-tipped hands of his sister laced around his neck. He watched soundlessly for several moments before turning away.

Ogden walked into the dark bathroom, the tiles of the floor even colder than the wood, his feet reacting, wanting to run. But he stood above the toilet, effortlessly reaching down and finding the handle in the dark. He flushed.

The sound of the water rushing through the pipes in the great old building echoed among the rooms, as surely as it must have in each of the flats in the building. Somewhere above them, perhaps Mr. Trykowski sat up in his bed and wondered who was awake at this hour. Below them, maybe old Miss Wright, who had taught them in kindergarten, woke from a sound sleep and shook her head in dismay.

When Ogden left the bathroom, he knew the sliver of shivering light from his sister's room would be gone, and the sounds would have stopped.

He was right.

                                             ✍ ✍ ✍

Mr. Horowitz died the morning Bernadette and Chase got on their airplane and flew to St. Croix.

"Oh, no," Ogden Smith said, arriving at the Hebrew Home.

Mrs. Newberg nodded. "Poor old war horse. He didn't want to go. He fought like an old tiger right to the end."

"This was this morning?"

"Yes. Very early. Before the sun was up. That was why he was fighting so, trying to hold back."

"I don't understand," said Ogden Smith.

"He said he wanted to see the sun, one last time," Mrs. Newberg explained.

"Oh," said Ogden.

"Very sad, really. But he'd lived a long time. A very long time. You were close to him, weren't you?"

But Ogden Smith wasn't listening. Somewhere overhead, an airplane passed, and it seemed as if the building shook.

The movie was *Horror of Dracula,* and there was a big sign for it underneath the marquee of the Palace. At night, lightbulbs around the sign were lit up, just like the lights up on the marquee. As a child, Ogden had loved coming to the Palace when it was all lit up, and he'd be there to see the latest Deanna Durbin picture, or Andy Hardy, or anything with Lana Turner. He and Bernie would troop down from their home, their father urging Bernie to hold Og's hand. "And come right home after the picture," he'd admonish them.

"Yes, Papa," they both would promise.

Only once did they disobey, and then Ogden got a spanking. They had stopped to talk with a boy from Ogden's class, a boy named Walter Moriarty, an Irish kid with red hair and lots of freckles and bowed legs. All the girls thought he was the cutest boy in the school. Bernie had the biggest crush on him of any of the girls. Ogden couldn't quite figure out why, but he secretly wished his hair was as red as Walter's, and that he had freckles all over his face, too. When Walter called over to them, of course they had stopped. Walter was eating a chocolate bar, and he asked if Bernie wanted a bite. Ogden wanted so much to taste the candy himself, but of course Walter would never ask him. Bernie had looked down at Ogden, who glared up at her with hard little nine-year-old eyes. "That'd be swell," Bernie had said, daringly, and Walter had held the candy bar in front of her face. She took a bite, right on the spot he had bitten himself just moments before, and she smiled broadly. "That tastes good," she boasted.

Later, at home, when Papa had asked why they were late, Ogden had gleefully squealed. "Bernie stopped to talk with a boy and she took a bite of the candy bar he was eating," he shrieked. Papa's face had turned red and he yanked Bernie without saying a word across his knee and beat her until she cried. Ogden got it next, for squealing. Then Papa stormed out of the house, not returning until the next day.

"Do you like vampire movies?"

Ogden was startled by the voice. He looked up from the poster and saw a man standing next to him, an older man, very distinguished-looking, much like the man in the movie poster, an actor whose name, he thought, was Cushing.

"Oh, I was simply—"

He felt his voice catch in his throat. The sun was setting. Bernie should have arrived in St. Croix by now.

"It's quite good," the man was saying. "But of course, they are allowed to show so much more on the screen these days. The Lugosi version was much tamer, but I think better. Have you seen it?"

He had a slight British accent, or at least Ogden thought he did. "No," he said. "Well, I don't remember. It's possible."

"And here I thought you were a vampire fan," the man said.

"Oh, no," Ogden said. "No, I'm not."

"Just curious then?"

"Yes." He made a polite smile. "Excuse me."

"The show is starting in a few minutes. Would you care to join me?"

"No," he said, too harshly, backing away. "No," he said again, catching himself, not wanting to appear impolite. "But thank you." He hurried away.

ও   ও   ও

The town at night was a blur of colors. The red and blue neon of Main Street shops and restaurants flashed on and off, and the streetlamps poured pale yellow light onto the street. It was a Tuesday night, not a busy night, but still couples strolled arm in arm, perhaps on their way to the movies, or to dinner. A gaggle of little girls in Girl Scout uniforms tagged behind an older woman, perhaps on their way home after a meeting. Ogden watched them as they crossed the street and all climbed into the back of a big black station wagon. To Ogden, it looked like a hearse.

"Oh, stop," he scolded himself. But as the shadows lengthened and the light blue of twilight melted in the deep purple of the evening, he dreaded returning to the empty flat. He sat there on the bench, facing the traffic of Main Street, lulled by the motion of the green and white buses and the golden orange of the taxicab lights, and fought against the tide of sleep that was trying to claim him. The bustle of people on the sidewalk behind him kept him awake, if not alert. Finally, overcome, he stood wearily and walked up the two blocks to his home.

He had considered sitting shivah for old Mr. Horowitz at the Hebrew Home, but something seemed not right about that. Not because he was a Christian, he told himself, but because Mr. Horowitz wasn't really dead; no, the corpse they had placed into the mausoleum this very day was just waiting, waiting for three nights from now, waiting to claw its way through the satin lining of the coffin and break free of its prison.

"Stop this nonsense," Ogden Smith told himself, and he placed both his hands down on the Formica top of the kitchen table and closed his eyes very tightly. "Stop this nonsense right now, Ogden Albert Smith."

When he opened them, he heard music: strange tinny music, as if from an old phonograph, somewhere in the building. It disturbed him, but he wasn't sure why. He opened the door of the old Kelvinator and removed a glass jar of milk. Unscrewing the cap, he poured himself a glass and allowed his eyes to wander through the gray kitchen. Behind the dull glass of the cupboard sat the old china with its faded blue flower pattern, the china that had been his mother's. Or so Papa had said. He decided they should use the china more: it was better than their old brown plates, which were getting chipped now and were shameful to serve to company. Even to Chase.

And the flat needed painting, Ogden decided. When was the last time it had been painted? Papa had painted it last, at least fifteen years ago, when he and Bernie had both been children. It had been eggshell white then; he remembered the name on the paint can. Now it was just gray. Everything was gray.

The tinny music seemed to have grown louder. Ogden placed his glass in the sink. He wished the music would die down; how would he sleep? He supposed he could tap on Miss Wright's door, but it probably wasn't her. It could be one of Mr. Trykowski's daughters, except they played rock and roll, and only on Saturdays, when their parents were out grocery shopping. He wasn't sure who could be playing this music. It seemed old, very old, as if it were coming from a Victrola—

"Stop it," he said to himself. He had flashed on an image: Mr. Horowitz as a young boy in Russia, with the great noble Count Alexei Petrovich Guchkov bent over, kissing his hand, a Victrola in the back, playing this very same music. "Stop it," he repeated, out loud, and his words made a curious echo in the kitchen. "Victrolas probably weren't even invented in 1868."

He went into Bernadette's bedroom and sat down on her neatly made bed. "Just three days," he whispered to himself, staring at his reflection in the mirror. "Just three nights," he heard another voice say, inside him. And in the glass, he thought he saw old Mr. Horowitz, chalk-white face and blood-red lips, rising up from behind him on the bed.

❧ ❧ ❧

"But that would not be possible," the man was saying. "Vampires cast no reflection."

"It was in my mind," he explained, not wanting him to think he was crazy. He couldn't be crazy if he knew he had imagined it.

"It is all patently impossible," the man said with finality, and Ogden wished he had never mentioned it. He hadn't intended the man to take his story seriously.

They had met again, quite by chance, at the counter of Henry's Diner, where Lois had just served Ogden a grilled cheese and a cup of tea. He had stopped here for lunch, as he often did, since the Hebrew Home was just up the block on Washington Street.

"Ah, my vampire friend," the man had said, sitting down on the stool next to him. The restaurant was not that crowded; there were other places he could have sat.

He said hello. He introduced himself. "I'm Stanley Kowalski," he said, then grinned: "Not that Stanley Kowalski." In fact, he said, his name was Stanislaus. He'd been born in Poland, but his parents came to America when he was just ten months old. He'd been Stanley ever since.

"Might I inquire as to your name?" he asked, in a gallant sort of way.

"Smith," he said. "Ogden Smith."

"Well, Mr. Smith, if I in any way offended you the other day, allow me to apologize."

He smiled a little. "No, there's no need to apologize. I was simply—" Ogden paused. "A man I knew had just passed away. I was a bit out of sorts."

And so Ogden told him the story of Mr. Samuel Horowitz.

Stanley Kowalski took a long sip of his coffee. "No, it's not possible," he said.

"Of course it's not," Ogden agreed, wishing he had never shared this with him, with this total stranger. He wanted to pay and leave. He wasn't hungry anymore. He tried to get Lois' attention, but she was pouring some more coffee for a man at the other end of the counter.

"I'll tell you why it's not possible. For a vampire to create another in his image, he must first *kill* his victim. If what Mr. Horowitz says is true, this Russian Count forgot about him, as vampires must do the majority of their victims, otherwise we'd be overrun with the creatures. The vampiric taint wears off, I assume. One would only become a vampire if the taint is in their blood at the time of their death, which would mean that they die of a vampire attack itself. Think of the Dracula story, my boy. Mina Harker was not going to turn into a vampire when she died. Poor Miss Lucy, on the other hand—she became a creature of the night because the Count sucked her dry, so to speak, and killed her."

Ogden Smith was shocked. It showed on his face.

"I'm sorry," Mr. Kowalski said at once. "Have I offended you?"

"I suppose I brought it on myself," he said, taking a breath. "I brought the horrible subject up."

"Are you all right? May I walk you home?"

"I'm fine," he insisted, getting off of his stool. "I've got to get back to work anyway."

"Let me pay for your lunch," Stanley Kowalski offered.

"No, no, absolutely not," he said. He handed two dollar bills across the counter to Lois. "Keep the change," he said hurriedly. Lois waved without turning around from the cash register. "Good afternoon, Mr. Kowalski," Ogden said, and rushed out the door.

In Mr. Horowitz's room that day, just as the sun began to sink lower in the sky, Ogden helped the other aides pack up the dead man's belongings. There was no family. Some of the personal items would be distributed among the other residents. The rest would be discarded.

There was a small icon of the Virgin Mary in Mr. Horowitz's jewelry box, along with a silver Star of David, its points still very shiny and quite sharp. Relics from the motherland, he supposed. Yet how odd that a Christian icon should be there as well.

"No one here will want that," said Mavis, a colored aide. "Do you think I could have it?"

Ogden wasn't sure. "You should ask Mrs. Newberg."

Mavis made a face. "She'll say no. Come on, Ogden. Who'll care?"

"All right," he said, handing over the icon to Mavis. She grinned when she got it, her eyes dancing.

That left the Star of David. Ogden stared at it for a few moments. Then he slipped it into his pocket. Who'd care?

The sun edged the horizon.

Two more nights.

He hoped he would sleep better tonight. How quiet the flat was. He had always known it was quiet, and had learned to live with it. He actually preferred the quiet to Bernie's moans and groans, which had started about eight months ago, when Chase had first come into their lives. Until then, there had been no men. They'd eat their meals together, maybe see a picture, maybe go down to Miss Wright's, their old kindergarten teacher, and watch her television set. She had been the first in the building to buy one, but now the Trykowskis had one, too. The Smith siblings had still not purchased a set.

Then Chase arrived. He was the brother of one of Bernie's pupils in her second-grade class. Bernie taught at the Edna Stillman School off Washington Street, just as Papa had hoped she would. Papa had saved all the money he made from the pool hall to send his children to college: Ogden to the Marcus T. Wilson School of Business and Bernadette to the State Teachers' School. But only Bernie had completed her studies: Ogden had left school after the first trimester. He preferred not to think about that.

Instead, he worked as an aide. First at St. Luke's, the Lutheran home, for a couple of years, where he tended to his own kind. But he never got a raise, and the Hebrew Home paid better wages. So just a few months ago, he had summoned all his courage and told the matron at St. Luke's that he was giving his notice, and two weeks later began his new career at the Hebrew Home, making thirty-five cents an hour more. The change prompted applause from Bernie. "Well," she'd smiled, "wouldn't Papa be proud how you asserted yourself."

But Ogden wondered if Papa would be as proud of Bernie. She had changed a great deal since she met Chase. Ogden thought it highly improper that she was dating the older brother of one of her pupils. But people hadn't really started talking yet, or if they had, Ogden hadn't heard them. But now that it was winter break, Bernie and Chase were carrying on with much less discretion. Ogden hated to think what Papa would have said.

But tonight, sitting on Bernie's bed, there was some small part of him that would have traded the relentless quiet for the sounds of his sister's passion. On his lap he cradled a pillow—the one Chase had slept on, he thought, just two nights before. What he really wanted to do, desperately, was push that pillow into his face and inhale; but he dared not. "Stop it," he scolded himself.

The music again. That same tinny music. From somewhere. Not above, not below. He flung the pillow to the floor and stood, pushing himself to the window and pressing his face up against the cold glass. The pane had fogged up too much to see outside. Where was the music coming from? What song did it play?

He paced the room. What time was it? Getting close to ten. He should go to sleep now. He had to be at the Hebrew Home by seven. Tomorrow was Thursday. Tomorrow he must pay the paper boy. And leave the money out for Mr. Otfinowski.

His stomach rumbled. "How silly of me," he said into the darkness. "I forgot to make myself dinner."

He stumbled into the kitchen and flicked on the overhead light. One of the bulbs had burned out; the glow was dim, not enough even to read by. He opened the cabinet next to the Kelvinator and considered a can of tuna fish. "It's too late to eat," he decided out loud, and closed the cabinet door.

At the window over the sink, something scratched at the glass.

He jumped. "Oh!" he cried, and narrowed his eyes to see what was there.

Three long scratches scarred the frost, scratches like fingernails.

"A squirrel," he told himself. "A squirrel."

It couldn't be anything else; it hadn't been three nights. It had only been two. And besides, Samuel Horowitz did not die from the bite of the vampire. The old man was wrong; the taint must have disappeared from his blood a long, long time ago. Ogden realized now that he had desperately tried to find some comfort in Mr. Kowalski's words. But Mr. Horowitz had been so sure—so sure he would rise again.

"Stop it," Ogden said to himself, turning out the light in the kitchen and quickly replacing it with the light in the hallway. This was brighter, more soothing. He passed by Bernie's room and turned into his own.

"I will sleep better tonight," he assured himself, getting undressed, "because last night I did not. I am tired enough tonight to fall asleep on a cold hard bench."

Standing there in only his underwear, long boxy polka-dotted shorts, looking at his plain round face in the mirror, he thought of the picture of his mother that Papa had kept hidden among his handkerchiefs in his top drawer, in this very room. This room had once been his, when Ogden and Bernadette had shared the other room. Ogden used Papa's bureau now, but in his top drawer the photograph of his mother, in its little tin oval frame, did not hide. It was burned long ago, shortly after Papa had died, when Ogden had tossed it, along with Papa's nightshirt, into the furnace.

He did not sleep as he had hoped. The music kept him awake, and the light he left burning beside the bed began to oppress him. At every little creak in the old building, he would start. He sat up finally, resting against his headboard, and tried to read. It was one of Bernie's trashy novels, *Peyton Place,* but Ogden couldn't abide it for very long. He heard the Trykowskis' great clock chime twelve from the other corner of the building, and then their own clock, out in the living room, also rang in the new day. Midnight.

"Why should midnight mean anything more than any other time?" he asked out loud.

And suddenly he thought of the Jewish cemetery out near Devil's Hopyard, that strange field where scaly hops grew yellow in the summer, where the Indians first heard unaccountable noises centuries ago, where the early English settlers, Ogden's ancestors among them, had pronounced the land the devil's own. The noises, scientists would later say, were merely the rumblings of a minor fault far beneath the surface of the earth; but might they not instead be coming from hell, Ogden thought now? The children of the town made up many stories regarding Devil's Hopyard, and sitting in bed this night, Ogden remembered them all. Worst of them were the tales of the cemeteries that ringed the hopyard: the flat, stark Jewish cemetery, where Mr. Horowitz's cold body lay in the mausoleum, waiting for the ground to thaw so it could be buried in the spring, and the hilly, ornate Protestant cemetery, where Ogden's mother had been interred these past twenty years.

"At night, the dead dance in Devil's Hopyard," Walter Moriarty had told them, and all the girls had squealed.

"Tell us more, Walter; tell us more!!"

"They crawl up out of their graves, the Jews and the Lutherans together, and they dance under the moon in the hopyard, to the sounds from the devil below," he'd intoned.

"No!"

Ogden covered his face with his hands. *Tell us no more,* Walter Moriarty. *I already know too much.* Mr. Horowitz's body does not wait to be buried in the earth; it waits to walk again, to suck the blood of the living, to find virgin blood under a cold black winter sky, with the snow overhead, anxious to fall.

❧   ❧   ❧

"I feel very foolish," Ogden Smith said to Stanley Kowalski.

"Please do not," he said.

They met at Henry's. Ogden had called him, having found his name in the phone book. Mr. Kowalski had been only too happy to meet him for lunch. This time they shared a booth. Ogden once again ordered a grilled cheese. "The usual," Lois smiled, scribbling onto her pad. Mr. Kowalski ordered a steak burger with onions, very rare.

"I must get this out of my head," Ogden told him.

"After tonight, the fear will be gone," Mr. Kowalski assured him.

"I certainly hope so. I didn't sleep at all last night." He was sure the other man could tell. The black rings under his eyes revealed his secret.

"Even if Mr. Horowitz really *is* a vampire, and even if tonight he really *does* rise," Mr. Kowalski said, "there's no reason to believe he would come for you. And even if he did, Mr. Smith, vampires must first be invited into a home before they can enter. You are perfectly safe."

Ogden didn't appear convinced.

"And vampires are not all-knowing. He doesn't even know where you live."

"Oh, he knows," Ogden told him. "I feel sure of that. There was something connecting us. He picked up on that. I was different, he said. I would *believe.*"

Mr. Kowalski raised an eyebrow. "And do you?"

Ogden hesitated. Lois brought over the grilled cheese, burned around the edges, with a thin wedge of pickle on the side. "Your steak burger will be out in a minute," she said.

"Thank you."

Ogden took a bite, then realized it was impolite to eat before the other person was served.

"Go ahead," Mr. Kowalski offered, but Ogden shook his head no.

"I'm not sure what I believe," he said. "I just wish my sister were not away. This wouldn't be happening if she were here."

"Is your sister some sort of magic talisman?"

"My sister wouldn't let anything bad happen," Ogden said. "She's very strong."

"And you?"

"Here's your steak burger," Lois interjected, thrusting the bloody flesh between them on a plate. "With extra onions. Will there be anything else?"

"No, thank you."

"Me?" Ogden said. "I used to be strong."

❧ ❧ ❧

He called the Hebrew Home after lunch and told them he had a headache, that he wouldn't be back. He wasn't lying.

"Come with me," Stanley Kowalski said. "My house is just over this way. I want to give you something."

He shouldn't go; he should just head home. Get this crazy notion out of his head. He shouldn't go to a strange man's house. But he followed.

Stanley Kowalski lived in a small, two-family house on Oak Avenue, on the second floor. The road was set two blocks past Ogden's own, off Main; there was a barbershop on the corner. Stanley waved to the barber inside, who was sharpening his razors.

It was a cold day. The wind was whipping, and Ogden's cheeks grew red and hard. He had misplaced his gloves, so he shoved his hands deep down into the pockets of his coat. The sky was a deep, dark gray. Snow beckoned.

The stairs that led to Stanley's apartment were highly polished wood, solid oak, and the smell of the carpeting reminded him of the way the Palace used to smell on the night of a premiere, back before television when they kept the theater clean for the Friday night crowds. There was a richness to the smell, heady, and it did something to Ogden: the deep scent of an obscure perfume that raised a tickle of memory way back in the unused part of his mind.

It was the rush of excitement of going to a premiere at the Palace that he felt, walking up Stanley Kowalski's stairs. For a moment, he forgot all about Samuel Horowitz the vampire, and the fact that Bernie and Chase were a thousand miles away, naked on some sunny beach.

"Here it is," Stanley said, opening his door. "My humble abode."

Inside, the smell was different: dry and dusty, faintly citrusy. A parakeet in a wire cage hung over a frayed soft chair in the living room. It chirped in greeting.

"Hello, Mrs. Tennyson," Stanley said to the bird, moving his face like a crazy man in front of the cage.

Ogden stood in his little foyer, unsure of whether he should proceed much further.

"Ah, Mr. Smith, do not be afraid," he smiled. "Please. Sit down."

"I shouldn't stay," he said.

"But I must give you what we came here for," Stanley said.

Ogden nodded.

Stanley Kowalski disappeared down the hall. Ogden looked around the room, at the newspapers on the floor, the plate full of crumbs and the empty Coke bottle next to the frayed overstuffed chair. Strange how Coke bottles always made him think of a woman: were they meant to? There was a television set, too, but much smaller than Miss Wright's, who'd bought one of the very first models back in 1951. Ogden had never seen one this small. Then he noticed the calendar on the wall: Jayne Mansfield, breasts bared, in a tiny fur-trimmed skirt and boots, shivering atop the hood of car surrounded by huge drifts of snow.

"Here we are," Mr. Kowalski said, coming down the hall. He had something in his hand. "You take this, Mr. Smith. Wear it around your neck. This will protect you."

It was a crucifix, a large wooden one on a silver chain.

"That will do no good," Ogden protested.

"But why not?"

"He was Jewish," Ogden said plainly.

"Ah," Mr. Kowalski said.

"But *this*," Ogden said, eyes lighting at the thought as he reached into the pocket of his coat, "this will work." He produced the Star of David. "May I take the chain?"

"But of course. Oh, this is splendid," Stanley said, clapping his hands.

Ogden felt better all ready. Why hadn't he thought of this before?

Mr. Kowalski slid the crucifix off the chain and proceeded to thread the chain through the small ring at the top of the star. "This was meant to be worn," he said. "May I put it on you?"

"Yes, please," Ogden said, turning his back to him.

Mr. Kowalski slipped the star around Ogden's neck. It dangled awkwardly over his coat.

"There," Stanley Kowalski said, and very quickly he slipped his arms around Ogden, pulling him in, nuzzling his neck.

"Mr. Kowalski!" Ogden shuddered.

"Oh, come, my dear," he soothed, gently biting at his earlobe. "You came willingly."

"No," he said, but Mr. Kowalski's arms only tightened around him. Ogden couldn't see his face, only hear his words and feel his warm lips pressed against his ear, his neck.

"Foolish boy, to think that vampires can be stopped by silly little trinkets, that they only walk about by night," Stanley Kowalski said, and now his hands, his cold hands, were unbuttoning the front of Ogden's shirt.

"No," he said again, but more meekly this time. "No, please."

Stanley Kowalski moved his cold hands under Ogden's shirt, finding the smooth warmth hidden there.

"Such a dear boy," Stanley said, his lips on Ogden's soft throat. "Such a sweet, innocent child—"

"No," Ogden said dreamily. "Not innocent . . ."

Mr. Kowalski laughed.

"There was a man—at the school—"

"Hush, hush, dear boy," Mr. Kowalski said. "There shall be no more men. Only me."

And with that, he bit Ogden Smith upon his neck.

It had begun to snow.

"It's true," Ogden said, coming out onto the sidewalk, his voice calm and full of wonder as he watched the fragile flakes accumulate on the black wool of his coat. "No two snowflakes *are* exactly the same."

He pulled his coat tighter around him. It had gotten very cold.

He would not recall the walk home except for the snowflakes. It was as if he walked in a lovely, untroubled dream.

Finally, back at his house, in the last slanting golden rays of the day, he put on a pot of tea and contemplated dinner. "Bernie will want stew," he said out loud. He opened the freezer and looked down into it. No stew meat.

"Oh, dear," he said to himself, and then the sunlight was gone, and the room, he realized, was a hazy shade of blue.

His sweet sense of dreamland faded away.

Bernie's away, Ogden remembered. *And it's the third night.*

The Star of David still hung around his neck. He clutched it and breathed.

"What should I do?" he said into the darkness, and he pressed his nose up against the windowpane, looking out across the rooftops in the direction of Devil's Hopyard, where he could see, in his mind, the great stone door of the mausoleum in the Jewish cemetery sliding back, and the demons dancing in the hopyard, bowing in strange homage to the returning Samuel Horowitz . . .

The teakettle was whistling, a piercing sound. Pierced through the heart. He poured some water over his tea bag and inhaled the bitter aroma. "Drink some tea," he told himself.

There it was: the tinny music again, the sound of a Victrola at the Russian Imperial Court, or the sound of an old phonograph spun by old Mr. Wilson, the dean of his school, who would sit there, all night, listening to its seductive sound, who sat there and watched Ogden cry without saying a word or ever moving from his chair. "Don't think your tears will keep you here, you pervert," he said.

There was a knock at the door.

Ogden tensed. He thought for a moment he should hide, but then decided against it. He took another sip of tea and then set the cup down on the table. The knock came again. He took a deep breath and walked over to the door. He spied through the hole.

It was Freddie. The paperboy.

He had forgotten.

"Good ev'nin', Mr. Smith," the boy said. His face looked bloated and distorted through the hole.

"Hello, Freddie."

He opened the door and stepped aside to let him enter.

Freddie seemed unsure, but he came inside. He was a tall youth, with long legs and a blond crew cut. He couldn't have been more than thirteen. There was a patch of acne on his chin. He wore a big shiny navy blue coat and a red-and-white scarf around his neck.

"Now where *is* that envelope my sister left for you?" Ogden mused. His voice was different: lighter, higher.

Freddie shifted his weight from his left foot to his right foot.

Ogden suddenly stopped his search and looked over at the boy, a broad smile on his face. "Freddie, would you like a cup of tea?"

"No, thanks, Mr. Smith. I've got to finish my route."

"It's snowing outside. And so very cold. Are you *sure?*"

"No, thanks. I don't drink tea."

Ogden smiled, approaching him. "Of course not. How silly of me. Boys don't drink tea."

Freddie made an uncomfortable sound.

Ogden touched the boy's cold hard cheeks with each of his forefingers. "I could make some hot cocoa," he tempted.

"No, thank you, Mr. Smith."

Ogden watched him for several seconds. Then Ogden's eyes seemed to change, and he looked away. "Here," he said, thrusting the envelope at him. "Go. Get out of here. This place is not safe. He's coming for me. Go. Run. Save yourself."

"Mr. Smith, are you——"

"Go, Freddie! *Run!*" he shouted, and the boy did. Ogden bolted the door behind him.

Heaving, he leaned up against the door. "At least I saved *him,*" he said, his eyes welling up with cold tears.

Ogden clasped his right hand around the Star of David again. He closed his eyes. Now old Samuel Horowitz was dancing in the hopyard in his floating white burial gown, his thick white hair cascading around him in the darkness. He left no tracks in the newly fallen snow; no one could trace him. He floated an inch above the snow, sometimes obscured in the swirl of snowflakes, but dancing all the while, a snow dance of death . . .

"Stop it," Ogden told himself, sitting down at the kitchen table, pressing his fingers into his temples.

"Bernie will be home tomorrow," he said, trying to convince himself of something, but what that was remained unclear. "Oh, why did she have to go away and leave me alone now?"

The vampire was closer. He floated over the snow, so white, so pure, so fresh, all the way into town from the hopyard: through the Polish neighborhoods near the river, past St. John the Baptist Church, all the way down Main Street, past the Hebrew Home, past Henry's Diner, past the Palace Theater, up the block toward Ogden's building . . .

"Stop it!" he screamed at himself, but then the music got louder, a scratchy old tune, one he knew but couldn't place, and the scratching was at the window again, and this time it was no squirrel, it was a hand, an old hand, a very old hand, long gnarled fingers scratching to get in . . .

Ogden Smith backed up into the cupboard in the dark kitchen, staring at the scratch marks in the frost on the window over the sink. "No," he said meekly. "Please don't."

The hand reappeared at the window, scratching away more of the frost.

"You don't want me," Ogden cried. "I'm not what you think. I've been defiled. You don't want me."

But the music only got louder. And when instead of a hand, a face appeared at the window—the face of old Samuel Horowitz, grinning wide and baring his fangs—Ogden screamed with every last vestige of what he once was. He screamed and screamed, but when that was over and no one had come, he finally looked up at the window and said, defeated, "Yes. All right, yes. You might as well come in."

And he tore the Star of David from around his neck, pressing it against his throat for just a moment before tossing it across the kitchen floor, where it clattered and rolled for several seconds, finally settling among the dust beneath the Kelvinator.

Then the window over the sink began to slide open, a screech of icy metal against wood, just as the Trykowskis' great old pendulum clock began to chime the hour, somewhere far off in the building.

"Miss Smith?"

"Yes."

"My name is Stanley Kowalski. No, not that Stanley Kowalski."

But Bernie didn't laugh.

The man became serious. "I came inquiring about your brother."

"Are you a friend?"

"I'd only just met him. We had lunch together on Thursday at Henry's Diner."

Bernadette Smith's eyes were still puffy. "And how did he seem to you?"

"Oh, fine, ma'am. Just fine."

"Then you have no clue as to what happened?"

"No, I'm afraid I don't, Miss Smith."

"Then why did you come here?"

"Just to tell you . . . to tell you what a fine lad your brother was."

Bernadette began to cry. "I should never have left him."

"There, there, my dear," Stanley said, taking the young woman into his arms. He held her in the doorway, stroking her hair.

"He relied on me," Bernadette said into his coat, her words muffled. "And I let him down." She trembled. The man's touch was cold. "Ogden's always been such a sensitive boy. Ever since what happened to him at the school—did he tell you about that?"

"He mentioned something about it."

"Oh, I'll just never forgive myself," Bernie cried.

"Poor dear," Stanley Kowalski said, petting her. "You can't blame yourself. We all wonder if we could have done something."

Bernie looked up at him. "How did you know something had happened?"

The man seemed uneasy for just a moment. "I—I came by in the morning. I saw the ambulance . . ."

"Oh, please, don't mention it again. Mr. Otfinowski has already described what he found when he came here, just as the sun was coming up, to deliver the milk . . . Oh, I should have been here!"

"I'm sorry, dear. I didn't mean to upset you again." Mr. Kowalski's eyes bore down on her. "Might I see him? Perhaps it would do him some good to spend some time with a friend. You *will* let me see him, won't you?"

"Yes," Bernie said, looking up at him. Her eyes seemed caught by his; she couldn't shake his stare. "Yes. Of course." She turned finally with difficulty and began walking inside the house, leaving the door open for Mr. Kowalski to follow.

"My dear," he called after her graciously. "First you must invite me in."

❧   ❧   ❧

In his room, Ogden Smith huddled under his blankets, his neck bandaged where Bernie said he had tried to slit his throat with the Star of David. He tried to shield his eyes from the light.

He was one of them now. Ogden knew he hadn't tried to slit his throat. The wound was from where the vampire had tasted of his blood.

Oh, how the light burned his eyes now. Such would be the way from now on. That much he knew. But for how long? Would old Samuel Horowitz come back for him tonight and kill him? Or would he, instead, make him wait, wait as he had, wait until he was one hundred and six, living only through sheer force of will, always afraid to answer the door, afraid that death would be on the other side, afraid that he would rise up and walk the earth as one of the undead, drinking the blood of the living?

Ogden Smith knew almost everything else, but that was the one thing he still didn't know.

The Perfect One

Greg Wharton

Our time is coming to an end, sweet one. I wish we could be together always, but like they say, if you love someone set them free and if they return . . . no, I guess that doesn't apply. I poke you with my elbow to make sure you realize it's a joke.

I knew when I first saw you at the club, your puka shells bouncing around your neck as you tried to keep up with the pounding beat of the bass, your skin bathed in perspiration and shining under the dance floor's lights, I knew we were meant for each other. How could I then resist your invitation?

"My name is Sean. Take me home. Come on . . . you know you want me."

Young, tall, thin, deep green eyes, pierced in all the right places, big cock. It didn't have to end this way. You used me, then I used you. We both knew what we wanted. I thought that we might both get it too. All's fair, I guess. You were nearly perfect. But the body is never quite as strong as the soul. It never seems to last as long as you want it to. Does it?

" . . . harder! Harder, baby! Yes . . . now let up just a . . . no, come on, I can't breathe! I can't breathe! You're hurting me . . ."

We've had two near-perfect weeks. I guess I should feel grateful. You lasted longer than most. Time to move on. The shells you always wore, I'll keep. The rest of you . . . oh, I always hate this part.

Through my tear-blurred vision, I carry you from the bed we have shared during your short stay with me and lay you softly on my favorite blanket on the kitchen floor. Your body looks so frail. And you smell. I'm not sure what I saw in you, how I thought you might be the one. I light a cigarette, dump the overflowing ashtray on your still, now grayish body and fix some coffee. I roll you up. Having made the tough decision we should part has caused me to lose interest, and folding your stiff body into the blue recycle bin takes more effort than I really want it to.

I pull on some shorts, realizing that I haven't dressed since you came home with me that first night. I drag you to the dumpster, toss you in, and decide to clean up a bit. It's been two weeks since I've been out. I need a shave and I want to make the apartment look nice; you never know when you'll meet the perfect one.

Fever

Victoria A. Brownworth

Unnatural, almost sickening. Or so it seemed to Lily Sakhret as she stood, a small sheaf of papers in one hand, a suitcase in the other, and a large leather bag containing a laptop computer slung over her shoulder, outside the lacy iron grillwork gates of the old convent on Ursulines at the very edge of the French Quarter.

"This heat. Unreal," she murmured as she set the suitcase on the damp slate walkway and wiped her face with the edge of her voile scarf. It had gone dark a good hour earlier, which only added to Lily's sense of unease. It should be a chill night, even cold, she thought, so near to Christmas, even if this was New Orleans. Instead the air was suffocatingly warm with a cloying humidity she had always associated with summer and death. So near to Christmas and here, in New Orleans, where it should have been a chill winter's night, it felt eerily, disturbingly hot. Like home, like Calcutta.

And it smelled like home. The dankness clung to Lily, the air a fetid, murky mix of heat, fog, mud, and something slightly rotten wafting in from the Mississippi River. At home, in Calcutta, it would have been the Ganges; that rotting smell would have been bodies and she would have fled. Had indeed fled. Was that not why she was *here* now, instead of at home, in India, watching the lepers decomposing in the side streets and all manner of filth floating along the river's edge?

Lily steadied herself against a wave of nausea. *A protracted Indian summer,* the National Weather Service had explained when she had checked before booking her flight. Not to *this* Indian, she thought. October, yes, even November would be protracted, she argued. Such heat—the heat of high summer—in December in this part of the world was something else, something sickening, unnatural, very close to evil. Yes, evil, Lily thought, for along with the heat came the lep-

157

rous, choleric pall that hung in the air and clung to every lamppost and shutter and doorknob, leaving nothing and no one immune from its fetid touch. No house would be passed over by this plague, this aura of putrefaction.

For that was it, the atmosphere, this unnatural heat, and that smell—what was it? rotting kelp? dying fish? oysters turned deadly by a red tide?—seemed to Lily indeed to be evil, as if Kali herself had had her bloody hand in somewhere.

What would her relatives think of these sacrilegious thoughts, she wondered, as she searched the grillwork for a bell to announce her arrival. "Sacred territory, the Ganges," her aunt would have admonished her, lighting incense and bowing low to the blue-faced god before her on the little kitchen shelf, reminding Lily of her good fortune at being brought the great distance from "that sinkhole, Lahore" to live awash in—though her aunt did not see this—the endless wave of filth, disease, poverty, and death that was Calcutta.

So many years later Lily could no longer remember Lahore, nor her mother, though she knew both had been beautiful. Nor could she recall the long trek away from her father's Pakistani family back to her mother's in Calcutta, which must have been for Indra, her mother, a journey daily deeper into hell. Indra, who had gone to bathe in the Ganges the night after she and Lily had arrived at the aunt's, at Vashti's, and had never returned. "Taken into Krishna's arms," her aunt had intoned. Even then the ten-year-old Lily had thought, *Someone's arms, certainly*. But she had doubted Krishna's. So there Lily had stayed, the girl child abandoned by two countries, dropped at the mouth of hell, suffocated for a decade by the miasma she had feared would be as inescapable as being born into the wrong caste. Yet escaped she had, long, long ago.

So why had Lily come here, where now as she stood in yet another foreign place in which she did not belong, searching for entry into yet another world that was not hers, all those memories washed their pungent unpleasantness over her as the fog slithered along the footpath like any common viper.

There. The bell lay nestled in a whorl of blackened metal, just above eye level where the convent gate met the high, blistered stone wall that surrounded the place. Pretty, but impractical, thought Lily as she pressed hard for longer than she would have done were she not overwhelmed by bad feelings bordering on premonition. Behind her, on Jackson Square, the carillon of St. Louis Cathedral began to chime the hour. Six o'clock, yet dark and still as death and midnight.

Beyond the gates the convent looked stark and unoccupied. A short stretch of dim gas-green luminaria lit a slate path to the place, but through the fog all she could see were cypress shutters of characteristic bottle green closed against the swell of heat and stench of—what? disease?—that subsumed everything.

Lily pressed the bell again, even longer this time, wondering why she had come, what she had been thinking, leaving her work to respond to some inchoate urgency in Monica's letters. The sheaf of pale blue onionskin papers wilting in her hand. The notes on—something—that Lily had pored over on the flight here as she tried to pinpoint what it could be that had made her feel she must leave London at once, putting the assistant she did not trust in charge, and come here to this place far too reminiscent of the home she had renounced over a decade ago to see the woman she had renounced over a year ago.

And yet the letters had compelled her. The letters in Monica's tight, small hand. The letters—Monica who hated e-mail, felt it lacked both privacy and grace, and used it only for memos and confirmations—which had begun suddenly and come in a flurry, written nearly daily, and then stopped. Stopped with as little apparent reason as they had begun but having revealed—

A door had opened in the near distance. Shutters had been flung back and a figure of indeterminate gender came toward the gate with a stride both languorous and purposeful. The woman, for as the person neared Lily saw it was indeed a woman, was tall and somewhat lean, clad in black trousers and a long black shirt that hung open at the neck, revealing a silver cross that glinted surprisingly brightly in the narrow yellow sliver cast by the quivering gaslight above the gate.

"Yes?" Neither query nor statement, the word betrayed an accent Lily could not place, enunciated with neither welcome nor reprimand.

The woman stood still, made no move to open the gate. Within the cadaverous light of the deepening fog she appeared somewhat ephem-

eral, her face its own pale light set in bold relief between the night sky
and her own black garments.

"I'm Dr. Lily Sakhret." Lily stretched her long fingers through the
gate. The woman did not raise her hand to meet Lily's. "I'm here to
see Monica—Dr. Graves. She wrote me she was here and requested
that I meet her. We are colleagues."

This must surely sound the lie it was, thought Lily, whose flair for
dissembling remained limited to work and sex, not the sort of subter-
fuge this odd setting seemed to warrant.

A hand slender as her own, yet pale as the rising moon, fluttered
against the gate, which opened slowly and with a melodramatic
groan, as if it were little used.

Lily felt laughter rise in her throat where minutes before fear and
nausea had lain. Suddenly the eeriness of the setting had gone comi-
cal, with the moaning of the gate and the "Who goes there?" tone of
the woman on the other side. Every Indian child, no matter how poor,
spends hours at the cinema, and Lily had been no exception, viewing
many an English import that reeked of just this sort of hyper-atmo-
spheric tension. No moor in sight, nor baying hounds, yet Lily's previous unease had been replaced by a rampant giddiness. *Why indeed had
she come?* This was true foolishness. Monica would think her mad—or
worse, mistake her intentions for something else. It was not too late to
claim error, leave with a bit of grace before it all fell flat.

And yet—

Fog curled around her feet, warm and enveloping. "I'm Sister
Stephania." The woman had extended her hand to Lily, who now caught
the unmistakable burr of Eastern Europe in the woman's clipped elo-
cution. "We have few guests. Excuse my surprise."

The suitcase seemed unbearably heavy as Lily crossed the threshold
of the convent grounds and Stephania closed the gate behind them. A
feeling of irrevocability descended upon Lily as they strode through
the thickening fog toward the dim light of the convent beyond. Was
Monica even here? Lily wondered as she followed Stephania's purposeful walk along the weathered slate path.

᠅   ᠅   ᠅

The first letter had come just as Lily had begun the stultifying task of organizing her data from the last epidemic in Congo. Well, not *epidemic,* she corrected herself. Only fifty-three had died this time in the short-lived outbreak. There had been no press whatsoever. Shocking, she had thought, as she had stood, masked and cloaked in protective gear in the tiny bush hospital outside Kikwit. But then the Western media had little appetite for anything but terrorism these days and few understood that the perils of Marburg virus were as deadly as Ebola and in some ways much more punishing. Had these fifty-three—all women and children this time—been infected in some small town in America by someone with her own ethnicity, the Western press would have swarmed the place despite risk of infection. Or had the name Osama bin Laden been whispered to a source, caught and spread like the bush fires that plagued Australia this time of year, had there been intimations that this little village was a testing ground, like Saddam Hussein's Kurdish experiment with sarin gas, the Western media would have found a way to field a satellite hookup right there amidst the rubber plants. This was terrorism, all right, she had thought, but only for those living with the terror.

No one had come and no mention had appeared, except for a small item in the Congolese paper she took when in Kinshasa. Perhaps for a continent so rife with wars and torn by desperation fifty-three lives taken within a matter of days, a tiny epidemic decimating a few families and then leaving as mysteriously as it had come, had no real resonance for any but those who lost their lives and those who loved them. There were no televisions here, no knowledge of planes flying into buildings. The extravagant pyrotechnics of the horror wrought in the West were unknown here; there were no points of comparison in a country where nearly three million had died in three years of an undeclared war between Rwandan rebels and Congolese militia. There were so very many dead and dying in Congo from diseases of a century ago—tuberculosis, malaria—who was there to notice fifty-three women and children dead in a few weeks from a disease almost no one had ever heard of, it was so new? Lily herself had been charting Marburg for only a decade, since some poor soul had gone into the rain forest and returned infected. Lily, who had come of age in the charnel house that was Calcutta, understood how slow exsanguination by Marburg seemed just another way of dying to a people bloodied by amputations at the machete-wielding hands of the Mau-Mau guerrillas.

No, the fifty-three deaths outside Kikwit registered no seismic tremor on Congo's disease Richter. Only the latest in a series of epidemics. As one young nurse had said as she shrouded a girl of nine in the blood-soaked sheet that would become her burial garment, "We didn't lose too many this time, did we Dr. Miss?"

Still, for weeks those fifty-three women and children had been Lily's primary and inescapable focus as she reviewed her data from the previous outbreaks of Marburg. Monica's first letter had lain atop a stack of index cards detailing medical histories of the first handful of victims.

Lily's assistant, Ian Blentham, an irritatingly officious clerk of an epidemiologist, had waved the letter at her. "Dr. Sakhret, is this data to be entered? It's not been opened." Blentham was so clearly of that class of Londoners who retained the belief that the Subcontinent, as they referred to both her parents' homelands, belonged to a British Empire they still imagined existed outside the British Museum's rooms full of colonializing plunder. When Blentham saw her, his superior, his *boss,* with her smoke-brown skin, snake-black hair and obsidian eyes, he saw a woman who should have been serving him a Tandoori take-out or stirring up a curry on a market stall. He could not see the prize-winning scientist who had charted eleven epidemics of the world's deadliest diseases and was currently England's foremost authority on leprosy. Blentham saw the scullery maid he thought she should be, and Lily never failed to hear the imperious tone of the Raj in his voice, whether his query was about when she wanted her daily tea or the proper intravenous hydration level necessary to delay total exsanguination from Ebola in a previously healthy adult.

"Dr. Sakhret," Blentham had intoned, the pale blue aerogram fluttering from his worm-white hand, "more data for me to enter or not?"

She had taken the set-aside letter from him; set aside because the hand had been unmistakable even if the return address had not.

Monica. "Something I must do myself," Lily had dismissed Blentham, to whom she never gave any personal ground. She had left the laboratory then, gone out for a stolen curry and Indian cigarette, the still-unopened letter her silent luncheon companion

It had been so oddly innocuous when she had finally had the will to open it after a too-hot cup of chai.

23 November 2001

Dearest Lily,

The rain has been unceasing for five days now, and I haven't been out for three. The weathercasters talk about stalled fronts in the Carribean and a hurricane brewing off Cuba. It's sloshing rain into the gulf at a fearful rate, though apparently it's much worse in Florida right now than here in New Orleans. But since we're below sea level and a virtual island, what with the lake and the Mississippi, there's never anywhere for the water to go but up and over levees.

I went to the market Friday and had to run an errand on Canal Street—the rain in torrents and I could barely see to drive. It was going on dusk, though not much past four. (The only thing I hate about winter are these shortened days, though conversely I love the longer nights!) Then right near Bourbon Street the most amazing sight: the sewer covers thrust up on fountains of water, spinning like dinner plates in a Chinese circus! I doubt I shall ever forget that—much more dramatic than that old Trevi Fountain we tossed our la dolce vita coins in, n'est-ce pas? Though not terrifying, like that monsoon in Bangladesh when we first met, mud was running rivers through the town. Of all the ways to die, suffocating in mud seems one of the more hellish.

That seems to threaten, here, though. There's mud everywhere now, what with the flooding. The convent actually has a basement, which is extraordinary, given when it was built and how few basements there are here. One of the sisters was telling me one year it flooded so badly that bodies were washed up out of the graves in the little cemetery behind the place. Now that has disease written all over it.

Which is, of course, why I am here, researching the current strange epidemiology which doesn't seem to have a correlative yet—No doubt you've heard some news of it over there? Some strain of influenza perhaps, though far worse than the A strain we charted three years ago or the Sydney component. And they seem to have ruled out anthrax (though it has similar properties) and pretty much decided it is not bioterroristic, though no one is saying 100 percent—it wouldn't be prudent, to quote the presidential père. But it's killing sporadically, though from my perspective as scientist the most intriguing thing is the deaths have all been in adults, none in children, none in the elderly. Totally contrary to the usual epidemic process we've charted in so many other places. In fact, I feel this quite eerie sense about the deaths; nearly every one has been a woman or man between twenty-five and forty. Were it not an immediate killer and were this Africa, you know what i'd say: AIDS. But it's not, of course. Can't be.

Right now I'm staying at this convent on the edge of the Vieux Carre, the French Quarter, which was a quarantine site a century ago. Though I've got precious little data on the new outbreak, it's undoubtedly some sort of influenza, pretty strong, of course. I'm comparing this current plague to the yellow fever epidemic in 1898, how epidemics are handled in the U.S. now with public health services and so forth, how we don't quarantine except in extreme and individual cases. The quarantines in the four corners during the hanta virus outbreak in 1993, or the quarantining of patients with multidrug-resistant TB in Belle Glade. Did you know the yellow fever epidemic (pandemic, really) killed nearly half the population? The entire city was quarantined, which was fairly simple, given the peninsula. (We could do it now, if it comes to that, though I can't imagine it would.) The army staked the place out for months. They were burning bodies on pyres. You would have felt right at home, all that suttee going on. Of course you know I think burning bodies is the best medicine in an epidemic; the Hindus had the right idea about that. Now if we could get them out of that bloody Ganges disease vector you and I loathe so much, even if it did bring us together. Who would have thought love would be born out of all that leprosy? But I digress . . .

Once I finish this project I am considering a book on religion and medicine. Or rather how one is substituted for the other in the poorest of places. Certainly that was the case for my little West Virginia snake-handling family and your Ganges-immersed relatives. Surviving religion, I sometimes think, is much like surviving an epidemic. Aren't we the lucky ones to be inoculated through our individuated autos-da-fe? I had feared being around all these nuns—I'm positive most are queer, special friendships and all that—might jes' tetch me with that ole time religion agin, but fortunately I haven't seen a snake, nor been to communion, despite continual urging. So I am safe from that bacterium, at least. As for what's transpiring elsewhere, we shall see. But then you know better than anyone how much I crave that danger-ous edge that epidemics lead one to.

Perhaps you'll write? The address is on the post. You know I still miss you.

Monica

There had been the references, of course, to their love affair. Five years full of the volatility of a febrile illness was how Lily remembered it. Monica Graves was an extraordinary scientist, gifted writer, impressive lover, and demonic to live with. They had met studying leprosy and Lily had always felt that insidious disease had been a heavy-handed metaphor for their relationship; something that blooms soft and pink as a blush in its early stages, then slowly decomposes the living body. She and Monica had worked together doggedly throughout Asia, had traveled to Africa and even done a short stint in the less romantic areas of Europe as they sought out their bacterial prey. Monica was good, but both she and Lily had known before long that Lily was better.

In the end, Lily had been worn down by the fighting that fueled Monica's ardor even as it staunched her growing professional jealousy; had found it by turns juvenile and incapacitating. Once Monica had struck her quite hard in the face and tossed a sheaf of papers—data jotted down in the field during a tularemia outbreak in a godforsaken village in Albania— onto the fire that warmed their tiny whitewashed room. Lily could have forgiven the slap and even all it signified, but the trashing of her work was a statement as unforgivable as it was irrevocable. She had gone the next day, leaving both project and Monica behind.

That had been just over a year ago, and except for a handful of curt telephone calls early on to determine the disposition of possessions and the London flat Lily had decided to keep when Monica returned to the States, there had been no contact, professional or otherwise, between them since.

Thus Monica's letter had been more than a surprise. Lily had eyed it on the stack of mail in her laboratory as if it carried the very anthrax spores Monica alluded to in her letter. What could Monica possibly want? They had seemed, both of them, silently, implicitly, to have chosen paths that would take their work and thus them as far away from each other as possible. Despite twenty years of living there, Monica had left London for good and all and Lily had been entirely sure it was to avoid her. In their profession the circles were far too small to maintain even a semblance of distance.

So why the letter? It had been the chattiness, the almost studied carefree element of it that had shaken Lily most. At thirty-six Lily had lived with few lovers and none for as long as she had with Monica. Previous lovers had found Lily's constant traveling tiresome, and not a few had been disturbed by the work she did; Lily had always found it ironic that the very women who balked at safe sex feared she might infect them with Ebola. Monica's complete understanding of both her lifestyle and her work had stoked Lily's passion as much as Monica's keen mind, milk-fed good looks, incendiary passion, and acerbic wit.

What was the letter about, really? Lily had pondered this over a sticky Indian drink in the dark little restaurant she always fled to when she needed to leave behind not just Blentham but London itself. Nair's was a hole in the wall with food from home; neither Londoners nor tourists frequented the place. Thick-aired and dimly lit, this was as far from a ploughman's lunch as she could get off the Kensington high street. Indian music whined behind her, and staccato clips of Hindi and Urdu thrummed the air like insects. There were no de-

mands on Lily at Nair's—a place not much larger than her Aunt
Vashti's Calcutta flat with smoke-brown faces like her own and the
peppering of language she rarely spoke but did not want to forget.

More than an hour later, Lily had returned to her work to find
Blentham absent and yet another blue envelope delivered with the afternoon post.

25 November 2001

Dearest Lily,
The rain depresses me. You know how it can get here in winter—some days it's
warm, others freezing. Perhaps if like you I'd been born into equatorial heat instead
of mountain cold I'd have no expectations of snow and the rain wouldn't distress me
so. But with Christmas just a month away I simply ache for a soft coverlet of fluffy
white and that blue-lit quiet that comes with a first snow. I know, hate the religion but
love the trappings.
The deaths continue here, though there appear to be fewer now. Not truly an epidemic, more an outbreak, if we must stick close to the technical. I had occasion to
speak with one of the nuns, the abbess here, actually, Sister Claire, last night about
the first cases she'd seen—she does some sort of laying on of hands work at charity
hospital. It's becoming common, you know, this melding of religion and medicine,
though I find it more common when the doctors don't know what the bloody hell
they're dealing with. Although to be fair, this is a nursing order of nuns. That's why
the convent was used during the yellow fever epidemic and before that to nurse sol-
diers in the Civil War. It's a small order, or so Sister Claire tells me as I actually
hadn't heard of it before coming here. They came to the U.S. from somewhere in
Europe just after the Louisiana Purchase, though they have little convents all over
the world, she tells me.
Anyway, according to the public health director, the first six cases were prostitutes. Now what does that sound like to you? AIDS again, of course, yet we know
AIDS doesn't kill within seventy-two hours, which is the time frame we're dealing
with here. Much like Ebola—no, more like Marburg. But I am wondering if there is
some kind of connection somehow. Blood-borne is blood-borne, after all, and it's
not like we haven't seen a lot of viral mutation in the past few years. Remember that
village in Burundi where everyone was infected and the time from seroconversion
to death was only about eleven months?
I asked Sister Claire details about the women and she gave me what she remembered—all mid-twenties, all but one black. Because of the order of their
deaths, no one could determine if they had perhaps been infected by the same
trick. One interesting thing, though. Sister told me—you would have loved the kind
of sotto voice way she leaned close to do so—one of the women was a lesbian and
didn't trick with men, just did sex jobs with women. Apparently she felt some sort of
need to confess to Sister Claire, who I must say has a bit of a butch affect about her.
So that adds another random aspect to the epidemiology, n'est-ce pas?

The letter had stopped there with no closure. After a space it had
begun again with a new date.

26 November 2001

Dearest Lily,

A woman came to the convent last night quite late. The rain was still torrential—it's been nearly a week now. As I've told you, it's a skeletal staff here right now, a handful of nuns. They travel a lot, sent to different places to do the nursing. This is sort of a terminal, a stopover. The woman was soaked through, of course. Umbrellas are useless in this kind of tropical storm. The rain comes sideways. I let her in because I was still awake and heard the bell. It's very eighteenth century, the bell, a strange kind of fog-toned clang of a thing. Oddly, none of the nuns seemed to hear it, for no one met me on the stairs as I went out to get the gate. I got soaked to the skin just running the hundred or so feet to the grounds' front.

So there she was, drenched, only a small black duffel like the nuns use here for travel. I just let her in, didn't think to do otherwise until we were nearly to the convent steps and then worried I was overstepping. I guess I had just assumed at that hour—it had just gone 2 a.m., I'd heard the chimes, you know I hate a watch at night—she was somehow expected. It seems this convent has always been some sort of novitiary transit site. Nuns come and go quite a bit, even in the month I've been here.

As we were both sodden, we hadn't run back, just walked briskly, I hadn't really looked at her, but as we got to the lighted doorway i was momentarily stunned—she looked bloody much like you, darling. You as a nun, of course, because I gathered that's who she was. March, she said her name was. Whether first or last, I wasn't clear. She thanked me for letting her in and just went on up the stairs as if she knew where she was going and had been here many times before. I hadn't asked her a bloody thing and for all I know she's going about stealing the silver (chalices) even as we speak.

27 November 2001

Lily, my dear,

Feeling hellish and the rain simply refuses to abate. And did I mention it is bloody hot here now as well?

March. Wasn't that the name of that butch item in that violently homophobic story by D. H. Lawrence? The Fox, I think. Didn't March cut a tree down and kill her lover, by metaphoric accident? There's also that maniacal march hare in Alice in Wonderland who's also a pathological character.

As I said, too befuddled by rain to think clearly. And I swear to god (see, this convent is infecting me) I have been coming down with some fever since the rain. Or since March. After all, she does so resemble you.

Now the letter was fully finished, but just stopped. Lily turned the page over, involuntarily. It was unlike Monica, a stickler for both manners and detail, to send an incomplete letter, to not even sign her name.

The London winter afternoon had faded into evening. The city had gone dark and now the laboratory windows stared dully obsidian in the twilight gloom, office buildings across the high street well-lit, yet empty. It was just past five but Lily wanted to pack it in and go home. She felt queasy from that too-sweet chai and had no more heart for details of death and dying, of mystery diseases and mystery women. The fifty-three souls from Congo would still lay on the marble counter in their index-card shrouds tomorrow. She put the two letters into her bag, tossed her coat back on, and left for the night.

The dream jolted Lily awake with the atavistic force of childhood nightmare. Had she screamed? She hoped not. The walls of the flat were thick enough but not so thick as to dispel her Paki looks and criminal suspicions from the minds of her very white neighbors. Now that Monica no longer lived here with her creamy-skinned, Irish-countryside looks, Lily, always quiet, found herself preternaturally aware of sound late at night or early in the morning. Mortgages in this part of town had been foreclosed for far less than a late-night scream from an already unwanted wog.

Lily switched on the small booklight on the bedstand and checked the clock. Just past midnight. Now she really hoped she hadn't screamed. She reached for her robe at the bottom of the bed; the room was bone chilling as only a London flat can be in winter. Lily had always thought the American poet Sylvia Plath had killed herself more from the desperate cold of a miserable London winter than anything else. Her head in the oven seemed metaphoric; perhaps it had been an error and she'd only been wanting a little warmth.

Softly padding across the bedroom, Lily went to the kitchen and turned on first the heat, then the kettle. *Tea.* What *had* the English done for solace before they stole it from us, she wondered. All these thoughts of racism and death were both unlike her and beside the point, Lily thought as she got the tea things ready and found herself some biscuits. She was avoiding the reason she was awake and fearing her neighbors' wrath. The dream. The dream and Monica's letters. Three missives within three days' time. Were there more to come?

She sat at the kitchen table, the mumble of the kettle and the lowing of the heat behind her. Before her lay the five newspapers she'd bought at the newsagent's on the way home last night: the two decent London papers, *The New York Times, The Washington Post* and, as the newsagent had proclaimed to her, a finger aside his nose in that knowing British male manner, a *Times-Picayune* from New Orleans that she was very lucky to get, as they rarely carried it, but a Mister from that part of the world had been ordering it for a fortnight and hadn't been in for two days, so yes, she might have them.

Lily poured the tea and milk, adding the honey and pepper while she ate a biscuit. She'd never acquired a taste for the weak way the English did their tea. Perhaps her only true memory of her mother was of the little half-glasses of tea she would give Lily on steamy Lahore afternoons. Sweet with honey, sharp with pepper, and thick with milk, shavings of cardamom dusting the top. Lily could see the little glasses so clearly, and her mother's dark olive hands, her deep blue sari. But not her face, never her face. Only the turn of the head, the dark hair piled high like any Indian woman's, the small area of middle back exposed between skirt and top. Any mother.

Lily drank her tea with a pang of loss and scanned the *Times* for mentions of the outbreak in New Orleans. It was there, where she knew it would be, the science section. Not very long and in the succinct style she had come to expect from the *Times'* science writer, whom she had met at conferences and by whom she had been interviewed on numerous occasions. Here a different kind of expertise was required; there were quotes from Laurie Garrett and Richard Preston, discussion of hot zones and influenzas of the past and present. Garrett, always smart, Lily thought, and always a step ahead for a journalist who wasn't a scientist, commented on the perils of influenza and how the strains had become stronger and deadlier over the years and should not be dismissed out of hand simply because "everyone gets the flu." For his part, Preston mentioned the avian viruses that had sprung up in China and other Asian vectors in recent years. Smart as they were, neither told her anything Monica hadn't already written in her letters. So this was a particularly bad flu, then? Or . . . ?

The Centers for Disease Control gave a crisp nonanswer that raised Lily's eyebrows and ire. AIDS had taught them nothing. The resurgence of tuberculosis had also been virtually ignored by them, except for one scientist whose mother had been in a TB sanatorium, which had left the son with emotional scars. There was news here in the

Times piece, but it was encrypted and Lily was too worn out for deciphering.

She had gone online when she'd gotten home, but there had been nothing on the Net worth her time about this mystery outbreak. Some crackpot commentary about everything from bioengineered food to terrorist-tainted oysters. All conspiracy theory signifying nothing.

The New Orleans paper was no *New York Times* nor *London Observer*. It gave the same CDC quotes. And a full three-column inches of interview with Dr. Monica Graves, formerly of the World Health Organization and acclaimed scientist in town researching the cataclysmic yellow fever epidemic of a century ago. Graves, the article noted, was on a presidential panel of epidemiologists consulting for the National Institutes of Health to study the impact of terrorism on disease vectors. Graves had been entreated by the NIH panel to use her specific expertise to aid local authorities in determining the source of the outbreak and its cause.

Monica had left these facts out of her letters, Lily presumed, because it would have sounded too competitive. She had also left out the numbers. Small, just like Lily's Congo outbreak, but equally lethal. Twenty-four people were confirmed dead of the mystery flulike disease in the past month. Not a lot, argued the CDC—in fact, fewer than would have been expected to have died of flu-related symptoms in any given winter in any urban center.

But what Monica had alluded to in her letters was clarified in the newspaper report. The unusual aspect of the disease was its victimology: Eighteen women and six men ranging in age from twenty-five to forty had died. Six were prostitutes but all the others were from various and, as the paper noted, legitimate professions, including mail carrier, which had brought the CDC and Office of Homeland Security into the mix because of the anthrax attacks in the East. Everyone had been deemed perfectly healthy prior to the onset of illness. The only other contiguous demographic factor: to a one the victims were all single, unmarried, and childless.

The kitchen clock read nearly two. Lily shut off the light and turned off the heat again. She walked back to bed, where she hoped the dream of a flaming city, a headless woman in a sari, and a corpse resembling Monica did not recur. She slipped beneath the duvet and willed herself to dreamless sleep after reciting the short prayer to Krishna her mother had taught her.

Sister Stephania opened the French doors that led into a sparsely furnished, high-ceilinged parlor whose only indicators of the twenty-first century were a CD player discreetly tucked into a bookshelf and a languidly whirring ceiling fan. The furniture—a large sofa in claret chintz, a trinity of matching chairs, and a Queen Anne-style coffee table in the center—was demurely serviceable and just a little worn. Bookshelves filled with volumes of indeterminate age and lineage lined the north wall; on the south were French doors, covered by the ubiquitous shutters. A discreet mahogany pre dieu topped with a small onyx Virgin, a single red votive lit before it, stood against the whitewashed plaster of the opposing wall. A wide, rounded doorway led into a foyer beyond which a spiral staircase curled into shadow.

Lily stood on a worn but still beautiful carpet of a pattern she recognized as Kurdish. In the distance, from somewhere deep in the house, she thought she could discern the susurration of chanting. Vespers, perhaps?

Sister Stephania had made no move to take Lily's bag nor to summon anyone else—Monica, the abbess, anyone. Stephania stood, somewhat awkward now that she was no longer in fluid movement, waiting, it seemed to Lily, for some signal from her.

Lily set her things on the carpet. "Is Dr. Graves available?" she asked.

"Dr. Graves is—" The awkwardness had escalated into a full-fledged anxiety, or so it appeared to Lily. Her earlier foreboding returned. "I will get Sister Claire. Please wait." Graceful in movement once more, Stephania strode off at a fair clip into the dark beyond the foyer doorway.

The chanting Lily had heard ceased. She walked over to the sofa and sat down, suddenly aware of the exhaustion her long flight and subsequent drive from the airport had engendered. At least her modest celebrity had saved her trouble in customs. She looked at her watch, still set on London time: it was after midnight and she'd been traveling for over twelve hours. Her stomach released a low growl. She'd like nothing more than a light supper and a long sleep. Despite her years of traveling, Lily had never learned how to conquer jetlag. What had she been thinking, coming directly here? She should have gotten a hotel room and come to the convent in daylight, rested, alert, and ready to face both Monica and whatever epidemiological mysteries she had uncovered. All this secrecy had made her somewhat overwrought. Monica had asked only that she perhaps write. She hadn't asked Lily to come seven thousand miles to New Orleans, hadn't asked her to leave the Congo project to Blentham, hadn't asked anything, really, save to reconnect with a former lover who shared her passion for virology.

Why was she here? What had sparked the foreboding she had felt? Did *she* have some need to see Monica, or did she simply want to investigate the virus Monica had happened upon? Had she really been propelled all this way on the merit of a handful of cryptic letters and some vague quotes in *The New York Times*? This was hardly the way she normally behaved. The last time—the only other time in her career—that she had left a project unfinished had been when she had left Monica in Albania. Something was wrong, very wrong, but it might simply be her own instincts.

Lily stood to leave. Nearly fifteen minutes had passed and neither Sister Stephania nor anyone else had appeared. She would go out as she had come. The fog had thickened but at least it wasn't raining, and she was certain as anyone who had spent over a decade navigating through London fogs that she could find her way to Jackson Square, a hotel, and a good night's sleep. She would reconsider what to do in the morning, once her head was clear.

She had just opened the French doors when a deep, throaty voice spoke behind her. "Oh, my dear, you must have felt totally abandoned down here to be considering leaving."

Lily turned. Sister Claire, the titular abbess of this transient's convent, wore the same flowing black pants and shirt as Stephania. The simple silver cross was the same as well. But replacing Stephania's broad Slavic features and short blonde hair was a deceptively youthful face of indeterminate ancestry, thick, slightly wavy, shoulder-length hair which may have once been the color of Lily's own but which was now equal parts iron gray and graying black. And looking straight at her with an expression Lily could not discern were eyes of a clear and unnaturally pale green. The eyes of an animal, rather than a person, thought Lily.

"I thought perhaps I had simply come at an inopportune time and without sufficient notice." Lily recovered the moment and her composure with the aplomb that had seen her through many far more harrowing moments than this. "My colleague, Dr. Graves, had requested I come to assist her during this outbreak. I'm Dr. Lily Sakhret; I'm with the Whitfield Laboratory in London, a division of the World Health Organization's infectious disease unit. I'm an epidemiologist. And I'm exhausted from traveling and thus babbling just a bit."

Lily'd seen it, she knew she had: a flicker in those animal eyes when she had said Monica's name. The abbess knew Monica hadn't sent for her, but Lily was not about to falter. She had the letters to wave in front of the abbess's face, if need be. But where, she wondered, was Monica?

"Of course, you must be exhausted," Sister Claire said, her voice almost lulling in its empathy. "It's an even longer flight from London this time of year with the head winds. And all this terrorism business makes the time spent in the airport itself nearly as long as the flight one is taking. Did you have any trouble in customs?"

Lily was certain Sister Claire implied no racial comment, and yet Lily felt it at the back of her neck and the base of her skull. No, no one had presumed her an Islamic terrorist, only a doctor with a mission to save lives.

"No," she responded in a tone slightly more clipped than her Cambridge education necessitated, "we're so used to the terrorism threats in London, the security has been monumental since Lockerbee— we've had many years to perfect the process." Lily had always hated flying anywhere in the West where she would have to stand in the interminable non-EEC customs lines full of brown-, black-, and yellow-skinned women and men. She would go through it again when she returned to England, her Indian passport, its pages crammed with stamps from countries the customs agent had never heard of, let alone been to, causing him to eye her suspiciously. Later that night he would complain to his wife about the bloody wogs coming in from all over the damn place taking jobs from decent folks.

They were still standing by the half-open French doors. Fog had slithered through and clung near the windows. With it had intruded the smell of the Ganges that Lily had noticed before. She felt her gorge rise a little. The abbess reached past Lily and shut the doors with a flourish. "We don't really want to let the fog in," she averred. "The unusual heat has set up a red tide and the smell from the river gets worse at night. Hot as it is, we need to keep the windows shut at night to keep the stench out." Sister Claire made a movement on the wall near the windows and the shutters clattered closed. "Technology. Great when a quick storm blows up. You'd be amazed how much rain can come in if the shutters are open, even if the windows are closed."

What was it that caused Lily to want to run her hand frantically along the wall, find the button to release the shutters, and flee, flee, run into the garden and through the gate and keep running until she was well shut of this convent and its eerie silence and strange, undiscovered link to epidemics. What was it that made her almost swoon under the touch of the abbess as she took Lily's arm and steered her in the direction of the shadowy foyer?

Lily found her voice before they crossed the threshold of the parlor into the unknown dark of the spiral staircase. "Abbess, you haven't told me where Monica is. Might I see her now?"

Sister Claire stopped, her hand light on Lily's forearm. "My dear, your friend isn't here at the moment. I'm afraid you'll have to accept my feeble hospitality until her return. She must not have known the exact time of your arrival or I'm certain she'd have been here to meet you. It's the research, you know. Some lead took her out of the city for a few days. We expect her back very soon."

The whole long flight from London Lily had dreaded the moment when she would see Monica again. Not a part of her had secretly thrilled at the idea. Rather, she had agonized over how she would explain her presence without implying romance or any other passionate emotion. She had been too raw and wary after Monica to be with anyone else, and a series of outbreaks had kept her busy. Soon after, the Whitfield appointment had sewn up every spare moment of her time. But the lack of a new lover did not lead her to want to rekindle the madness with Monica. That was over the day she saw her research incinerated into ash. So why did the abbess's pronouncement that Monica was not here leave her feeling nearly distraught?

"Well, it must have been something urgent." Lily tried to keep her own feelings of urgency from her voice. "Monica had written me and I thought it was clear when I would arrive." This last sounded far too vague, but exhaustion was keeping her from thinking clearly. That, and the oppressive heat. It had become virtually airless in the room since Sister Claire had arrived. Lily thought if she didn't lie down she might very well faint.

Her unsteadiness did not go unnoticed. "Let's get you upstairs to a room that's a little cooler so you can rest," Sister Claire said soothingly. "Would you like some food? The best way to avert terrible jet lag is food, a glass of wine, an aspirin, and about nine hours' sleep."

"This heat is odd, isn't it?" Lily asked the abbess. "Almost unnatural." She again dabbed her scarf across her forehead.

"I've spent an interminable number of years here," Sister Claire answered, her tone mildly ironic. "I'm older than dirt, as my grandmother would say. New Orleans has the most erratic climate. I remember my very first winter here, I had arrived just before Thanksgiving and it felt like summertime. I was so disoriented. I had only heavy woolen clothes, and it must have been ninety degrees. So, unnatural? It's difficult to say. Unusual for this late in the season, perhaps, but in a week it could snow a bit. One of the joys of this city is its many surprises."

Sister Claire bent to pick up Lily's suitcase. "Come with me, my dear. Let's get you taken care of."

≈   ≈   ≈

There had been no more dreams—at least none she could re-call—that night after Lily had drunk her tea and prayed to Krishna, which she always thought of as praying to her mother. But she had awoken to a burring alarm and a buzzing headache, as if she'd drunk gin instead of tea before bed.

She'd showered till there was no hot water left, a hideous waste, she knew, and yet it had brought her around. A thick coffee followed by a tomato juice with lemon and Worcestershire as if she'd actually been hungover snapped her to. It wouldn't do to face Blentham without her fullest wits about her. That boy just ached to find the tiny crack he could worry to a fissure.

The tube took far longer than the three stops warranted, but the crush of Londoners—Indians, Pakistanis, South Africans, Nigerians, Chinese mixed in among Scots, Irish, Canadians, and the native En-glish—made her feel less isolated than her English-only mews had done.

The infernal noise of the morning rush and the breathtaking climb up the hundreds of steps at Russell Square, where the ancient lift was out again, disallowed her any thoughts of Monica and her letters. Climbing in Nepal had never been as arduous as this bloody Russell Square staircase, she was certain. But she'd been only twenty then and middle age was creeping up on her now, plus she'd had that bad night. Still, she could almost chart the age demographic of those around her by how quickly they took the high-hewn steps and how much breath it took them. Could she keep science out of nothing?

The rush of chill gray winter morning took what was left of Lily's breath away as she entered onto the high street. She pulled her scarf across her face after she stopped to buy the morning paper at the newsagents. Monica's letters were coming back. What was this dis-ease she had uncovered? Had the government sent her there? The New Orleans paper had implied as much, with its discussion of her part on the terrorism study. It seemed she had come bidden, research on yellow fever aside or perhaps just a cover.

The walk to the office was rife with unanswerable questions. What had prompted Monica to write? Was she looking for Lily's expertise or imparting her own? There had been a year's silence between them. Why break it? Had Monica wanted to gloat, wouldn't she have sent Lily some sort of notice of her appointment, rather than letters that deliberately avoided mention of it? Certainly when Lily had won the Whitfield Prize she had contemplated sending Monica a formal notice, but then decided Monica would read of it and the subsequent appointment in some journal or another or hear of it through a colleague. No need for statements of what they both knew to be obvious, that Lily had surpassed Monica professionally, despite being a decade younger.

Professional wrangling aside, Lily couldn't shake the sense of foreboding that had tainted the letters. Something about the arrival of the nun in the proverbial dark and stormy middle of the night had been the stuff of gothic tales. That combined with the mystery illness added to the eeriness, yet Lily had read the accountings herself in the newspaper. Not only was Monica not exaggerating, she had written primarily as a scientist, a virologist seeking answers. Perhaps she had merely wanted Lily to volunteer her own perspective without having to ask for her help. Perhaps it was that simple.

But as she took the lift to her fourth-floor laboratory in the Whitfield building and involuntarily steeled herself to meet Blentham, Lily remembered those last lines, the ramshackle delirium just around the periphery. And no signature. Simply not the Monica she knew and, despite their year apart, of one thing she was certain: Monica was as rigid a creature as one could ever come to know. When Monica acted out of character, it was for a reason. The question Lily had now was: What reason?

"I'm not going to have to carry you up the stairs, am I, my dear?" The abbess's voice came to Lily as if through a scrim. She was unbelievably exhausted. So exhausted she was unsure if she could indeed climb the staircase that loomed before them, spiraling up into what seemed an unending and incalculable summit.

"I'm suddenly simply knackered." Lily tried to get her voice back to its proper English-educated, pull-yourself-up-by-your-bootstraps, girl, you're a scientist not a swooning first-form self, but failing that settled for getting the words out without garbling them. "I think the combination of the heat, travel, and lack of food has just come over me all at once," she averred. "Do tell me it's not as far as it looks?"

The abbess laughed the same throaty chortle that had tinged her earlier description of herself as—what had she told Lily?—"older than dirt"? What an odd turn of phrase. Perhaps some rural American saying Lily'd have no way of knowing. There were so many idioms everywhere. . . . God, she was tired.

"It's only one flight up—it looks worse than it is. Here, let me take your other bag. You just get yourself up the stairs. I'm well rested and you aren't, but I'm afraid you can't spend the night down here, you'll suffocate in the heat. The upper rooms are air-cooled. The ceilings are too high down here to do it, plus we have to adhere to certain historic codes due to the age of the convent. On a night like this you can see why people died of the heat not so long ago."

Now, it seemed to Lily, it was Sister Claire who was babbling. She took hold of the dark wood banister and pulled herself up step by step as if she were climbing up some steep cliff back home. Sweat dripped under her arms and beaded on her forehead. A cool shower and a long sleep, she thought. Food seemed utterly out of the question. She hadn't the strength to chew and swallow. She'd eat in the morning.

Suddenly they were there. A long narrow hallway, almost like a balcony, extended into another chimeric range of shadow. Lily tried to take in her surroundings but everything seemed blurred at the edges, as if the fog had muddled everything. There stood a chair with a high back against a wall whitewashed like those downstairs. And there— a painting, dark, some religious theme perhaps? A saint slaying something or other. Then another little pre dieu, this one below a rough-hewn crucifix, still the single votive burning dark red.

They had reached the end of the balcony part of the hallway. There it turned into a wider thoroughfare. At the first door past the turn Sister Claire stopped and placed Lily's things on the floor. A blue carpet of intricate design—Pakistani?—ran the length of what Lily now saw was a short, wide hallway with doors on either side, all closed.

"Your friend's room is just across the hall, there," Sister Claire half-turned and gestured toward a door a few feet opposite her own. Closed like the others, Lily wondered fleetingly if it were locked as well. Perhaps there was something in Monica's room to tell her—

"A bathroom adjoins this room." Sister Claire was speaking as she withdrew a long key from her pants pocket and unlocked the door to Lily's room. The key, Lily noted, was old and silver, like the little crosses the nuns wore, and the keyhole on her door was of the sort popular in the eighteenth century. If Monica's door were locked, there'd be little chance of entry without that key.

Sister Claire was still talking to her. "The nun on the other side of you, Sister March, shares it as well, but she isn't here at the moment, though she is expected soon."

At the mention of the mystery nun Lily came around from her daze. So the March woman was indeed a nun. But where had she gone off to so soon after arriving the last time—only a week ago, according to Monica's letter?

Sister Claire entered the room and pushed a switch near the doorway. The room came slowly to dim, golden light, while above them a ceiling fan began its languorous turn. The abbess put Lily's laptop on a small escritoire against the far wall and placed her suitcase on a cedar chest at the bottom of the narrow bed. Lily dropped her purse to the floor where she stood. Sister Claire took it and placed it on the high-backed Shaker-style chair that stood against the wall next to the bed.

The room was plain but lovely. Opposite the chair a window— more like a glass-paned door—opened onto a large balcony which Lily presumed overlooked a garden, but it was too dark and foggy to tell. The narrow bed was of the same deep cherrywood as the staircase and pre dieus, some sort of mahogany, she thought. An ivory matelassé coverlet, simple but elegant, enshrouded bed and pillows. A crucifix similar to the one she had seen in the hallway hung over the headboard. On the bedstand stood a nineteenth-century-style handleless etched-glass pitcher with a matching glass upended, covering its mouth. Two small books were stacked next to the pitcher. Prayer books, no doubt.

Feeling faint once more, Lily sat heavily on the chair near the bed. Her Hindu aunt had taught her never to sit where one slept in one's street clothes. Lily's own charting of disease had formalized this tradition. One's street clothes were as filthy as one's shoes, they simply didn't look it. Might as well sleep in the streets like beggars, her aunt had said.

The abbess stood a few feet from Lily, eying her with an expression Lily failed to read.

"I appreciate your allowing me to spend the night," Lily said, her voice quavering slightly from tiredness. "If Monica hasn't returned by tomorrow I'll find myself a hotel room in the Quarter. I simply can't presume on your hospitality in her absence."

"Of course you won't leave here," the abbess said with a firmness Lily imagined had chastened many a young novitiate. "We are used to guests here, to a certain transitoriness. It would be shockingly bad manners of me to let you go before your friend returns when you've come all this way to aid her research."

Sister Claire walked across the room to one of two doors opposite the bed. She opened the one on the left and touched a switch inside the room. The pale blue bathroom glowed invitingly. The abbess opened the other door, reached up into the recesses beyond, brought out two towels, and laid them on the edge of the bed.

"No doubt you'll want a shower after all that traveling," she said simply. "You'll find everything else you might need in the bath above the sink. Don't be alarmed if you hear someone else in there in the night—Sister March has a tendency to arrive at odd hours and one never knows when she will turn up. I'm going down to the kitchen to get you a little something to eat"—at Lily's murmured protestation she waved her hand—"you must have something or you'll become ill. I'll also bring you some bottled water and that glass of wine I suggested. Port might be best for sleeping, despite the heat. I trust you find this room cooler than our parlor?"

The room was remarkably cooler; Lily had noticed the difference immediately. The smell from the outside was gone as well, replaced by a scent reminiscent of crisp, fresh laundry. Lily glanced at her watch. Nearly two a.m., her time. She stood, still somewhat shaky, and moved toward the bathroom.

"Thank you for everything, Abbess. If it's not too much of an imposition, would you set the food and water on the bedstand? I am going to shower and crawl into bed before I collapse. I can't imagine why I am this tired. It must be crossing time in the opposite direction—I'm more used to traveling east than west. Somehow it tires me more this way." She stood near her suitcase, waiting for the abbess to leave.

"I'd be happy to leave a tray for you here, dear," she said, her tone once again conciliatory and nurturing. She put her hand lightly on Lily's shoulder. "We keep the doors locked here at night. Convent rule. No doubt you'll think it antiquated but I hope you don't mind." She slid the silver key from her pants pocket once more and handed it to Lily. "Do lock the door when you go to bed. You'll find this key also locks the bathroom door from your side. Sister March has a different key for hers. I have keys to all the rooms in case of emergencies," she responded to Lily's slightly raised eyebrow. "Our dress may be modern but our values are of a different time. We still follow the rules set by the order centuries ago, even though some, like this, may seem old-fashioned."

Lily wondered if the locked-door rule was to inhibit sexual intrigue. She remembered Monica's comments that all the nuns at the convent seemed lesbian to her and how Sister Claire seemed particularly butch. But Lily also remembered something else from Monica's letters and wondered if everyone followed the abbess's rule.

"Of course," Lily said simply. "If you don't mind, however, it's nearly two for me and I'd like to get to bed soon."

The abbess stood still for a moment, looking directly at Lily with her clear animal-like eyes, searching briefly. "I'll get that meal for you." Suddenly she reached for Lily's hand, taking her left—something no good Hindu should ever allow, Lily thought fleetingly. The right hand was for eating, the left for excreting. "We're very pleased to have a woman of your stature here," the abbess said, her tone almost deprecating. "I hope you and your friend will be able to find the source of this disease that is killing so many young women . . . and men." Her grip on Lily's hand tightened briefly, then released. "Should I not see you again tonight, matins are in the chapel, which is at the end of this hall, at six a.m. You are welcome to join or not, but I thought you should be aware that you'll hear us, regardless. Breakfast follows in the refectory downstairs, though you may want to sleep in, given your trip. Should your friend return, I'll tell her where you are."

The Abbess strode to the door, then turned back, a look Lily could not decipher on her face. "Do remember to lock up, dear. Pleasant dreams, then." She left and Lily opened her suitcase and began to unpack. Until Monica returned she would not be leaving the convent.

Blentham stood over the morning post as Lily entered the laboratory. From the doorway she could see as he apportioned the letters, mailers, and magazines that atop what she knew to be her pile was another pale-blue aerogram. Monica. Four letters in less than a week from a woman known to all as the world's worst correspondent. A frisson of fear raced along the ridge of her spine. Something was indeed wrong. Perhaps if she called the NIH they could give her a number where Monica could be reached.

"Morning, Blentham. You left early yesterday. Feeling all right?" Lily walked briskly to the mail on the counter, fully aware of the barely disguised anger she had just engendered in her assistant. *Bugger him,* she thought. *Officious prat.*

"There were some data to log in the basement," Blentham was nearly stammering. "I thought you knew where I'd be. I hope you didn't need me for anything."

"No," she murmured, taking her post and going into her side office. "Is the tea on? Would you mind getting me a cup?"

Had she a female assistant, Lily would never have asked the woman to wait on her. It was Blentham. He simply encouraged her to bully and humiliate him. He'd come with the position; she'd had to keep him. His obvious—and racist—dislike of her had made her think he'd leave soon after she'd arrived. But that had been nine months and three epidemics ago and he was still here, by turns insolent and groveling. A plodder by nature, he got the work done, but he'd none of the imagination that had so excited her when she worked with Monica.

She glanced cursorily at the mail. Nothing pressing. But there was not one but two aerogrammes from Monica. After Blentham had delivered the tea and she'd set him to a new research task, she opened both, glanced at the dates and began to read.

29 November 2001

Lily, dear Lily,

I've come down with something. All the rain, no doubt, and this place has the worst setup for bad and hot weather. It's a thousand degrees downstairs and then freezing up here. Isn't heat supposed to rise? The cooling system doesn't run downstairs so it's almost unbearable to be there, especially at night when we are bolted in to protect the virgin nuns from god-knows-what. Anyway, I seem to have caught something, though lord knows I am always sick for Christmas, just like clockwork. I've had just terrible night sweats the past three nights and then I am freezing in the day and if I doze off I have the most dramatic dreams of the sort associated I think with psychosis, which since I never dream, as you know, has been both interesting and just the least little bit harrowing.

Remember how you told me when you were at Cambridge you got pneumonia one term and thought you'd die because your dormer was so chill? That's how this is. I have no symptoms but the night sweats, chills, and fever. No nausea or diarrhea, though I have absolutely no appetite for food. Sister Claire keeps force-feeding me, though, with broths and toast and tea. Very English, really. And then the—right, that's what the shrinks call them—"vivid" dreams. Don't be alarmed, dear, but they all appear to be of you. You and some strange disease metaphors like a city on fire and corpses lying about, all headless. Then I wake up in a sweat and it's over, but I feel terribly drained.

Lily put the letter down for a moment and sipped the tea Blentham had brought her. She detected just the slightest tremor in her hand as she raised the delicate cup to her lips. Her dream of the night before, the one that had awoken her and set her nearly screaming—it was the same as Monica's. How was that possible? Unlike Monica, Lily dreamed nightly, but rarely dreams of the troubling, almost nightmarish sort she'd had last night. Lily had never been one to put much stock in dreams. She took the post-Freudian view that most dreams were a subconscious revisiting of the day's events, somewhat laced with metaphor but usually just a way to let off emotional steam. Which was why the dream she'd had seemed so alien and disturbing. Now as she read the repetition of the imagery in Monica's letter she felt a chill the tea would not slake. This was not like her—nor

Monica—but then her former lover had the excuse of fever and Lily did not. What had the dream meant and why had it so made her think of her own mother? The foreboding Lily had fought yesterday when she had read Monica's first letters returned in a wave. She stood, walked to the window, and looked out onto the high street, searching for some grounding in the dailiness of the pedestrian traffic and the cars careening through the intersection below. She returned to her desk, sat, and resumed reading.

30 November 2001

Lily, dearest,

I was due to fly up to Washington for a meeting on Monday but I can't see how even with the weekend to rest I shall feel up to it. I've been doing some consulting about this epidemic for NIH—I may not have mentioned this before—anyway, I called and laughed and told them I'd a bit of a flu. No one ever gets my humor, save you, darling. I was asked if I needed to be quarantined and I said no, of course not, my fever has barely crested 100, it just feels much hotter because of this bloody weather. So I seemed to quell their fears. You don't think I've picked up something? Sister Claire has actually tended to eight of the victims and she's fine, even though she has to be sixty-ish. She makes out she's a lot older but I can't see it. She acts and even looks younger than I but then this place seems to be aging me, you know how poorly I do in the heat. Why I chose the profession I did, averse to heat as I am, god knows. But Sister Claire never breaks a sweat.

I caught a glimpse of myself in the bathroom mirror yesterday—the bloody place has no mirrors of course, vanity being a sin. I look like right hell. This would not be the week for me to try to lie about my age. I'd be hard pressed to pass for several years older than I am, let alone younger.

2 December 2001

Lily, Lily,

It's actually about three a.m. and I just woke up from the most fearful dream. I do hope you are all right as I keep dreaming of you and doesn't that mean something—Jungian forebodings and the like? My mother—yes, I know I only mention her once a millennium—when she was dying after the damned snakebite—had similar delirium dreams. Did I tell you it took her six days to die? Some sort of medical anomaly of course, since cottonmouths are supposed to be lethal within thirty-six hours. She had the three bites—that was Daddy's doing; he handed her the snake wrong—on her arm, cheek, and breast. The one side of her turned black over the next day and then she puffed up like a whippoorwill. Of course I was all of nine and had yet to discover my true calling so I could do nothing but pray as we were supposed to and put cold compresses on her. She must have been in agony with the venom destroying her kidneys and liver, but she prayed along with Daddy and me and the rest of the church folks. What an insane time that was! Thank god I escaped it. I think if she hadn't died and the social services folks hadn't got wind of it I'd be doing that snake dance myself right about now in some godforsaken backwater with a coal miner moonshiner for a husband and a zillion rickets-ridden children. Maybe that's what Mother was praying for instead of her own life—mine.

3 December 2001

Dearest Lily,

I'm a little better today. Of course, because I told them I couldn't fly up today. Terrible dreams and night sweats last night, but that March woman came in and tended to me as all good nursing nuns are supposed to do. It's eerie how she resembles you. If she didn't have this strange accent that is just totally not yours and short hair instead of that tail you whip about, I'd swear she was you. Don't have a twin stashed somewhere, do you?

3/4 December 2001

Lily darling,

It's the middle of the night again and my fever is back with a vengeance. I just took a shower because I was soaked through as it was and all I could smell was this awful odor that's been permeating the city over the past week. It's the smell of death, of course, though death of what is unclear. They've minimized it on the news, say it's down to heat and dead fish and all that but you and I know better about these things. My mother smelled like that even before she was actually dead. The gangrenous rotting. It's unmistakable.

I've been too ill to really work. They called me in to the health department yesterday, but I looked so terrible they seemed a bit afraid of me. This heat is sucking the life out of me. I know you think me vain, but Lily, I swear I have aged a decade in the weeks I've been here. I hope I'll recover once I'm shut of this place and will look—and feel—more like myself.

March came with me for support. She's a pathologist, of all things. I asked how someone in a nursing order ended up dealing with the dead, but she only laughed. She doesn't talk about herself much. One of those listener types—you tell her everything, she tells you nothing. Just like you, darling.

I'm more confused than ever about what's happening here. Five more women have died since I took ill. That's twenty-nine dead all told—that we know of. I told the health department folks that we need to autopsy other suspicious or similar deaths from before the delineating point where the epidemic seemed to begin but they say we have neither the resources nor funds to do it. But I think there have been quite a few more deaths attributable to whatever this is. Of course I've been so bloody sick the past few days myself I have really been a little afraid I might be among them. I was going to draw my blood and do some testing but I'm too wrung out. I told the abbess this and she told me I just have been working too hard and have picked up a virus. It feels malarial to me, but I doubt it is. She's probably right. But the heat makes everything so much worse.

5 December 2001

Lily, dear,

Miracle recovery. I woke up this morning and felt fine. I ate well and feel totally steady on my feet, which I haven't done in a week. I got a call from Washington. They want me to check out the possibility of another outbreak near Lake Charles, which is at the northern part of the state and rather isolated. It's hard to imagine they're related outbreaks unless someone took this thing from here to there. Unless it's the reverse and it started there and came here. Funny thing—March was there just a week ago. There's a tiny little convent up there. It has only two nuns, both visiting nurses who work the entire swampy area up there. Lots of backwoods inbreds living with no medical care. I might go. I haven't decided. I need to catch up here and it's pretty clear this outbreak has nothing to do with terrorism, so I think the Office of Homeland Security need not be involved (nor give me orders like I'm in the army!). I'm more interested in staying here and looking at these new deaths and trying to get a handle on just what is causing this.

The rain's finally stopped, but with the heat the smell is that much worse. I'm going down to look at some bodies this afternoon. Maybe take my pathologist friend with me. Something is definitely rotten here, but I can't pinpoint it somehow. Fever really addled me, but I'm coming round. This is really your thing, darling. You'd have this sussed out in no time. Now that I'm well again I could kick myself for not taking my blood when I was ill. The abbess can be very convincing.

Wish me luck, dear—Monica

Lily put down the letters and picked up the phone. Late night in the States got her an endless phone tree before she was given specifics on how to find Monica by the lobster shift staff. But her call to the convent went unanswered. Lily was surprised there was no answering machine, particularly given Monica's recounting of the nuns' work in nursing. Surprised and not a little concerned. She dialed another number, booking the first flights she could get to New York connecting to New Orleans. Ten hours of flying with some stopover time and she would be in New Orleans. Perhaps she had read too much into Monica's letters. Or perhaps Monica simply could not bring herself to say what her letters so clearly stated: Trouble lay in New Orleans. Trouble, an epidemic of unknown origin, and something Lily could not quite discern. Of one thing she was certain, Monica was no alarmist; yet all she had written—and the mere fact of her writing—meant something ominous. Lily had to see for herself what was going on in New Orleans.

Blentham must have been thrilled to be put in charge of the Congo project for now. A new outbreak, Lily explained. She'd be back in a few days, possibly a week, but too long to let the data sit, she'd told him. He was to e-mail her if there were any problems, but she doubted she'd hear from him before she checked in. She hoped she wouldn't regret the decision, but it didn't matter, really. She had something just as mysterious and much more pressing at hand. She packed up her laptop, took Monica's most recent letters, and headed home to pack.

❧ ❧ ❧

The dream seemed to suffocate her. A myriad of images, some surreal, some blatantly sexual, others frightening, detailing disease and death. The flaming city again, and the corpses, Monica's among them. But now a new face had entered the dream, insinuating herself between the headless body clothed in a too-blue sari much like her mother's. Indian like herself, but different, dressed in a black sari shot with gold threads glinting in the orange glow of the city on fire. Lily was so hot and the woman in the sari held something, a little glass of tea which she knew would cool her, if she could only reach it. But the bodies kept piling up before her, faster than they could be set on the pyres. And then the abbess was there, holding out the silver key, her eyes fairly glowing. *"Lock the door,"* she whispered. *"Lock the door."* But another woman, much like the one in the black sari, except dressed like the abbess, took the key. She came toward Lily, holding the key in her outstretched hand. She had an expression Lily could not read on her face, yet Lily felt compelled to go to her despite the abbess's protestations.

Lily jolted awake as if she'd been struck. A pale blue light suffused the room. *Where was she?* She sat up and looked at her watch. Two? Could it be two in the afternoon? She looked toward the window and the unmistakable light of dawn breaking. She was in New Orleans, but her watch was still set on London time. Not for the first did she wish she'd gotten herself one of those dual-face watches; she could use one now, set to London time and this, seven hours earlier.

The events of yesterday—last night—came back. Lily was fully awake now and began to register the sounds of morning in the convent. The matins must be the sound she heard just beyond her bedroom door, and from outside, past the garden she knew to be there, came a sudden chiming. The carillon of St. Louis Cathedral in Jackson Square, as Monica had mentioned. Seven. Had she really slept ten hours? She hadn't slept so long at one time since school. And yet she felt logy and somewhat ill, as if she hadn't slept at all. Involuntarily one hand went to her forehead to feel for fever. Hot and dry. Likely just the radical shift in climate and the jet lag she always suffered from, Lily cautioned herself. Yet she could tell her pulse was racing even though she was barely sitting up in the bed. The aftereffects of the nightmarish dream, no doubt. She'd had that sensation before, in London. Some tea and another shower and she'd be all right.

. Lily swung her legs over the side of the ascetic little bed, and as she moved to stand she felt a concomitant wave of nausea and dizziness that sat her back down. Slowly she returned herself to a prone position. Surely she wasn't ill; she had always worried after long flights when she flew coach, as she had yesterday. She curled around and felt her ankles; not swollen. She palpated her calves, then thighs. Nothing that might signal a slight clotting, the pooling of the blood in the extremities that could lead, as well she knew, to embolism and sudden death. But fever never accompanied such trauma, nor did dizziness. More likely several nights of interrupted sleep and her concern for Monica had literally made her ill. That and ten hours of recirculated air from God-knows-where, she thought grimly. It was best people didn't know the real danger in flying lay in the air and the terrible diseases from TB to Ebola she knew it carried, rather than the possibilities of crashes or terrorist takeovers.

She must get up, however. She needed to take another shower, get dressed, drink something, make some phone calls from her mobile. She needed to locate Monica. Slowly this time, she raised her head from the stiff little pillow and sat. She flexed her wrists and ankles to get the blood flowing and lowered her head between her knees to ward against another rush of faintness. Gingerly she raised it and then began to stand. She stood still at the side of the bed as another wave of dizziness nearly felled her, then took the little key from the bedstand and walked to the bathroom.

The face in the mirror shook her. Surely a couple of bad nights hadn't wreaked this kind of havoc on her normally quite handsome face? Or was it the lighting that made her appear suddenly older and a trifle wizened? She leaned forward and touched her skin, feeling once again the hot dryness, so unfamiliar. Had she always had these sharpish lines and simply been too busy to notice them? She would be thirty-seven in a few months' time but thought that, like most Asian women, she was aging well. Not today, certainly. She'd be lucky to pass for forty or a bit more, when usually people thought her little more than thirty.

She ran the tap and splashed cold water on her face, feeling surprisingly stunned by the sensation. It was almost as if steam were rising from her face with the cold meeting the heat of her skin. Krishna, she *was* sick. Perhaps she had been before leaving London, and this had in part fueled her mania to see Monica and check out this epidemic for herself. The shower served only to make her feel weaker. She dressed, applied just enough makeup to render her less haggard, and piled her long hair into a chignon. She sat on the chest at the bottom of the bed and wondered if she had the strength to walk down the hall, take the stairs, and search for the refectory and the breakfast the abbess had mentioned the night before.

A knock on her door startled her despite its softness. She took the key and went to answer it.

Across the threshold stood a woman so strikingly like Monica that Lily came close to involuntarily embracing her. Tall, curvaceous even beneath the shapeless black shirt and pants of the order, with reddish blonde hair, creamy white skin, and eyes the color of Delft, she could be Monica's twin, but wasn't. A long-fingered hand extended over the chasm between them, "March," the woman said in a voice equally startling, holding as it did the odd admixture of accents Monica had acquired over the years: the West Virginia twang from her childhood melded with the British clip of years in London sprinkled with a touch of Asian lilt from extended stays in India and Bangladesh. *March.* Hadn't Monica written that the woman reminded her of Lily? This nun looked as much like her as Sister Stephania, which is to say not at all. How very odd. But then Monica had had a fever and by her own admission had been in a state of semidelirium. Still.

"Dr. Sakhret—Lily." She met March's hand with her own. "Excuse my rudeness, but of course you look so much like—"

"Someone you know well?" March laughed Monica's deep throaty chortle. "I get that a lot. I came to escort you to breakfast if you're up for it. Abbess said you'd had a bad trip here and might not want to get up, but I see you've been awake for a while. But you look a tad rocky, if you don't mind my saying so. Would you prefer I bring you a tray—wait, are you all right?"

Lily felt herself swoon and grabbed to steady herself against the doorjamb. March leaped forward, just catching her as she began to slide to the floor. Lily felt only half-conscious as the surprisingly strong March carried her to the little monk's bed. "Monica—" The name escaped Lily's lips unbidden, ill and vulnerable as she was and unable to shake the unsettling sensation that this woman who called herself March actually *was* Monica.

"I'm afraid your friend is still up at Lake Charles, Dr. Sakhret." March had taken off Lily's short boots and socks and was now undoing the belt of her trousers, unzipping the pants, pulling them over her slender hips. Lily felt an extraordinary wave of sexual heat course through her. March stood and turned toward the French windows, pulling closed the thick, dark-blue drapes, blotting out the low rose light of the early winter morning. She stood over Lily. "Where is your key, Dr. Sakhret?"

Was it the room or merely she that was so hot, Lily wondered as she lay, half naked, in a kind of stupor, on the bed which seemed barely wide enough to hold her, let alone March/Monica, who had taken Lily's silver key from her trouser pocket, locked the door, and now lowered herself beside Lily.

"Who are you?" Lily whispered from what seemed an extraordinary distance as March deftly unbuttoned her silk shirt, sliding it out from under her, unfastened her bra, and lay both items on the Shaker chair beside the bed. Naked except for her watch, earrings, and the little silver Krishna she always wore around her neck, Lily could feel the dampness between her legs and a concomitant intensity of desire as March disrobed.

"We've met before, Dr. Sakhret. Don't you recall?" Was Lily imagining the change in March's voice? Could she have missed the unmistakable lilt of Hindi when they had first spoken, or had she merely been so taken aback by the uncanny similarity between Monica and March that she hadn't heard it, had heard instead Monica's voice? Met before? When had they met before? Would she not have remembered a woman so closely resembling her former lover as to *be* her?

"When?" Lily asked, but March put her hand over Lily's mouth, stifling her voice but heightening her eroticism almost unbearably. Monica had done this, Monica whose expertise in bed had overwhelmed even the well-traveled Lily. Monica had placed her hands around Lily's throat, as if to throttle her, but had applied only the merest pressure, enough to make Lily swoon a bit as she had done in the doorway a few minutes before, but when Monica released her, had placed the pressure elsewhere, it had made Lily come with an intensity she had never before experienced.

It was like that when Monica put her hand over Lily's mouth when they made love. She could barely breathe, but Monica would talk into her ear and cover Lily's mouth with her whole hand, pressing her fingers between Lily's lips as she pressed herself between Lily's thighs.

Lily and March were both naked now, in the dim light which appeared blue, as if it were three in the morning rather than the three in the afternoon that registered on Lily's watch. *Day for night* it was called in filmmaking, Lily suddenly thought for no reason other than that the last time she had been in New Orleans she had experienced this same sort of light in her hotel room. Her lover at the time, Françoise, a filmmaker, had told her directors would shoot in daylight and alter the print to make it appear to be night on film. Lily could not remember the lovely succinctness of the French, could only recall "day for night." She whispered the phrase now to March, who laughed a small laugh that was not Monica's, not like that of any other woman she had known, a laugh that made her shiver with either desire or fear, she was unsure which.

"May I take this off?" March asked as she put her slender fingers around Lily's neck and began to unclasp the Krishna. "Oh, don't," Lily breathed into March's ear. "It was my mother's; I haven't taken it off since she . . . died." Had her mother died? Aunt Vashti had always said so. "Taken into Krishna's arms," she had lamented and touched the tiny amulet around Lily's neck. But Lily had never believed her mother had died. Rather, she had believed that the youthfully widowed Indra had left her young daughter and sought a new life elsewhere, unencumbered by child or past, sought another man or perhaps even a woman, in Calcutta or elsewhere. Lily never believed

Indra had died, even though to believe otherwise meant to believe she had been abandoned by her mother, as she had been by the father who had died so suddenly of the infected machete wound he had suffered clearing brush near their home in Lahore.

"My mother made me promise never to take it off," Lily told March as her own hands covered those of the other woman, gently guiding them away from her neck. March paused; Lily could feel March's breath, surprisingly cool against her own throat, could hear her breath, slow and rhythmic, no hint of the intensity of the moment between them.

March's face was over hers now. In the bluish light Lily could barely discern her features, but knew now that she looked just like Monica, could in fact feel, as she traced March's face with her fingers, Monica's face beneath her hands. It had been several months since Lily had been to bed with anyone. Since Monica there had been no steady lover, but a series of casual encounters with women met at clubs or the music venues Lily occasionally frequented when she just couldn't bear any more work. Each had been pleasant but only that; the desire had been fleeting, as had the satisfaction. But now she could feel desire building in her to an almost excruciating intensity. She ached to have March touch her, kiss her, fondle her, ravish her, take her in ways she had only ever enjoyed with Monica. A deep sigh escaped her lips as March lowered her body onto Lily's, and she spread her legs wide, wrapping them around March's back. From the far distance of the consciousness that Lily was fast leaving behind as she sank deeper and deeper into the erotic miasma March was enveloping her in, Lily was asking herself the same questions again and again: *What has come over me? How and why is this happening? Has March seduced Monica as well? And where are the other nuns and the abbess while all this is going on? Is this the reason for the locking of the doors?*

Suddenly Lily tried to struggle her way back from March's hold over her. This simply wasn't right. She had come here to find Monica and ascertain that she was okay as well as to try to track an insidious epidemic. Whatever had transpired between her and Monica, there had still been something important between them, something to which Lily felt she owed some allegiance. And beyond that, they were colleagues, and Lily owed Monica the professional courtesy of helping her with this crisis.

March could sense Lily pulling away from her, trying to quell the incredible heat that had built between them in just a few minutes of inchoate passion. Like an animal sensing its prey might elude and escape it, March pushed her body hard against Lily's, thrusting her strong hand between Lily's thighs, entering Lily with a force she had rarely experienced and which literally took her breath away. Thoughts of Monica, the convent, the epidemic all began to fade, subsumed by the power of March's hands on her and in her. Animal sounds of pleasure and pain cascaded from her, only to be silenced by March's lips on hers, kissing her, biting her, filling her mouth with the metallic taste of blood. Her own hands grabbed at March, clutching at her back, her buttocks. She slid her hand down between March's thighs, tried to find an entry point between her legs, but March scissored her away, pressing harder and more frantically against Lily until Lily was consumed by a wave of orgasm so deep and intense she fainted, her hand on her own throat, Krishna gripped tightly in her fist.

Lily awoke to find a dark-skinned woman sitting on the side of the bed, holding her hand. "Are you all right?" Her voice held the lilt of Hindi, and in the half-light Lily imagined it was someone she knew, imagined for a moment that it was her mother, Indra, finally returned for her.

"I'm Gita." The woman's voice was clearly Indian and Lily felt a wave of longing for everything she had ever lost—her parents, her home, even Monica. *Monica.* Lily had had such a strange and terrible dream; Monica and March had become one, and March had—

"I'm one of the nuns here at the convent," Gita continued, her voice low and quick like her Aunt Vashti's. "I arrived yesterday from Delhi and Abbess thought, as you had been ill for several days, you might feel more comfortable with a familiar face and voice. She meant Indian, of course. Don't think her racist. She means very well, she's just an old woman, and there are many things that are new to her now that we are living in a global village."

The sound of Gita's voice felt soothing to Lily even as the words washed over her with a barely discernible meaning. Ill? For several days? Lily tried to get her wits about her. She remembered the night of her arrival and then the next morning feeling terribly sick, meeting the other nun, March, and then—nothing.

"What day *is* it?" Lily asked, her voice husky as if from disuse. Her throat felt raw and bruised, as if she'd been throttled. Now, as she began to be more awake, more aware of herself and her surroundings, she could tell she still had fever. Her skin was hot, her muscles ached, and she felt an incredible weakness and ennui.

"It's December 13," Gita responded. "St. Lucy's Day. Our patron saint, actually. Do you know St. Lucy? Oh, how rude of me, of course not. I see from your Krishna that you are Hindu. Please forgive my insensitivity. We are not a proselytizing order, you must understand."

The words had come in a small torrent, so reminiscent of the way women spoke at home that Lily once again felt a deep pang, an ache for her own mother, to be surrounded by Indian women, to be bathed in water scented with lilies and sandalwood, and to smell the incense that always burned beneath the statue of Vishnu that her aunt prayed to.

"You haven't offended me, really." Lily's voice sounded so alien to her. "I've managed to resist conversion all these years. But I'm not offended by people talking of their own religion. I *do* understand that this is a convent, after all. But please, tell me what has become of my friend, Dr. Graves. When I arrived she was out of town on research, and I have obviously been ill for a week's time. Do I have some sort of fever? Has a physician been in to examine me? I feel quite weak and febrile. Do tell me—" Lily put her hand on Gita's in entreaty, "what has happened to me and to Monica?"

Gita rose from the bed and walked in semidarkness to what Lily remembered was the French window. "Close your eyes," she said to Lily as she pulled back the dark blue drapes. Light suffused the room, but it was the waning light of a late winter afternoon. From somewhere far off Lily heard the call of a foghorn, and then the clear pealing of the cathedral carillon. Four. Late afternoon on St. Lucy's Day and she'd been comatose for a week and Monica was still not here.

"Abbess thought it best I tell you all that has happened, even though I just returned and was not here and you do not know me any better than you know Sister Claire." Gita paused and returned to sit by Lily's side. She wore a variation on the order's habit: a black shirt and pants, but close up Lily could see the outfit was distinctly Indian. The shirt was long, with a Nehru collar, and the pants blousy like those from home. An almost imperceptible gold thread was shot through the fabric. It glinted slightly as Gita moved closer to Lily and put her cool dark hand on Lily's brow. Gita's hair was much like Lily's own, but hung long in a thick braid down her back. At her throat hung a small cross of the sort the abbess and Stephania had worn, except Gita's was gold, not silver. She touched the cross, then made its sign over her quickly as she began to speak.

"I'm sorry to tell you your friend, Dr. Graves, has succumbed to the fever that has claimed the lives of close to fifty women and eight men in the past month. We had been terribly afraid you would be next. Sister Claire was with you much of the time, caring for you and trying to keep you from dying. She probably didn't tell you, she never tells anyone, she's so schooled to be modest, but she is a physician, has been one for literally ever. To hear her talk, of course, she's been with this order since the founding of the group here in the States, but since that would make her close to two hundred years old, we all laugh when she says something like it. 'Older than dirt,' she calls herself— quaint American expression, isn't it? But the point is, she's spent all her time nursing you this past week, hardly doing anything else. She's slept in your room on the floor near the door, which for a woman her age is certainly a hardship. But I think she'd never have forgiven herself if you had died, since she felt responsible for your friend as well. It was at her urging, you see, that Dr. Graves came here to do her study."

Lily couldn't quite take it in. Monica dead? She was only forty-eight and had been in such excellent health. How terrible was this plague that it had killed this woman who never got ill and who had faced seemingly far more terrible diseases in far worse places on the globe? A strangled cry escaped Lily, and tears came unbidden down her cheeks. This was *her* fault for not finding Monica right away, getting her out of this place. Lily had known as she stood at that gate that something had been very wrong in this city. That smell had been the most potent portent of death she'd experienced in some time. And now Monica was dead, and Lily had, if Gita was to be believed, nearly gone with her.

"Has anyone determined what it was that killed her—that has killed all these people?" Lily's voice was vivid with anger. Gita moved back a bit, flinching involuntarily at Lily's tone.

"The abbess can tell you more," she said, her voice less calm than it had been. "She wanted me to break the news to you. Dr. Graves died in Lake Charles. The place was quarantined immediately after. The CDC decided to burn the bodies. I believe an autopsy was done, but the abbess will have to tell you more. I will go and get her before vespers begin. Can I get you anything else? There is some juice and cold tea there on the nightstand, and some ice chips in a dish. This is what we've been feeding you. If you are feeling stronger later I could help you bathe if you would like."

The spate of words subsided and Gita rose. She turned to face Lily and put her small brown hand on Lily's shoulder. "I'm deeply regretful about your friend," she said. "I have lost many of those I love to disease in India. It never gets easier, I know. Please accept—" Lily saw tears welling in the woman's eyes. She turned and left the room. Lily heard the key in the lock and then the soft padding of footfalls leading away down the hall.

It was going dark now. The sky looked riven, as if a wound had been sliced across the horizon, bleeding out the day. Since she was born Lily had faced down disease and managed to cheat death. She had held that in common with Monica; Monica who had watched her mother die from a snakebite inflicted during the bizarre religious ritual of the small Christian sect her parents had belonged to. Monica who had survived malaria, dysentery, even dengue fever, and who had chased down more epidemics than almost any other epidemiologist alive. How had she died? What *was* this disease?

Lily pulled herself to sitting and then tried to stand. Too weak. She began to cry, a feeling of real terror and inexplicable loss cresting over her. Suddenly she heard the key turning once again in the lock. Before her stood the abbess, a small tray with covered plates in her hand.

"I cannot tell you how grateful I am to see you sitting up," she said, her eyes inscrutable as they had been that first night. She reached for the dimmer switch and turned the room gold against the purpling light of encroaching night. "After Gita spoke to me I thought you should try a little food." The abbess placed the tray on the table and sat on the chair beside the bed. She uncovered the plates and turned to Lily. "Shall I help you or do you think you can feed yourself? You must be very weak. You've spent over a week in veritable coma."

Lily felt a surge of anger, near rage, sweep over her. As the abbess stuck a fork into a small bowl of what looked to be a gray-brown rice, Lily clamped her hand hard on the woman's arm. Kernels of rice went flying, and the abbess swung around to face Lily, her eyes wary but impassive.

"Why am I not in a hospital if I am so ill?" demanded Lily. "What really happened to my friend, and where is Sister March, who was the last person I remember seeing before my alleged coma ensued? What the bloody hell is going on here, Abbess, and why should I not call the authorities immediately and press charges against you?"

Lily could see it all now in Sister Claire's eyes. It was beyond the question of knowing more than she would say. Lily saw now what the abbess meant when she said she was older than dirt. She had seen this look before in the eyes of men in India whose claim to be well over a hundred years old could be substantiated by nothing but faith. Yet she knew somehow in some almost preternatural kind of knowing, that the abbess was more and less than she seemed. Perhaps she had indeed been on this ground, this pestilential ground, since the Louisiana Purchase. Lily still had a fever, but it wasn't delirium that led her to know what she saw move behind those unnaturally pale green eyes was true.

"Who—what—are you?" Lily hissed at the abbess, her grip still tight on the woman's arm, but Sister Claire made no move to extricate herself.

"What is it you need to know, my dear?" The woman's voice was measured. Neither cold nor warm, simply inquiring. "Do you need to know how your friend died or why you did not?"

Lily let the abbess's arm go. She pulled herself up in the bed, her head swimming with dizziness. She fought to sit rigidly straight against the bed frame. For the first time she looked at her own body. She seemed to have lost a stone since her fever. Her arms were thin, the skin ashen. Now she also noticed her dress: she wore the same black shirt and pants as the nuns. All that differed was that around her neck still hung the tiny Krishna from her mother, in place of the small crosses the nuns wore.

"Am I one of you now?" Lily asked, her eyes traveling from her own garb to that of the abbess.

"Actually, yes," declared Sister Claire. "Those who survive become one of the Order, those who do not—well, that's a story for another time. Here, my dear, please eat. You must build up your strength." She handed Lily a small blue dish with the grey-brown rice and red and black beans. "You must have protein," the abbess added. "There is no meat. We are vegetarians here, just like you."

"When did it begin?" Lily asked, taking a small fork and the bowl from the abbess with an unsteady hand.

"How long really isn't the issue," Sister Claire began. "Let us say simply that the fight between good and evil has gone on for all time and each of us enters the fray in our own way at our own pace. I have been here on this spot for many, many years. Before I came here I was elsewhere. But I have been a member of this order, the order of St. Lucy, for quite longer than you could imagine." The abbess must have registered Lily's skeptical air because she continued, "I am purpose-fully vague, my dear, because I must be. You are a woman of science and science is so often at war with—with what else exists in the world. In my faith we still skirt the line between science and superstition. Do we send the man complaining of demons to a psychiatrist or exorcist? Sometimes one is more helpful than the other."

"How did my friend die?" Lily could feel the tears rising again be-hind her eyes, and with them the rage flooding back. She ate another bite of beans and rice—surprisingly spicy and delicious—and thought of her dead lover.

"There are many beings in this world who skirt that line of which I just spoke," the abbess said, looking off toward the now-black sky outside the window. "Sister March is one of them. It is our blessing and our curse to have her as part of our order. She, and several others like her, test us in our faith and our determination to survive. And to heal, which is our mission."

She paused, reached for a glass on the tray and took a sip of a dark red liquid. Port perhaps, thought Lily. The abbess turned and handed it to Lily. "Sip this slowly," she admonished. "You must have it." Lily held it to her lips, then drank. The hot, dense liquid flooded her chest with warmth. It was no port.

"In the Middle Ages we called them succubi and incubi." The abbess spoke low, yet with a strong voice, as if this were a narrative she had told at the bedsides of many a woman like herself. "Demons who came in the night and fed on the desires of humans, sucking the life from them, aging them, withering them, bleeding them of their life force. The only antidote to death—of the body and the soul—was faith. This"—the abbess touched the little Krishna around Lily's neck—"these"—she touched the cross around her own—"are the talismans that signal to those who would steal our souls that they are not for barter. Your friend—"

Lily knew now. It had been there in the letters. The nuns had tried to protect her, abjured her to come to communion, to return to the Christian fold. Had they known Monica's history, perhaps they would have found a way to convince her. But they had not known. And she had succumbed to March, the shape-shifting sensualist who each night entered through the adjoining room and sucked a little more life from Monica under the guise of Lily's features, just as she had attempted to leech Lily's soul from her by appearing as Monica, with all her sensual allure.

"My friend's mother was killed by the accoutrements of Christianity," Lily said bluntly. "She and Monica's father were members of a small cult of fundamentalists. They handled snakes. No doubt it's an ancient form of faith with which you are familiar." She tried to keep the sarcasm from welling into her voice. "She gave up Christianity—any religion—when she was nine and watched her mother die a hideous death from snakebites. They prayed over her for the six days she suffered. When she died, so did Monica's faith. From then on her faith lay in science. She had a will to save people, but it was by science only, not faith."

The abbess sighed softly. "I invited her here to chart our history. I didn't realize at first she would be at so much risk. March was away, but she came back one night when I was at the hospital and your friend did not lock her door."

Realization dawned on Lily. She put aside her half-finished meal. "The epidemics. These aren't fevers, are they? The reason they cannot be defined is because—"

"March, and before her, others. You see who the victims are. The willing, the enterprising, the vulnerable. We lost close to a hundred this time, and you nearly among them. It will be some time before another epidemic strikes us. March has gone elsewhere for a time and the other, the one in Lake Charles, she will not survive much longer; her reign is drawing to an end."

The women sat together in silence. The abbess handed Lily another glass. This time the liquid was a deep amber. "Drink," she said.

Snow dusted the sidewalk outside the Whitfield building as Lily walked toward the tube. Tomorrow would be Christmas Eve. Monica would have liked to see this light snowfall, Lily thought, but tomorrow Lily would be on her way east, far from snow or even cold. She was going to Lahore and then Calcutta. A pilgrimage, her friend Françoise had said when they had met for dinner after she returned from New Orleans. "Your friend dies in the epidemic in the States and you must memorialize your parents, n'est-ce pas? What is that about, cherie? Do you want so much to go back? Forward would be better, non?"

But back Lily must go. Back to lay flowers and burn incense where her father died and back to visit Vashti and float flowers in the Ganges for her mother, and to go to the temple of Krishna and give thanks for her life.

It was near seven, and somewhere nearby a church bell tolled the hour. She looked at her watch, dual-faced. Only noon in New Orleans, where the epidemic, it was reported, had stopped as suddenly as it had begun. In January noted virologist and infectious disease specialist Dr. Lily Sakhret would take a sabbatical from her work with the World Health Organization and come to New Orleans to research the recent outbreak and investigate a series of smaller outbreaks that had been uncovered in nearby rural areas.

Lily looked up into the drifting snow, light and cool on her face as she stood outside the Russell Square tube stop. A busker was playing "Ave Maria" on a flute. She dropped a five-pound note into the case before her. "Merry Christmas, Monica," she whispered into the night air and turned into the station, the door shutting on the plaintive notes of the flute, a small squall blowing past her, into the night.

About the Editor

Greg Herren is a New Orleans author/editor who lives three blocks and about three million dollars from Anne Rice. He is the author of the novels *Murder in the Rue Dauphine, Bourbon Street Blues,* and the forthcoming *Jackson Square Jazz* (spring 2004) and *Murder in the Rue St. Ann* (fall 2004). He has edited the anthology *Full Body Contact: Sexy, Sweaty Men of Sport,* and is currently working on two more.

Contributors

Victoria A. Brownworth is an award-winning author of eight books, including *Too Queer: Essays from a Radical Life,* and editor of ten, including *Coming Out of Cancer: Writings from the Lesbian Cancer Epidemic,* which won the Lambda Literary Award. She was among *OUT* magazine's 100 gay success stories for 2001. Brownworth is a columnist and critic for several magazines and newspapers. She teaches writing and film at the University of the Arts in Philadelphia, where she lives with her four cats.

M. Christian's stories can be seen in *Best American Erotica, Best Gay Erotica, Best Lesbian Erotica, Best Fetish Erotica,* and over 150 other books, magazines, and Web sites. He's the editor of over twelve anthologies, including *The Burning Pen, Guilty Pleasures,* and *Best S/M Erotica.* His first gay collection, *Dirty Words,* was nominated for a Lambda Literary Award, and his lesbian collection, *Speaking Parts,* is available now from Alyson Books. For more information, see <www. mchristian.com>.

Richard Hall was a novelist *(Family Fictions),* an acclaimed short story writer (the collections *Fidelities: A Book of Stories* and *Letters from a Great-Uncle*), and a widely produced playwright. He was a longtime member of the National Book Critics Circle, and his reviews and essays have appeared in *The New York Times Book Review, The New Republic, The Advocate, San Francisco Chronicle,* and *The Village Voice.* Hall passed away from AIDS complications in 1993, but his work lives on.

Quentin Harrington is a longtime fan of horror whose favorite scary movie is *Showgirls.* He has written three unpublished horror novels for young adults (any takers out there?) and is currently working on his fourth novel, *The Nightwatchers.* He lives in New Orleans and swears he didn't sleep with the editor to get "The Troll in the Basement," his first published story, into this anthology.

William J. Mann is the author of the novels *The Biograph Girl*, *The Men from the Boys*, and the forthcoming *Where the Boys Are*, as well as the nonfiction studies *Behind the Screen: How Gays and Lesbians Shaped Hollywood* and *Wisecracker: The Life and Times of William Haines*.

David McConnell is a New York-based writer/journalist whose work has appeared in *Lambda Book Report*, the *James White Review*, and *The Gay & Lesbian Review Worldwide*, among others. His first novel, *The Firebrat*, will be released in fall 2003 from Attagirl Press.

Marshall Moore came up with the idea for "Sic Gloria Transit" while riding on the Barcelona metro. When he's not tramping around the globe he makes his home in Northern California. His debut novel, *The Concrete Sky*, was published by Harrington Park Press in early 2003. He is working on both a second novel and a collection of short fiction, one of which should appear in 2004. For more information about Marshall and his writing, please visit <www.marshallmoore.net>.

J. M. Redmann has written four novels, all featuring New Orleans private detective Michele "Micky" Knight. The most recent of these, *Lost Daughters*, was published by W. W. Norton in the summer of 1999. Her third book, *The Intersection of Law and Desire*, won a Lambda Literary Award. The first two books in the series, *Death by the Riverside* and *Deaths of Jocasta*, have been recently republished by Bella Books. A Mississippi native, Ms. Redmann now lives, works, and frolics in that city in a swamp, New Orleans.

Carol Rosenfeld is a New York City-based writer and poet. Her work appears in *Best Lesbian Erotica 1999* (Cleis) and *Poetry Nation* (Vehicule). She will have a story included in *Back to Basics: A Butch/Femme Erotic Journey*, to be published by Bella Books in 2004. Carol wants to thank Greg Herren for giving her the opportunity to be published with such a distinguished group of writers and for providing her with a reason to avoid working on her novel, *Fool's Mushroom*.

Lawrence Schimel is a full-time author and anthologist who's published over fifty titles, including *The Drag Queen of Elfland, Things Invisible to See: Gay and Lesbian Tales of Magic Realism, Camelot Fantastic, Kosher Meat, The Mammoth Book of Gay Erotica,* and *Streets of Blood: Vampire Stories from New York City,* among numerous others. His *PoMoSexuals: Challenging Assumptions About Gender and Sexuality* (with Carol Queen) won a Lambda Literary Award, and he has been a finalist for that award on numerous occasions for other books. Born in New York City in 1971, he currently lives in Madrid, Spain.

Therese Szymanski's first three books (the Brett Higgins mysteries *When the Dancing Stops, When the Dead Speak,* and *When Some Body Disappears*) are available from Naiad Press, while her latest books, including *When Evil Changes Face,* which was a Lambda Literary Award finalist in 2001 for best lesbian mystery, were published by Bella Books. Her short stories have appeared in numerous anthologies (including the Naiad anthologies *The Very Thought of You* and *The Touch of Your Hand*), and she has also written literary reviews, humor columns, political essays, and other items for various publications along the way. An award-winning playwright residing in Washington, DC, she believes in erotic freedom and maximizing the erotic content of life. She wrote "The Morning After" one fateful night when the power went out after she had spent all day watching horror movies.

Jess Wells is the author of twelve volumes of work, including the novels *AfterShocks,* recently reissued as a Triangle Classic by Insight-Out Books, and *The Price of Passion.* She is the editor of *Home Fronts: Controversies in Nontraditional Parenting* and *Lesbians Raising Sons,* both published by Alyson Books. A three-time finalist for the Lambda Literary Award, she has published five collections of short fiction.

Greg Wharton is the publisher of Suspect Thoughts Press and the editor of two Web magazines, *suspect thoughts: a journal of subversive writing* and *Velvet Mafia* (with Sean Meriwether). He is the editor of the anthologies *The Best of the Best Meat Erotica, Law of Desire* (with Ian

Philips), *The Love That Dare Not Speak Its Name, Love Under Foot* (with M. Christian), and *Of the Flesh. Johnie Was and Other Tall Tales,* a collection of Wharton's short fiction, will be released in 2004 by Suspect Thoughts Press.